DEAD IN THE RING

ADVANCED PRAISE
DEAD IN THE RING
by Jay Ridler

"***DEAD IN THE RING*** plunges the reader into the surreal, fantastical, and brutal world of professional wrestling, following a determined—and deeply damaged—hero pursuing the truth in an arena sustained by illusion. Ridler's visceral prose and ability to create larger-than-life characters that still sweat, bleed, and suffer make this mystery compulsively readable from the opening pages to when the last body drops."

> **—Kate Alice Marshall**, bestselling author of ***WHAT LIES IN THE WOODS***

"Set in the relentless world of pro wrestling at its zenith (or nadir, depending on your point of view), Jason Ridler's ***DEAD IN THE RING*** is a brutal, intoxicating novel that grabs you in a chokehold and doesn't let go. Hardcore noir at its finest."

> — NYT-Bestselling author **Elizabeth Hand**, author of ***GENERATION LOSS*** (Cass Neary)

"Nobody does hybrid quite like Jason Ridler. Part mother-and-child reunion, part epistolary, part adventures on the mat, ***DEAD IN THE RING*** challenges the tropes of storytelling, an iconoclast's fast-paced, no-hold's barred blend of noir and mystery; a love letter to the lost art of wrestling."

> **—Joe Clifford**, award-winning author of ***SAY MY NAME***.

JASON RIDLER

DEAD IN THE RING

A NOVEL

DEAD IN THE RING
Text copyright © 2026 Jay Ridler.

Published by **Shotgun Honey Books**

1808 Huber Road
Charleston, WV 25314
www.ShotgunHoney.com

Cover Design by Bad Fido.

ISBN: 978-1-956957-92-1 (eBook)
ISBN: 978-1-956957-90-7 (Paperback)

10 9 8 7 6 5 4 3 2 1   26 25 24 23 22 21

*Dedicated to the Workers, Jobbers, and Shooters
who lived and died for our entertainment; often before sixty.
You were the true sons of Achilles:*

*"Let me, this instant, rush into the fields,
And reap what glory life's short harvest yields."*

The Iliad

DEAD IN THE RING

PART ONE
MYSTIFICATION

ONE

SCREWJOB

December 5th, 1983.

"He's not dead."

For a hitman, such words are fatal. For a wrestling journalist, they were worse.

Sinus agony and Rat's last tab of speed hidden in a hollowed-out copy of *Fear of Flying* meant I hadn't slept in three days, so fuck if I knew what Val was talking about from behind his stained oak desk.

"Mr. Weston is very upset. You must come to the home office." That's what Ted had said. Words that dragged me to Long Island from my railroad apartment three hours ago. NyQuil tendrils ate my attention span.

"Hear me?" Val said, pinching out another Winston from the open pack on his table, next to a half-eaten ham sandwich and photos slated for the next issue. His raw face reminded me of a blood-stained urinal. His ducktail haircut was frazzled and twenty years out of fashion and had been last seen on Burt Ward, Batman's side kick, on a Very Special Episode of Family Feud. "He called me, alive. He thinks I killed him on purpose. Instead, we just fucked his career to death."

The haze shattered and rumbled down to my guts.

I had been dragged to the Long Island office of *Amazing Wrestling!* from East 10th to be told my last obituary was a hoax.

Val grunted. "Hey, Sully? You speak English still?"

Shit. I couldn't lash out. Sarcasm would sink me. I took my dad's tone when discussing Edgar Allan Poe's importance to American Letters. "Sadistic Stan Rapowski, master of the flying knee-drop, is alive and well?" Fuck, I sounded like Gordon Solie at a funeral.

Val wiped his thin eyebrows with his palm. "Asking this once. You do this to screw with me?"

Fuck, no! Writing "fake" articles about "real" pro wrestling is the easiest gig in the world, why would I fuck the dog now, you retard? But I said, "No," then chewed my molars. Val could swear in his office. Not some soaked punk looking like he'd just finished huffing Sterno on the train.

"It's a bad thing," said a voice that made my shit itch. Ugh.

I barely registered Ted in the back corner of the office next to the giant newsprint poster of Buddy Rogers. The black and white shot failed to snag Roger's coffee-grade tan and peroxide locks. Ted sat on a plush leather seat and chewed thin-sliced baby carrot after baby carrot from a paper bag, his latest fad. Swore it would heal his bad knee. A strawberry blond comb-over was plastered with sweat and Vitalis over his bulging lobe. "We told a lot of people he was dead," Ted said.

We? The little shit was even taking credit for my mistake. "Look, it's an easy fix," I said, wanting to kill this conversation. These geezers would not shut up. "I'll write another piece. Make Stan look amazing. Dedicate an entire issue to his resurrection. We'll say it's a conspiracy, that Dr. Fung spread a death rumor, so he lost a title shot in the NWA. Say that Ric Flair paid Freddie Flashman to write the obituary, to—"

"Smarten up," Val said, breathing smoke. "You're being played, Sully." Ted nodded. It hurt to ping pong between them. My sinuses were filled with green ants. "*Someone* is fucking with Stan, *through* you, and making *me* look like a mark. Who the fuck did you talk to?"

I hugged myself, wishing Rat hadn't pawned my leather jacket before he vanished. Flannel couldn't keep out December on Long Island. "I called and talked to Smokey, Mid-South, and Florida. I spoke to three reps in the NWA and then did AAW. None knew anything but didn't doubt what Dutch Mackrell said when he called you, Val. Stan was dead. Leukemia. Died in Barbados."

"Did you talk to the Mahones?" Ted said, the wet paper bag the same sheen as his undertaker skin.

"No." The most powerful family in New York, promoters of the Global Wrestling Association. GWA, the big independent promotion that ran New York and the Eastern Seaboard. And those rich shits ignored me. Ted had been sucking wrestling's dick for thirteen years, especially in New York. Remember the Charles Atlas ads on the back of DC comics? Ted was the one getting sand in his face. But instead of hitting the weights and turning *into* Charles Atlas, he snapped pictures of his bullies at Madison Square Garden to make them his friends. In return, they took him backstage and made them their mascot: The Unmasked Loser. "They wouldn't talk to me. And you know it."

Ted's jaw drooped, carrot remains on his thick bottom lip. "What does that mean? Sully, I'm trying to help."

Bang. It was clear. Ted had set me up. All my contacts? I got them through Ted. I was the new guy, filling a dead man's shoes. And now I'd been suckered by the veteran who wanted me to look like an idiot. And take all five of my jobs. Five popular columns left vacant by Peter Kardassopoulos, whose pennames I'd inherited after he choked on a chicken wing at Pang's Noodle House on Mott. Five issues singing with a dead man's voice andno one suspected a thing. I was golden. Now I was golden shit.

Next move would kill me or save me. I couldn't implicate Ted. He was bulletproof. But I could feed Val's paranoia. "Well, it all started with Ron Mace."

Ted's lips puckered like a virgin asshole before the plunge. "Ron?

He's a friend of Stan's."

"But he's a loyal soldier to the GWA."

"You just said GWA wouldn't talk to you," Val said.

Val had one weakness. It was paranoia about wrestlers fucking with him, especially GWA guys. Especially now. They were expanding their talent pool, poaching younger talent, and they never felt we covered them enough … meaning covering them alone. "Stan was going to try and revive himself in the AAW," I said. "The only people that benefit from us screwing up talent for the AAW? New York. Face it, Val, GWA played us through Ron Mace."

"That doesn't sound like the Old Man," Ted said.

"No, you dumb shit," Val said to Ted. "But it sounds like Little Junior."

Cassidy "Little Junior" Mahone was the heir apparent to the NYC wrestling scene. Rumor was he wanted to be a wrestler but daddy wouldn't let him. Instead, he did everything else: ring crew, accounts, booking, announcing, and now specialty shows and super cards with boxers and karate guys that were boring as hell but made money. Val hated his love of spectacle and bringing in heavy metal bands and other outsiders into the biz. Worse? He hated that Little Junior was making a mint doing it.

"Ted, cancel Japan. You're staying in NYC and covering every fucking show the GWA does. Make them know we love them best. Front row shots. Bug everyone for locker room poses. Lie about their Christmas ranking if you have to. I want details. Anything weird. Anything odd. Anything different."

"But Val," Ted said sheepishly, "the Mahones would never do this—"

"Did I all of a sudden need a photographer to tell me how the business works?" Ted flinched. "Sully?" I kept nodding to stay awake and not sneeze, agreeing to everything that was coming out of his grimacing lips. "You're from Minneapolis, right?" Fucking hell. I nodded, the itch in my nose too great to stop. "I'm sending you to AAW." He grinned.

I nodded, *NO NO NO.*

"I got a lead," Val said. "The Swede has a new protégé he's pushing for children. The Atomic Kid. Hear of him?"

"Sure," I said. Then nothing. What little I knew was that he was a strong man with some nuclear makeup or some shit. I hadn't covered AAW since Val and the Swede had some beef. Which suited me fine. No way I was going back.

"They're giving him the strap. They're turning him into a star. Big push. We get in now and I can wipe away the stain of GWA screwing with me. Do a big feature. Make him the next Gorgeous George"

"He's barely Sully's age," Ted said.

"Why are you still talking? Sully, ach of your pen names will be talking about the Atomic Kid. Interviews. Analysis. Complete with photos."

"Photos?" Ted said.

"Shut the fuck up!" Val scribbled on a piece of paper, then handed it to me. "Here's a stringer in the Twin Cities. Do this right and I'll forget you killed Stan."

My face clenched.

"Kid, don't make me repeat myself."

I screeched as I sneezed. Green snot flew at Val's desk and blasted his ashtray, muttering "fuck no.".

"Diseased shit," he said, crumpling up the paper and then throwing it. "What did you say?"

"I can't go."

"You have job interview at CBGBs?" he said, plain and clear. "You'll go."

I pinched my nose and tried to take a weaker tone, like a whipped kid locked in the hole. "Val, please, I don't know anyone in Swede's promotion. Ted does. He's best friends with all those guys. I'm just a writer, not a photographer. I'll look like some mark from New York."

"But Sully," Ted said, crossing his legs, the blue trousers still soaked from the snow. I hated the way he smiled. It looked happy.

The little shit saw something. "You *do* know people in the Swede's promotion."

Val tugged out another Winston, enjoying the show. "Huh."

"No. I don't."

"Well, one person. Though I understand she's retired."

"I don't know *anyone*."

Ted's face went slack. "But isn't your mother Black Widow Moscow?"

Val's head turned slow. "What in the name of all that is holy … Sully, is this true?"

My anger coiled. I wanted to pinch Val's twelfth Winston and stab Ted's left cornea until his dying screams shocked his comb-over white as newsprint.

"Answer me!"

"She—"

"—lives in Dinky Town," Ted said, placing his bag of carrots on the floor. He stood and pulled out a burgundy wallet. "She's a mall cop, I believe. I've got an address for you."

"Shove it up your ass," I said, chest thrumming.

"Zip it," Val said. "You want to go back to washing dishes at Wang's and playing bars for spit and eggrolls?"

I did. I really did. I wanted to say take this job and shove it and karate kick Ted's face before tossing the desk and releasing the dogs of hell and shit down everyone's neck.

But I didn't.

My anger was pre-punk, a dead end I'd stuffed down in my cell at Red Wing.

"Last chance," Val said.

Ted handed me a card.

Black embossed letters on glossy vanilla cardboard said "Katey Moscowitz, Security Management." All business until the bottom. A tiny black spider with a red hourglass body.

Ted had kept this ace in his back pocket.

I wiped my palms on my brown cords and counted to five like

one of the shrinks at Red Wing beat into me. I took it.

"Yeah, Val. I'm the son of the Black Widow."

Apparently, she wasn't dead, either.

TWO

DEAD MAN WALKING

IN MEMORIAM: PETER KARDASSOPOULOS (1942-1982)

The family at Amazing Wrestling is deeply saddened by the loss of writer and editor Peter Kardassopoulos. Peter "The Golden Greek" wasn't one for the spotlight. He was a man who worked behind the scenes to make Amazing Wrestling great. A friend to many wrestlers, managers, and promoters, Peter's keen eye for detail and bottomless laughs helped make Amazing Wrestling the #1 magazine for all your wrestling needs. The entire staff of Amazing Wrestling miss our Greek hero and offer his wife and children our condolences. Next month we will be featuring tributes from the greatest wrestlers in the world, but it is the staff here at Amazing Wrestling that knew him best. Here are some recollections of The Golden Greek.

Val Weston, Publisher

Poets are better suited to tell you how rotten it is to lose such a talent, and I'm sure that no-account Flashman will spend many ten-dollar words trying to do just that. I'm just a cub journalist who's seen men destroy each other in the ring every day of my life. Only those men get back up to fight another day. Losing Peter is like showing up to work and instead of mayhem there's just silence. Peter made everyone's day better by being tougher, smarter, and funnier than the entire cast of Saturday Night Live (except that kid who plays Buckwheat).

Warren Wexter, Chief Journalist, Amazing Wrestling

"That is not dead which can eternal lie,
And with strange aeons even death may die." E. A. Poe.

Even the most primitive intellects who "read" this magazine, minus the Neanderthals who just enjoy the pictures, know that the end comes for us all. No man can escape the vice-grip of Lady Death as she bequeaths us the gift of release from our mortal coil. Not even the "Golden Greek" Peter Kardassopoulos (whose name, I dare say, no one in this magazine but I can spell without the aid of a Greek dictionary or the local Gyros merchant). Peter was a rare creature, not unlike me: an intelligent fan of professional wrestling. We spent many afternoons deconstructing heroic archetypes (that's Princeton talk you will never understand) over flaming ouzo and fresh baba ganoush, and placing non-monetary bets on the Sport of Gods (he was almost as accurate as me). I shall miss having someone around whose intelligence was almost as high as mine, and infinitely superior to anyone reading this condolence. Νάρκη με ειρήνη.

Frederick Flashman III, Esquire

Damn, foo'. Forty be too young to die, even for a jive talking cracker like Peter K. Wonder who he ticked off in this crooked game of chumps and thugs, where the real men are exploited, demoted, or ejected. I smell a conspiracy, youngbloods. Whoever is responsible, you better hope I don't find you in Harlem, Turkey. Shame you became a victim of a rigged system, Peter K. A rat-low, no-good shame.

Leroy LeBull

Given my perpetual travels around the world, I rarely got to work with Peter directly, but he was only a long-distance call away. He knew all the best Chinese restaurants from Toronto to Java, and he was the greatest editor I ever worked for. Here was a man who knew the art of the interview, the right questions to ask and the ones to avoid, which wrestlers to test and which ones to grill, and the need to always check their stories against the facts. I'll miss having you on the other end of the line, Peter. Godspeed.

Charles Clifford, writing from Pago Pago,
American Samoa

My heart broke upon hearing of the death of my dear friend Peter. A warm laugh and good person are hard to find in this business. Peter had both, and he found a place for this double-tough gal from Buffalo Chips, Nebraska to tell her stories and spotlight all the hair-pulling and crotch-snatching actions in the thriving apartment scene. Will miss our monthly poker games at the Caboose Lounge in New Jersey. You always made my heart submit. Kisses and head-locks, Peter.

Wendy Waves

Peter was a wonderful man and editor. Simply irreplaceable. He laughed at my corny jokes and even my crass attempts at sketch comedy around the office, always offering the same suggestion. "Great stuff, Teddy, but next time try to make it funny!" No one can fill your shoes, Golden Greek. We will miss you.

Ted Filkers

THREE

LITTLE NUKE

Princeton, New Jersey, December 10th, 1983.

Outside Dad's house, my fist was tight. Scattering wisps of snow annoyed my face. I huffed breath. Didn't want to open my fist. Or open the door.

Inside, a voice sang about wrestlers from *Bad Streets, USA.* Throaty and scuzzy like Michael "P.S." Hayes.

I jammed my hand in my pocket. The fist relaxed and the card breathed in the dark. I plucked my house key from my brown cords and they dug against my skin with a burr. I opened the door and was hit with yellow light.

"Special delivery," I said, walking through the kitchen.

From the living room to the right came the butchered singing voice. "Sully?"

I blew my nose into a well stained McDonald's napkin, then tossed the plastic bag full of wrestling mags. Kara ducked and screamed on the plush green couch as if I'd catapulted napalm. "Incoming!" I yelled.

"What's your damage?" she said, all smiles and giggles. She was rail thin in the old Columbia sweatshirt Dad had bought me. "Are there old ones?"

"Mostly. Picked the bloodiest covers I could."

"Grody!"

I sat next to her on the couch we called Rhino. Camel smoke rose in the air. Covering her mouth, Kara did her little cough. The one that would grow. Winter was murder on her lungs. She wheezed like a piano-man from Greenwich who lived on Century Sams and toilet gin, but she was the happiest person I knew. "Am I in time for *AAW* on ESPN?" I asked.

She looked up from the mags, pale as the moon through a grease-smudged window "Five minutes! Hey, are you staying for dinner, or are you on deadline?"

"Actually, I need your help."

"You still don't have a TV, do you?"

"Nope." Most of my facts came from calling promoters, listening to Val, bugging Peter, reading other mags or, when I was desperate, talking to Ted. And talking to Ted got me into this mess. "I also need to ask your advice on a top secret project."

"Seriously? Like, for real?" Another little cough, straight out of Dickens. "Gnarly!"

"Yeah. Gnarly." I got up and walked over to the *Fangoria* mags littering the coffee table. The cover sported what looked like mutant Shanghai Noodles bursting out of a two-hundred-pound TV. A Cronenberg flick called *Videodrome* that I hadn't seen. Being five writers ate most of my time and kept me from the Liberty Theater. Hell, I hadn't seen *Return of the Jedi* yet (though apparently Darth Vader got thrased by some teddy bears so I guess I wasn't missing much). Few people craved gore like Kara. In these slasher and wrestling mags were monsters. But ones she could face. Demons she could banish. Devils that didn't live in her pulmonary system.

I grabbed the TV's knob and turned hard. The thud and click continued until Kara said "Stop!" and I heard ESPN groan about real sports stats. "It's not on yet! Tell me what you need!" I crossed my arms. "Swear not to tell a soul?"

She crossed fingers on both hands. "Double swear. Not even Dad."

"Perfect." I reached in my back pocket for my moleskin, then took a stray ballpoint from the table. "What can you tell me about the Atomic Kid?"

One gasp and four minutes later, I had it all.

Six-foot-tall, dense and strong, but not a muscle idiot from Venice Beach. "He can wrestle, Sully. He knows moves from Japan. Top rope stuff. Holds and counters. But when you make him mad, he explodes!" Like an atomic bomb. A one-man Hiroshima with only a single casualty, his opponent. Their fate was *Idiot Assured Destruction!*

AK, as the marks chanted, was the newest star, poached from Calgary Stampede Wrestling, a weirdo Canadian league where TV Psycho had been the main attraction until AK showed up. AK got booted because, according to Kara, "he's too much of a rebel, more rock and roll than country."

Rock and roll? That was different.

Rock and roll had crept into wrestling about forty years late. So much of rasslin' was Southern and stupid, and the old promoters hated new shit unless it was a one-time attraction. GWA was trying to rope in big-name metal bands, but most of the Black Sabbaths of the world still gawked. So Junior Cassidy had dropped them for boxers and karate men. Now AAW was tuning into teen headbanger culture? Like GWA, AAW was an independent promotion. Innovative since the 1950s. The Swede had been one of the great wrestlers of his day. Legit tough guy. Even played in the NFL for the Denver Broncos before he realized he had more fun in the ring. But the NWA didn't think he would put asses in seats like Lou Thesz, so the Swede said "fuck it" and started his own promotion in the Midwest. Like the Mahones in New York, an independent spirit against the other promotions – and it thrived.

AAW was fun. There were matches with ladders and chairs, there were steel cages and tournaments of wrestlers from around the world. The Swede didn't do spectacle like Little Junior. No bears. No midgets. No boxers and kung fu people (except for the alleged signing of Bruce Lee right before the master died). The core was still "wrestling," but around it was a wild ride of *characters*. Larger than life but not full cartoons. Unless those cartoons looked like they could slap you to death on the docks.

But AAW's problem was on the covers. The gods of the 1970s had saggy guts and dyed hairlines receding like roaches against lamplight. But the Swede knew it. Kara called a lot of the talent "the New Breed," younger guys from around the world and many local faves, like the Swede's talented but goddamn boring son, Alan. But the leading light was AK, who according to Val was going to lead the company and beat their champ, Nathaniel Princeton, the self-proclaimed "smartest man in wrestling" who was part-femme, part-aristocrat, and apparently a real tough guy if Val was to be believed.

"Princeton keeps getting disqualified," Kara said, yanking a few mags to her lap"so he never loses the belt to AK."

"Well," I said, already tired but not wanting to haul ass to the Greyhound station, "titles only change hands in pin-falls or submissions."

"I know that, doofus! And AK's submission move is so rad, Sully. It's called the Tarantula Death Lock!"

A Japanese wrestling move. Looks painful, as if the tangling of legs and bending of back is crippling the dude's tendons, knees, and spine. Does zilch, other than massage your spleen. A perfect wrestling move. "Sounds like you're a fan."

"I am! And it's on!"

Kara coughed, harder, but kept bouncing as I took a seat next to her. Favorite thing about being with Kara? She doesn't care who I am. I don't have to be funny. I don't have to be mean. I don't have to cop an attitude or be an adult. I can just *be*. 1

Techno synth played against a vacant cosmos when BOOM! All of a sudden a wrestling ring crashed into the screen and the old-school logo of the AAW appears: two blue and white cartoon men pretzeling each other. *"All American Wrestling is on the Airwaves!"*

And then a moderately filled arena was alive with screaming fans.

"Coming to you live from the St. Paul Auditorium, it's Main Event Super Card! Good evening everyone, I'm—"

"Tony Masters!" we said in unison with his stiff Midwest high school coach pitch, Kara excited, me in rote. A chunky man in a yellow sport coat and red tie with mid-forties sideburns stood next to a splotch-tanned man dressed in purple spandex, rainbow costume jewelry, and sunglasses. White-blond hair leaked beneath the rim of his beret like frayed spaghetti. *"Joining me as always is the Champion of Style, and five-time former AAW tag-team champion, Doctor Aces."*

Aces smiled with a snarl. At Ming's Noodle Hut, Peter had once said, "I love Ace. Fat as fuck and can do a two-hour Broadway in the ring with all those muscle heads and leave them gasping. The slob lives on white lightning and fried chicken and can keep up with any cardio machine, and what a talker. Like Little Richard gave birth to a white baby from Daytona. Nice guy. Actually will do an interview if you call him. Just drop my name."

"Listen up Tony Baloney because the Ace in this Place and the King of all Space is only going to say this once... to Your Face! Tonight, we are going to see history made in front of all these fans and a million or so out in TV-Land. Because here, tonight, this evening, we will see a dynasty made live when the Atomic Kid—"

The roar of the crowd lit itself on fire. My ears trembled. I'd played in a hundred shit bars with crooked PA systems and crowds ranging from sad to psychotic. Could read them like Spider-Man read danger. Only I didn't get "smell lines" around my head. Just eardrum shakes. And *this* crowd was livid. Raw and loud and distorted. Most audience reactions were canned or "sweetened." Not here.

Aces cranked up his volume to match the crowd and the mutual distortion tangled so that his voice could barely be decoded. *"See, Masters? The people know I ain't lying! To-night the Atomic Kid is finally going to best that pest with the belt of the best, Nathaniel*

Princeton!" Cold as my knuckles were, they were rosy compared to the crowd's frostbitten boos. *"Tonight, the AK is going to be champion, okay? AK, Okay!"*

Masters pulled the mic to himself as the crowd chanted "AK! OK!" *"That's our main event, so don'tcha dare miss it later in the program. Right now, back to the ring and Earl Flowers!"*

Mid-card matches rolled on. I nodded as Kara commentated better than Masters and almost as good as Aces. Wrestlers hustled their move sets while my right hand smushed against the crumpled card in my pocket. Bodies crashed. Eyes poked. Punches and slaps and slingshots into the ropes. I knew their ring names, real names, and backstories, all gifts from Peter who was easy to work with in a way Val wasn't allowed to be. But right now I didn't give a shit. I had a weird gig to "spotlight" the Atomic Kid or lose my livelihood.

Two weeks in the state where my dead mom lived.

Kara crunched graham crackers as she talked until a thunder of metal guitars injected itself into the crowd. Not rock and roll. Metal. Like Black Sabbath with Ozzy. Good stuff. "That's it! That's his theme music!"

"Coming down the aisle," Tony said, *"weighing two-hundred and seventy-five pounds, hailing from FinchTowne, Minnesota, he is the number one contender for the AAW Heavyweight Champion—"*

Then it was white noise as the curtains spread.

He jogged to the ring. Big. Cultivated muscle. Wild eyed stare at the dead center of black grease paint smeared around his eyes. Manic energy like a Dead Boys show. Limber, not weighted down and slow like most strong men, and his face ... white as a ghost except for two letters etched in his forehead in black—

AK.

"The Atomic Kid!"

Then he smiled. Big, bright, and knowing. Missing one of his canines. Goofy and menacing. The crowd loved it. He owned it.

My hand coiled around the card in my pocket.

"That's him, Sully!"

The number one contender.
AKA: AK. AKA: The Atomic Kid
AKA …
Robbie Varhooven.
My cell mate at Red Wing.

FOUR

THE MINNESOTA MODEL

MINNESOTA STATE TRAINING SCHOOL
1079 County 292 Blvd, Red Wing, MN 55066

September 28, 1973
To: Mr. Alexander
Concerning: Final Incident

Dear Mr. Alexander,

This letter follows up the discussion Dr. Stinson had with you this week. I regret to inform you of the latest incident concerning your son, Sully Alexander, at our facility at Red Wing.

Five days ago, Sully and another inmate were involved in what I can only call a bizarre wrestling game. It involved attacks on other students and garish costumes and women's make up. Several suffered serious injuries. When we spoke last month about Sully's own injuries, I had taken your son's word at face value that they were from general roughhousing during fitness breaks. I now see a larger pattern. When this "game" was discovered, Sully and the other inmate resisted confinement in quarters. Many guards were needed to restrain them and some received injury. Sully is currently in quiet confinement until the next step of his rehabilitation has been decided. This decision has not been made lightly, nor is it my preferred method of correction, but I am entrusted with the safety of both inmates and staff at Red Wing. Including that of your son.

Sully is a weak boy. It has been my professional stance since our first conversation that his criminal acts, outward aggression, and de-socialized behavior are a direct result of his mother's absence and unorthodox employment. Indeed, Sully threatened guards and social workers with violent retribution from the "Black Widow," a reference to his mother's wrestling persona. In short, he remains an abnormal child. He has difficulty in separating fantasy from reality. He also wishes for his mother to return and protect him, instead of developing the ego and maturity to function in such normative environments as school or employment. What's worse is that he is corrupting others. We have segregated them into different blocks as a first step towards rehabilitation, but Sully's leadership in this anti-social behavior has led us to consider far more severe consequences to his actions, especially given the violent nature of his arrival.

Sully will soon be reassigned to Block 9 for more intensive work and rehabilitation. It is my belief that separation from others, isolation from popular culture, and an increased focus on skills and compliance will help him complete his sentence without further incident. However, this is also Sully's last chance. Further obstruction or abnormal behavior will result in greater restriction and possible relocation to an adult correctional facility. I do not like writing this letter to you, as I feel that the failures here are strictly with his mother. But you are his father and responsibility rests with you.

Our board of directors has agreed to a single phone call with you before his term of reassignment begins. I strongly suggest you take this opportunity to influence Sully's behavior in a positive light.

Dr. Jack Palate

FIVE

MEMENTO MORI

Across Robbie Varhooven's ghost-white and massive chest was a black mushroom cloud. Or a tree. Couldn't tell because he didn't stop moving, spinning, and twisting to see the fans. His eyes were also blacked out like an old-school mask. Paint or ink, he looked like Gene Simmons from KISS if he had spent the past ten years lifting trucks instead of getting VD from anything with a pulse.

It was Robbie. That missing tooth made him look like a giant kid, but the wide eyes gave the childish mouth a maniacal twist. Under the spotlight and next to the ref, he looked like he had become Gonzo Achilles again, founding member of the Night Shift, our "tag team" name for the tournament we ran in the showers and yard and bathroom at Red Wing. Gonzo Achilles and me … The Demon.

Robbie spun in the ring and pointed at the crowd while I tried to shove the image of his gap-toothed and wild-eyed younger self onto this one. I had no pictures of him. Red Wing didn't allow us to take them. His face on TV was déjà vu kicking my balls.

"I bet he could slam Moab the Giant," Kara said, then coughed.

Last time I saw him he was being dragged away by two guards, the shoe polish mask on his face still shiny. "Stay gold, Demon!" he screamed. That line was from the only book he'd ever read. They made a movie out of it, full of pretty Hollywood boys. The Demon? He would have knifed the screen. Gonzo would have taken a dump in the aisles.

"And now coming down the aisle, accompanied by his manager Gary "The Genius" Sheen, he is the AAW World Champion ... Nathaniel Princeton!"

"Gag me with a spoon!" Kara coughed through a Valley Girl accent she'd picked up from her weekly viewing of *Square Pegs.* "And dad says he's not alumni."

Nathaniel Princeton's robe dragged behind him like a purple-and-white rhinestone wedding dress. The colors of Roman nobility (thanks, elective humanities courses). In the sand and sword days, a returning general would have a slave in his chariot. The slave knew one phrase in Latin.

Memento Mori. "Remember: you will die." A reminder that no matter how hard you thought you were, one arrow through the heart and you are worm shit.

In wrestling, it was the reverse.

"Shut up you apes," Gary the Genius yelled as he walked in front of Princeton. *"This man is a god! Immortal! Hands off the robe, peasant!"*

Princeton was cut from the 70s mold. Thick-muscled with zero attention paid to his diet. There was steak in that belly, beer in those arms, and his blond moustache didn't match his well-groomed and blown, moderately long black locks.

"This is sure to be an instant classic!" said Tony Masters, right before a key jostled the front door.

"What?" Kara said. "No! He said he was working late! I can't miss this!"

Leaning forward, I grabbed the wrestling mags and shoved them under my ass while Kara crossed her arms. The bell rang. The door opened.

He stood five-foot-eleven, and he inhabited every bit of it as he dusted off an inch of snow from shoulders, hat, and what he called "rubbers." He weighed about two hundred pounds thanks to Dunkin Donuts being his breakfast since forever. He hailed from Omaha, Nebraska but now resided in Princeton, New Jersey. He is the current tenure-tracked professor whose work on Edgar Alan Poe has earned him a legion of weird and depressing fans. He is Damon "The Raven" Alexander!

"Kara? Dinner." He bashed the snow off his green puffy coat with his hat. Dad's black hair was rich with sweat, snow, and pomade. In his left brown glove was a soaking McDonald's takeout bag and a briefcase with one lock missing. "Kara? Why are there wet tracks through the kitchen?" Kara said nothing, eyes on the match. AK and Princeton were sizing each other up as the ref held the sixteen-pound gold-and-diamond belt between them.

"Kara?" Then he saw me. "Oh." The burgers looked ready to drop out of the bag's saggy ass. "You didn't call." He walked into the kitchen, rubbers still on, tracing the steps I took. Dad had the kind of five o'clock shadow actors in the 1950s used to show they were "alcoholics." He stood between the kitchen table and the counter with the knives. The bag swayed.

"Can't stay long," I said. "Wanted to see you two before I left."

"Left?" Kara said. "Where you going?"

AK got jumped by Princeton. "Kara." Dad said, with a frown at the television.

"I wanted to watch it," I said.

Dad's smug professor smile emerged. "Then you can turn it off."

Kara's mouth shook, but this wasn't my house. And I needed something.

A flurry of punches from The Atomic Kid had the fans going apeshit as I strode over to the table, wrestling mag sticking to my ass, and twisted the knob. The TV died.

"No! Sully, you can't do that!"

"Kara" Dad said, soft as a library whisper. "Enough."

Silence hummed between us. Dad took heavy steps into the family room and put the bag on the table. "Eat your dinner."

An Alexander family standoff. Dad stood before his kill, likely cheeseburgers and fries by the smell. Dad could wait. Stay still. Old Iron Spine got a kick out of being a sentinel. Kara's power was to suffer. Hunger strike. Make him feel bad for being the only one who could care for her. Me? I was the ghost. But I couldn't vanish yet. "Go on," I said. "Eat. I'll tell you who wins later."

"Not the same," she whispered, then reached for the bag.

Dad blinked, keeping his insults to himself, then walked past me. "My office." He walked to his bedroom. I mimed eating a burger. Kara shook her head and mouthed a question. I made the *shhh* finger, followed Dad.

He walked into the dark of the room, then hit the light. Shadows plastered the walls. Old Spice and weeks of undone laundry fought for the prize of dominant odor. The twin bed was made. The tiny wooden writing desk with its electric typewriter was neat. Alongside one wall was stacked a collection of hardback books, mostly with POE on the spine in some gothic or slick printing. Dad was allergic to anything written after The Mexican-American War. Nothing hung from the walls. Not even a mirror. The bedroom of a man who had given up fucking.

"Shut the door."

I did.

Dad turned and unzipped his winter jacket. "How much?"

"I don't need money."

"You don't do social calls," he said, draping the jacket on his work chair. "You look sick."

"I have a cold."

"I bet. We had a deal. Keep that junk out of Kara's sight."

My voice always turned weak around Dad. So I tried Belushi, RIP: wide eyed surprise and slow burn fuse. "I get them for free, from a job *you* got me, man."

"Friend," he said, warming his hands together in mock prayer, "I helped you get admitted. You found that degenerate internship. Not me." Dad had two terms. "Sport" meant he liked you like Gatsby liked Nick Calloway. "Friend" was for tolerating a malignant peer. "Don't bring that trash here."

For a handful of times as a teen, I had to sit in on dad's university lectures, sucking on a mushed piece of Red Delicious apple he'd cut with a butter knife. Here's what I learned. Poe was America's greatest writer because he emerged out of the gutter of gothic lit. He cranked out stories about living houses, crazy birds, and torture. But the class angle? Of being better than his genre? That's what appealed to the fat kid from Nebraska.

To me, Poe's life was pathetic. And his stories were boring. But his journalism? Gonzo.

The West Point loser who wrote "The Raven" started as a journalist. But he was lazy. He turned a bunch of his gothic nightmares into "true" tales about balloon journeys to the moon and hypnotists that froze people between life and death. He blended bullshit and reality. Dad called it "mystification." I call it pro wrestling for the 19th century. Americans liked to be fooled by fantastical crap, and then loved being righteous about it being fake. Dad pulled a string and got me into Columbia's journalism department. He didn't think I had what it took to be a writer, or a teacher, but slumming among the normal? Maybe that was the best I could do. My payback? I found a supervisor who was punk enough to be interested in "mystifications." Nikola Kardassopoulos was a former city crime reporter in Boston and pop culture freak. His classrooms were always full because he'd reference Star Wars as much as Woodward and Bernstein. Nik was Peter's kid brother, youngest of five, the respectable one who didn't do side gigs writing wrestling trash or porn novels with titles like *Father Fucks Best* or *Lesbian Dick Challenge*. "Talk to Pete," Nik had said. "He works in mystification on a daily basis! He's fighting a rebellion against the Dark Side of reality." I dropped out before that thesis turned into an abstract. When Acid Shit broke up Peter took pity. Mystification was how I paid my rent. Barely.

Dad breathed exclusively through his nose. "You broke your deal."

It consisted of three rules. One, never use my real name. It would ruin his reputation as a scholar of Poe. Two, never, ever bring wrestling shit to Kara. Three, never surprise him. For three years I'd been good. Drugged out and alone, but the rules were sacred. Now?

"Just wanted to bring her a gift."

"You missed her last two birthdays."

"Because of the rules you made."

"Don't talk back."

I thought she'd like them."

"Sully. I want you to leave."

"That's why I'm here." I reached into my pocket. Dad stopped blinking. Hands loose at his sides, basic training still in his academic brain. Just in case. "Don't freak," I said, drawing out the crumpled card.I held it in front. "This true?"

He leaned forward, examined. Teeth set. "Where'd you get that?"

"She's not dead?"

His big mitten hand rose, then rubbed his neck as he turned his back. "Quiet."

"That means yes," I said, loud enough so Kara could hear me all the way from the living room.

That turned him around. "I said *quiet*."

"Answer the question."

"What do you want? An apology?"

"Ten birthdays. Christmases. Mother's Days."

"You're being dramatic."

"You conned me."

"Listen to you. I can't believe that mag pays you to write."

I put the card in my pocket. "You said she died."

"She did. From our lives."

"God, you sound as bad as my writing."

"She was no good, friend. I did you a favor. She did you a favor staying the hell away."

I snorted. "Explains why I turned out so great."

"Blame yourself. You're a goddamn adult acting like a street kid, too smart for his own good and yet no spine to do the work to make a life for yourself."

I laughed. "You should work for Hallmark. You'd be a real hit on graduation day."

Dad leaned. "Get out." Rye laced his breath, mean and real. The preferred drink of angry farmers and their bookish children. Pete said the witches of Salem were likely drunk on bad grain in their bread. Low embers of anger flickered in my dad's eyes. "Now."

"I'm going to see her. It's for work."

He grinned. "Why do I care?"

"Kara might."

Fury flushed his cheeks. The war in my dad's eyes wanted out. But like his Great God Poe, Dad was a thinker as well as a feeler. He'd led me into this room. To beat the shit out of me if I pulled something. Kara outside the blast radius he believed was inside me like a bomb built in hell. But Kara still needed protecting. We'd been fed the same lie.

"Fine," Dad said, smooth and low. "You want money for dope, or glue, or whatever the scabs you run with do?" He lifted a mattress and took out the yellow envelope we all knew he hid. "Take as much as you want, you degenerate."

"Don't need your money. I want your jacket."

"What?"

"I don't have a jacket that can handle real cold."

"Just take the money and buy one."

I shook my head. "Your jacket. Flask included. And I'll leave." His lip shook. "Quietly."

He returned the envelope. When the mattress went down I felt a rush of power that made me feel electric. He grabbed his jacket, then glared. " You're going to Minnesota?"

"Yep."

"To see her?"

"Yep yep."

He snorted, handed me the jacket, then pulled it back in a pathetic attempt to control me. "Not a word to Kara. Or I'll make sure you never see her again."

"Dad? Gimme the fucking jacket."

He shot his fist out. My eyes winced, but I didn't move. His punch held the jacket before my chest. I took it. He clenched tighter before letting go. "Don't come back."

Screams broke our glares.

He shoved me aside. I rebounded off the bed like ring ropes, bouncing back to follow him into the white light of the rest of the house.

"Kara?" Dad said. "What's wrong?"

She was wheezing, pointing at the screen, left hand shaking her inhaler. She'd turned the TV back on, but killed the volume.

Dozens of people flooded the ring. Men in regular clothes. Security. Princeton was pale. Eyes shocked. Refs and security huddled around one figure.

The Atomic Kid lay on the canvas. Medics deadlifted one side of him, then slid a gurney underneath. Face slack. Eyes wide as if electrocuted. No peace. Kara wheezed while Robbie's mouth hung open.

"He's dead! He's *dead!*"

PART TWO

MARKS

SIX

MY LITTLE MONSTER

June 5ᵗʰ, 1968

Hey Kid Kong! How's my little monster? Your daddy said you're Prince Valiant of the school yard. That's my boy! Always go after the big and nasty ones and show them they can't push you around. Go for the wrists like I showed you. Pinch hard and never be scared to scratch their eyes or knee them in the "no no" place.

Are you still enjoying Bewitched? One of the ladies I'm beating up across America is one of those witches! This piece of work is called Alice Nightshade and she rides a broomstick to the ring! Don't worry, though, your momma's tougher than any old witch. Right now I'm in Alabama. Do you know where that is? Go find it on the map I left you and put a pin in a city called "Mobile." I'm meeting all kinds of interesting people. There's a cowboy named Bob who talks funny and has a big beard. He's real nice. There's a woman named Mildred who claims she was born on a spaceship and talks like a hippie. She's help-ing me share the drive as I beat up Nightshade in every town. And of course you remember those rascally midgets, Flip and Flop. They all say hello and wish you a happy birthday (sorry this is so late!). There's a restaurant out here called Waffle House and I think you'd like it. Do you like waffles? I'll make you some when I come back. I love them, but they don't build much muscle. Watch your sugar, Kid Kong.

Help your daddy around the house. You have my permission to steal the scary books he collects in the basement! And know your momma loves you very much. When I come home, I promise it will be ice cream and cake for a week! Plus, by then, your momma will be champion! Bear hug from the road!

M

March 3rd, 1970

Hey Kid Kong! Happy Valentine's Day from Anaheim! How are you? I'm trying like heck to get home for your birthday, but when you're a champion you're fighting all the time. I'm sorry I couldn't get you out here to Disneyland, but enjoy these pictures. Doesn't Mickey look funny with my championship belt? For a giant mouse he sure is weak, though. Cried out loud when I slapped on my chicken wing!

Guess where I'm going next? Canada! Do you know where it is? Look for a place called Vancouver (not the lousy town in Washington State, but the nice one in British Columbia). Then I'm going across the Rockies to Calgary, that's where Canada has cowboys. Remember Bob, the Cowboy? He's from there and I'm going to see him and so many other characters like those Samoan Bros, that Bruce Lee guy, and this goofy army guy called Corporal Punishment. They're like your funny book characters come to life (or do you still want me to call them comics?). Sometimes we ride together and I swear to Christ it looks like the Munsters are in town. Keep putting in those pins in your map and you'll know where I am and what I'm doing.

Time to go to the gym and work off this road food. I know you must think it's all glamor and waffles, but your momma is working all the time and sending back checks. Remember why I do this, my little monster.

M

PS: Don't listen to your dad about fighting. That's a lot of non-sense. Long as you're beating up people who are mean, your momma is in your corner. And if they get too nasty, tag me in!

January, 1972

I don't even know why I'm writing you. I should write your dad but he's impossible to talk to because he won't listen. Funny thing about men with fancy degrees, just because they're smart at one thing they think they know everything.

Maybe that's why. You always listen, don't you? You always help. You don't get it, thank Christ, but you help. He used to tell me when you'd see me on TV and cry when some Angel was slapping the shit out of me. You care. I know you do. I can feel it. Even far away. I know you're watching and cheering me. Each pin you put in the map, I can feel it. I do feel it. I feel everything. Why does no one get that? It's why I do it. For them. For you. It's what makes the miles and bumps and the stuff that crawls into my nightmares go away. You're my number one fan. And I never see you or your pins. I probably won't recognize you when I come home. Shit, you'll probably get a driver's license, hit the road, and I'll never see you again. God, I'm a rotten mother. Never wanted the fucking job, but that's not your fault. Why do you think I'm on the road? You don't want me around, trust me, but your idiot father thinks differently and pulled a goddamn fast one and now it looks like I'm coming home to stay. Fucking idiot just ruined your life, too. I had it all figured out, Kid Kong. Was going to bankroll your future. They were going to make a movie about me. Me. Not your dad or Poe and loser shit no one reads anymore. I was going to make your future so goddamn plush and easy you'd never know hunger, you'd never know how cold it really gets in St. Paul. Instead I've got a present I can't get rid of and need to bring it back to you guys. Little nuclear time bomb that killed my career.

Whatever happens, know this much. I tried.

M

PS: Burn this after reading.

SEVEN

SLEEPER

The sour heat and clank of the Dinky ride to the Junction kept me awake. I shuffled in the warmth of Dad's jacket past the huddled masses of red-faced and raw humanity that bundled around the bus station, belly full of a cold Big Mac.

"Change, brudd-a?"

"Light?"

"You hold'n?"

Got an overnight. Mainlining the 80 to Chicago, then the 90, then 94 through the wasteland of the flyover states. Twenty-seven hours starting with a redeye Greyhound. A toxic sardine tin packed with the working poor's sweat- and snow-slapped faces. A touring band that hated each other but said nothing but grunts, silent farts, and mutters of the way things used to be.

I'd left Dad's house the night AK died, after consoling Kara and saying something very, very stupid. Even a few swigs of the cherry – or maybe I should say red, because the flavor was as natural as a Penthouse model's tits – NyQuil I'd swiped from Dad's bathroom couldn't erase it from my memory.

"I'll find out what happened," I'd said.

Dad told me to shut up but Kara's wet eyes were glued to me.

"I'm going back. To Minnesota. That's why I needed you to tell me about AK. Now I'm going to find out what happened. And you'll be the first one I tell, Kara. You're Watson, I'm Sherlock."

Dad told me to stop. For him, the great detective was Poe's August Dupain, a little computer in the shape of a midget Frenchman who had no emotions and solved things by thinking like a calculator. The kind of asshole who tells a pretty girl her ghost story is horse-shit, it's just the wind.

I put on my best Peter O'Toole. "I say, do you get me, dear Watson?"

Her tears stabilized. Kara nodded. "You're really going back?"

I'd promised I'd keep her up to date on my investigation. If there was any foul play, she'd be the first to know.

"Bet it was Princeton."

"Kara, that's enough," Dad said. "He's probably fine."

What he didn't say, what I heard every time I watched wrestling, was that it was *fake*. It was pretend. It was bullshit. A ruse. Phony. I'd received lectures on the stupidity of the masses and how grown-ups fell for this junk like headlines in the Enquirer or thinking soap operas were real. It was delusion for the idiots of the world. A load of bunk. Dad made sure to I was not among the intellectually inferior scabs of the world since I was about eight years old. But not Kara.

I knew wrestling was made up, but pretended otherwise. For every argument Dad made I had a counter-hold. Why don't their noses break when punched ten times? They're tougher than you, Dad! Why do they slap their legs when they do a kick? To wake up strained muscles! Why do the good guys never look behind them? Because they have a code of honor and expect the villains to fight fair!

Of course, I knew it was bullshit. It was just easier to be a smart man's dumb kid than find a better identity. Plus, you couldn't out-smart dumb. No matter how well or clever the argument, no matter how convincing the evidence, I could just say "You don't get it, Dad. You just don't get it."

But Kara? She was still a mark. Santa Claus was bullshit but wrestling was still as real as school and asthma attacks, and often more important—if less serious.

The trump card of reality sat in my pocket. I could shatter his lie. Instead, I kept up kayfabe. "It might be," I said. "I'll see what I can dig up on him. Thanks for the help, Watson."

Then I raided the medicine cabinet and called a cab Dad paid for to get me to the station.

On the bus, snores issuing from men of many colors filled the dark. They became the soundtrack for my numbness. Twisting the cap of red knockout juice, I wasn't sad Robbie was dead. I cared more that the mother I thought dead was still alive.

I pulled a heavy and hard swig. Liquid licorice mixed with menthol splashed my lips as I settled in for the long haul, hoping the chemicals would drown my dreams and I'd awake in a frozen land of bad memories and dead friends.

"Hey, man?"

Shut up, I thought at the darkness.

"Hey, I don't mean to bug you. But aren't you famous?"

No.

"Yeah, you are. Didn't I see you on TV?"

Nope. Never.

"C'mon, it must be that."

Look, I just want to sleep.

"Yeah, we've seen you. On TV. You're that lady wrestler."

What?

"Shhh. Easy. Don't struggle so hard. It's only going to get worse. Yeah, we like you."

Mmm—

"Feel that, lady wrestler? That's just one bar. We got a dozen. You make a sound and we do a chain gang. You'll be pissing blood for a week. You that tough, lady? Yeah, I didn't think so. Just be real quiet, lady. Just submit and it will get better. Yeah. We thought so.

"Welcome to Red Wing, lady."

EIGHT

KAYFABE

Transcript from ABC Consumer Program CULTURE WATCH, Episode 187, "The Real Deal About ... Professional Wrestling, Part II."

Voice Over (VO): For years, professional wrestling has entertained thousands of Americans across the country. It makes millions of dollars. And it seems to be growing into pop culture. Comedian Andy Kaufman's confrontation with Jerry Lawler on the David Letterman Show was violent, rude, and ratings gold. But was it real? Is wrestling *real*? Chief investigative reporter George Strombone went into the heart of the ring to separate fact from fiction.

George Strombone: You'd think with names like Killer Joe, the Rusty Gears, and Sergeant Massacre that professional wrestlers wouldn't be afraid of answering some questions. But it turns out that to these brawny daredevils with bad attitudes, there is nothing more terrifying than the truth. And as you will see, the truth gets ugly. Here we talk to the men of the Global Wrestling Alliance, New York's biggest promotion, and what they say … well, it wasn't pretty.

GS (VO): I caught up with Killer Joe Pulch, whose tag team partner, the Skeeter Livy, had told me in our first segment that while wrestlers are real athletes, much of what we see is scripted.

KJP: You got questions, little man? Speak up so I can hear you up here where real men can see you eye-to-eye!

GS: Yeah, I got a question, why this job?

KJP: Why this job?

GS: You heard me.

KJP: Better watch yourself, TV man. You're in my world now. And in my world it's the law of the jungle, red in tooth and claw, and you couldn't last three seconds here if I didn't want you to.

GS: Is that why you became a wrestler?

KJP: Damn right. I don't walk around with a buncha sissies. My world is for the tough. You got another question? Do you?

GS: Sure. Skeeter Livy answered this one.

KJP: So what? You're talking to *me* now, TV man. Hurry up as I got business.

GS: Fine. I think this stuff is fake.

KJP: Fake? You calling me fake?

Killer Joe slaps Strombone, dropping him to the floor.

KJP: Did you feel that? Was that fake? That's a Samoan open palm slap. You think it's fake now?

Strombone stands.

KJP: That smart lip ain't so smart is it. Fake?

Strombone is slapped again. He stumbles and walks away as Killer Joe stalks him down the locker room hallway.

KJP: If it's fake, why are you running, boy?

NINE

THE BLACK HOLE OF MINNEAPOLIS

Red stains in my eyes were burned white with sun reflecting off snow.

"Hope I didn't wake you."

No one had sat next to me in the bus as it pulled out of Trenton. Just the ghosts in my head who had turned sleep into nightmares and pushed out a few liters of sweat into my now-damp clothes. Outside, on some freeway, Volvos and trucks slushed through the elements to whatever fucking stretch of Ohio I was burning through.

I turned. Someone was sitting next to me now.

She was plump and thirty. Perfumed and made up with K-mart cosmetics that you tend to see on schoolteachers who need to make a good impression every day. Faux leather boots, black tights, a thick beige skirt.

I rolled my shoulders and felt fresh aches. "Wasn't really sleeping," I said.

"Oh, god, I'm so glad. I'm visiting family in St. Paul."

Fuck if I missed NYC's FU attitude to other people's lives, but a

Midwestern reflex kicked in. "Oh really?"

"Oh yeah," and that Minnesota accent was like a scalpel against my skull. "I love Columbus fine, the schools are great and I swear to god there's always an Applebee's around the corner when I need one, but home is home." She smiled with thick, dull lip tar.

I smiled back. Big mistake.

"Where you from?" she asked.

"New York," I said.

"There's only one reason anyone from New York goes to Minnesota, and the State Fair isn't until July, so where are you from originally?"

"Minneapolis."

"That's so wonderful."

If Mrs. St. Paul had been my English teacher when I was twelve, my fantasy life of riding her like a roller coaster would pop with her screaming "that's so wonderful."

I tried silence, but Minnesotans call that an invitation.

"Are you in a band? You look like a musician."

"Worse. I'm a journalist."

"Wow, a real Woodard or Bernstein."

Deep Throat. Is that what I was going to look like in the Swede's locker room? I tried not to laugh.

She leaned in, warm and flowery. "Is this about that wrestler?"

What the fuck?

"What wrestler?"

"Oh, I heard it on the radio. Some guy died. In the ring. Can you believe it?"

Shit. Until then, I half-wished Dad was right. That AK was OK. "I don't believe anything about that stuff. You know it's fake, right?"

She giggled. And then a familiar scent behind the Minnesota Nice. Orange and vodka. Warm and inviting. "Oh, you are a hoot. Say, wanna enjoy some morning sunshine with me?" And her smile curled. From her purse, those dark brandy nails pulled out a red and white thermos. Six inches of screwdriver later, I was rubbing through her tights while she panted, biting her lip as she stroked me to the disgust of every fart-machine on the bus. She kept eying the bathroom door until an old man shuffled out. "We need room. You go. Leave it unlocked. Sit tight."

Her attempt at sexy-talk reversed every hormone in my body, but I obliged.

Stepping across the rumbling path of the aisle, disdain met me from the Greyhounders. I had one virtue here. I was cute. Not handsome. Cute. Unthreatening. Cute. And once about every three years something like this would happen. I'd be a boy toy to an aggressive woman who liked to take what she wanted.

I opened the door, held my breath …

Before me was a little prison room, smaller than a pauper's grave. Smelled of shit and encroaching death.

Fingers clawing the plastic door frame, I shook before the dark hole of the toilet. The world moved me forward and this image remained still. Blood and shit. A prison made of blood and shit, a taste of iron and brine—

My eyes bugged a second before the inevitable.

Cheeks filled with vomit, I launched my head inside the stall. Acid ate my mouth, but my feet would not step inside.

Robbie called that room at Red Wing the Black Hole of Minnesota. Solitary. A blanket thinner than your calluses. Ants walked between the hairs of your forearm like Tarzan swinging through the jungle. He said the Black Hole would pull you in if your will was not strong. That that's where they shoved the kids who could never be saved. A hole of dead children, orphaned by their families. A bottomless grave ready for the next suicide.

"Are you going in, or what?" said an accent without a body behind me. "Some of us know how to use a toilet without our parents."

My heart snarled before I screamed. Sick chunks of quarter-pounder with cheese soaked in a screwdriver blew past my lip. A scatter gun of vomit painted the toilet before dripping down on my shoes, over as soon as it began. A chorus of quiet boos came from the other passengers. I wiped orange goo from my lip and turned. "Is that how you use it, Daddy?"

Some thirty-year-old asshole in a pink ski jacket and a clean shave stared back. "Oh my god."

"Did I do well, Daddy?"

His nose crinkled as he turned around. "We should have taken the train, Beth."

I sniff-laughed, then walked back to my seat.

My school-time day-dream had fresh make up and an aghast look to match. "God, I meet one New Yorker and he can't hold his liquor."

She let me in, and I sat, all interest now on her trashed copy of Danielle Steele's *Crossings*. I swore I could smell her pussy on the white pages. What was left of the screwdriver lulled me back to sleep without thinking of the Black Hole ...

Lights flickered like my apartment hallway and for a half-sec I thought I was back in New York—

"Hawthorne Street Bus Terminal!" Mouth like sandpaper, I breathed in heat while the glass against my cheek burned cool. "This is the final stop for those heading to Minneapolis. For those transferring to St. Paul, your bus will be at Terminal five. We'd like to thank ... almost everyone for riding Greyhound."

I snickered at the joke, then heard it.

Silence.

No joy. No relief at being out of this iced sardine vehicle. No yawns. No quiet chitter. No kids sniffing. As if a pact had been struck before I passed out to give Sully Alexander the silent treatment. After three beers I used to bore Rat with my big idea: the entire world is high school. It's the god structure of life. It is reality boiled down to its essentials. Rat would usually punch my ear and say "Stop talking like your old man, man!" before shoving a fistful of pills in my mouth.

Everyone got up.

Then I smelled it.

Fetid. As if the whole fucking bus had been holding in their shit and now they were leaking farts.

They stuffed only one lane to get out and marched like overweight marshmallows dragging kids and suitcases and duffle bags while I stayed cozy. Some shot glances. Old ladies grimaced. One tsked about "manners." I smiled. I waved. "Thanks for coming. Bon voyage. Enjoy your stay. Hope you dug the inflight movie."

My English-teacher crush was not amused.

By the time I watched her backside follow the trail out, I realized my legs were lead.

"Last stop," yelled the faceless voice from the driver's seat. "Sir, you have to get off ."

I laughed. "I tried that earlier. Failed spectacularly."

"Sir? You have to get off the bus now. We need to clean it."

I massaged my legs. "Right, sorry. Just gotta get the pins and needles out. Complete accident, by the way."

"Sir, if you don't leave, I'll have to call security."

"What the fuck for?"

"You are not leaving the bus."

"I am too."

"Last time, sir."

I stood, yanked my bag from the luggage rack. "Look, see? Leaving. Stop giving me shit, man. I'm sick."

"I'm sorry to hear that, now please, exit the bus."

I swaggered up to the front. The driver was black, and smiling. "Thank you," he said.

"Don't thank me, man. I'm the asshole who graffitied your shitter. I'm the last person you should be thanking."

But he kept on smiling. Gave me creeps. Who smiles at trash?

I dropped the steps like a rock star on tour, expecting a ring of bus patrons waiting to tear my hide off. Winter infected my skin, woke me, then settled. All of the riders were hustling toward a bathroom with a very long line.

"Hey asshole," said a voice behind me. I turned.

There was Buddy Ski Jacket.

"Sorry, sir, the Alps are that way," as I pointed into the bright night sky with my middle finger.

He pushed me and I staggered back.

"You did that on purpose, you stupid punk."

"Fuck, man, don't start shit."

But he pushed me again. Harder.

"You little rat shits are always making life harder for everyone. Because you're all losers."

The bus's door closed. The driver was smiling. And the security guard turned his back, buried himself in his newspaper. The patrons in line looked on.

All of them.

Conspiracy job. Landed in Minneapolis and made enemies before I had a place to stay.

Then he grabbed me by the collar of Dad's jacket.

"Someone needs to teach you some manners."

How I wished Rat was there. My point had been proven. Every day is high school.

I smiled as my nerves twitched and I could taste the violence between us. "Be my guest, hero."

He drew back a punch and I prepared to tear off his lips with my teeth—

"Stop," came a hard, harsh voice. One washed through a metal strainer and bathed in broken glass and nicotine. Almost mechanical if not for the wheeze.

Its owner wore a long dark brown coat. Thick black boots with metal tips and salt stains older than my underwear. Red hair in a short perm. Face pale, lips red like old blood.

Buddy Ski Jacket turned.

I didn't need to.

The Black Widow Markowitz strode closer, cigarette burning in her right hand at her side. "Let go of my kid, doll."

TEN

UNCONTESTED

Damon,

You win. Asshole. The document you sent is here. I can't believe you got the law involved. You limp dick bastard, hiding behind books and lawyers and you know I'm on the comeback. You know I could make a difference. And you're taking that away from me. Fine. See how well you do without me. I hope Sully is the monster you think he is. I hope he rips your arm off and beats you within an inch of your life. And my baby girl? Every time she says "Where's Mommy" I hope it skins a year off of your cock. You have taken everything. My career. My movie. My life. And you don't have the guts or the patience to just wait, sit tight, and let me bring it home like I said I would. You never believed in me, Damon. You fucking popped a hole in a rubber to tie me down and now as soon as I'm back being who I really am, kill the baby fat you gave me, you take what's mine away. You are the devil's fuck toy and I will never, ever forgive you for making me do this. You'll regret it.

I, Ekatarina Moskowitz Alexander, being of sound mind and body, hereby do relinquish all parental and guardian rights to my children Sully and Kara Alexander to my former husband their father, Damon Alexander.

March 9th, 1975

ELEVEN

MALL QUEEN

Her voice had more authority than her body. She was shorter than I remembered. And the asshole gripping me was a well-fed six-foot-something. She raised her smoking hand. "Did I stutter?"

"Jesus," he said, "you got your mother to fight for you?"

I laughed. "First time for everything."

She shuffled forward. Her visage was pancaked with make-up, but long scars protruded her forehead like a sci-fi alien. Bottle-red hair covered cauliflower ears. At first blush she was a career barfly who had gone legit and now managed a JC Penney. The miles of thos years gave her weight. "Last time I ask." She closed into striking distance, then pointed with her smoke and I noticed … she wasn't wearing gloves. "Hands off."

He dropped me and turned to her. "I feel sorry for you. Birthing a shit like this."

Before I could think to swing a fist, the Black Widow's left hand darted out with her fingers in V formation, jabbing his eyes.

His hands shot up to his face. The cigarette jammed into his right hand and he screamed, stumbling back. "Psycho bitch!"

Quesque c'est, I thought, as the Black Widow walked slow and he backed off fast. "Goddamn right. Now head back to the ski lodge you came from off before I beat you in front of your adoring crowd," she sneered through the window. "Show's over, losers."

Her back to me, I looked for a cab to dive into. No dice. All the traffic was on Hawthorne Street. I'd have to go past her.

She turned. "Sully, you smell like a plugged toilet."

"I come by it honestly. Dad tell you I was coming?"

"More like warned me. He's still scared of you. Never understood it."

You'd have to have been around to understand it, I thought. "He say why I'm here?"

"Didn't need to," she said, digging into her pocket for a fresh cigarette. "But I know. And it ain't because I'm back from the grave."

An old reflex flexed. She was the master of redirection. She wanted me to ask her questions. Instead, I turned and walked away.

"The dead kid in the Swede's ring," she said and I stopped. "You're working for a Weston mag. Biggest thing to happen in wrestling since that Kaufman kid got pimp-slapped on Letterman last year." She had a fresh smoke in her mouth.

"Really?"

She dug out a Zippo lighter she'd been given by some Calgary Cowboy wrestler. She snapped the cap, hit the ignition and took a drag. "And the Swede's on lockdown."

"You talked to Teddy."

She smiled. "Funny little bastard called me. Took a walk down memory lane. He always took great photos of me on the road. I was in Milwaukee with Witch Hazel this one time, at the –"

I walked toward the glass doors to the station.

"Hey, rube! Where do you think you're going?"

"Motel."

"Downtown? Good luck. Place is booked."

"Why?"

"Holidays. Sales convention. Oh, and a dead kid in the ring. NBC, ABC, and CBS vans are plugging down First Avenue near the Swede's office"

"I'll find a place."

"Kid, it's three-thirty in the morning. You don't have a car. You have no place to stay. And you smell like a dog's breakfast. Who the hell would take you in?"

Emergency rooms, and Val's photographer, and if I had to get blitzed and tossed into the county tank, fine. The one thing I wasn't going to do was stay with this dead woman. "Thanks for the assist." I pulled the door.

Heat from the Greyhound station washed over me like a fever. I cut through the line as people muttered beneath their breath. Guts empty, I was hurting for a meal.

I dug in my bag for Val's contact, the photographer C. Ludstone. But he'd given me a number, no address. Shit.

I found the payphones that smelled of filthy boots and mop water. Then I called.

Busy signal.

I waited, tried again.

Busy signal.

I cracked open the white pages and flipped until the Ls. Nothing. I cradled the receiver and looked around.

She was gone.

The itch in my nerves eased.

I punched "0."

"Operator. Can I help you?"

"Yes, I'm trying to find the address for a C. Ludstone at the following phone number."

I gave it. Several clicks.

"This number is out of service."

"Yeah, but what address *was* it?"

"We have none on file."

"What? A phone is attached to a house."

"I'm sorry, but that's all the information I have."

"Can you even say what neighborhood was around it? I need to get there tonight."

"I'm sorry, sir, but that is all the information I have."

"Can you prove you're not a robot by speaking to me like a human being? What would you do if you were me?"

"I'm sorry, sir, but that is all the information I have."

"Do you have a name?"

"…"

"My name is Sully. I'm hungry. I have nowhere to go. This is the way I'll get out of the elements. The streets here kill people. You know that, right? You're from here?"

"…"

"I'm going to call you Donna. I'm asking you, as someone who does not want to die tonight, Donna, please. Help me. I just need an address. That's it. Happy to put in another quarter if that helps."

There was a hiss and click. I took it for a gentle laugh.

"Donna? Are you still there?"

"I'm still here, sir. Hold please."

I sucked in breath.

"You're at the Greyhound station on Hawthorne?"

"Yes, Donna."

"I can give you directions—"

"Thank you! Oh fuck, thank you Donna!"

"—to the local homeless shelter."

I hung up. Frigid, I walked through the bus shelter, past its orange seats and over its black-stained floors. The air was damp, wet, and sick.

I pushed open the door to Hawthorne Street. The cold was no longer amusing. One car sat in the cabbie lane, a blue Pontiac painted with rust, exhaust puffing out its ass. The high beams flashed before it pulled up.

I got in. The ashtray was clean, minus a single crushed butt. But the air was thick as a bar at closing time. The pine air freshener hung from the rearview mirror, dancing as I sat, yet what I smelled was warmth and rum. Christmas. That had been the last day I saw her. She'd worn a fur coat. And smelled like this car. The plastic in the seats creaked and creased under my ass.

"Told ya," she said, pulled out of the lane and drove into the dark of the city I hadn't given five shits about in over a decade. The ride didn't change my opinion. Minneapolis seemed to be in love with art deco, at least downtown. Neon signs. Big marquees. And a sense that we were all being dragged toward a river. Like a shitty Vegas covered in snow.

Vans with national TV logos surrounded the downtown office of the AAW. Fort Swede.

"Told ya."

The windshield clouded in smoke before the heater blew it away.

"You would have been out on the street," she said, "or sleeping in the Skyway."

"Instead, we're going to Dinkey Town."

"Well, look who bought his P. I. License."

"Your friend Teddy told me."

"Yeah, shocked the hell out of me when he said you were working for Val. Didn't take you for being like your old man."

All I had to do was wait.

"Bet you have lots of questions," she said

There it was. The focus was now back on the star of the show.

"And I want to give you answers, but I'm still on the clock."

"Someone break into the Mall of America?"

"That what Teddy told you? That I was the Queen of the Mall? That sweet talker."

Say nothing.

"Not yet. But I do have to do a storefront check before I call it quits. Had to fire one of my elves." Because it's all about her. "Was stealing candy bars of all the goddamn things. So much short-term thinking. Kid kissed away a real job for a ten Baby Ruths."

It was annoying that there was old smoke and yet the warmth ebbed.

"Mind if I listen to the radio?" she said, while turning the knob to some tweedy pedal steel. "That's my music."

"Your music is shit."

She wheezed, then laughed. "You may have your dad's job, but you got my mouth. And I'll take this compared to the snot-nosed noise I suspect you're into. Hell, I was still touring when the Sex Pistols played in Texas in 1978. You think those skin and bones are scary? God, I've fought midgets with more balls. Ever tell you the one about the Chinese Indian?"

"Did it happen after you died?"

"I told you I would talk about that later. It's a long story. I need time."

"I'm just establishing cause and effect. If it was after 1975, you told some other kid."

She grimaced, then laughed. "Smart ass."

"Better than a dumb ass."

She laughed. "A good line. I'm stealing it. Now let's enjoy some silence. I need to get in work mode." She turned up the volume. A castrated cowboy warbled about missing someone so bad it turned his heart to glass. I think he owed Blondie a check. Drifting to sleep, my breath hissed as I slid into a swoon, praying it was dreamless, the slush of tires against snow like the prelude to the flu.

TWELVE

LETTERS FROM THE BLACK HOLE

Hey Demon!

I called your dad and said I was from Red Wing, so he gave me your address. New York? Big time! I hope you're enjoying "wasting your time" as your dad called it. Hope music makes you happy.

I'm in a work house right now in PARTS UNKNOWN! It's not bad. Learning to build cabinets. But these fools don't know I'm saving up for wrestling school. And that's why I'm writing.

I feel sick asking. But, brother, I am lost. I need to find a way out of here. I think if I stay it will kill me. And I know I can make it. I got what it takes. I proved it at Red Wing. You know I don't lie.

And I make you this promise: this will be the only thing I ever ask you for.

Do you know anyone that knew your Mom in the business?

You hate me now. I know it. But I swear I don't have other options.

Please, if you can help, tell me who to call. A name. A person. A place.

I need your help, Demon. Like you needed mine in Red Wing.

Hope you're keeping it sleazy.

Robbie.

PS: Keep this top secret. Send it to Penny. She's back home and helping me with stuff here.

THIRTEEN

GHOST SIGNS

I woke. Dark purple sky was turning blue. Sweat ran off my nose in rivulets, lungs dry. Car was idling. She was gone.

"Fuck."

I was at a four-way stop. Thick snow-covered vehicles on each side, gutters from tires gently filled with black and white slush. To my right was a stone Lutheran church. University Church of Hope. Big. Grey. Flanked by suburbs. Stone steps led to … a large hole … the door was open, leaving a mouth of darkness.

The keys dangled from the ignition, swinging from the hot breath of the heater, under the little green tree freshener. Abandoned. That didn't take long-

A thud.

From the church.

"Fuck."

I yanked the keys out and opened the door. My skin sank fifty degrees, sweat like crystals, eyes starting to freeze. I slammed the door and moved before Minnesota tried to kill me.

The earth was ice and grit, and it took three near-falls until my body woke. Then I hustled up the steps, face numb, frostbite seconds away as another thud came from the dark.

I plunged inside, feeling nothing, and slammed into the inner door.

Godfuckingdamn it.

I grabbed a metal handle that almost fused to my skin. I yanked.

Gloomy lighting filled a vast, empty church, and down by the dais were two swirling figures.

Sliding the keys between my knuckles, I ran.

The swirling figures danced, awkwardly, until they stumbled into the front pew. "Gah!" a male voice cried. "Stupid fucking—"

Whatever warmth the church had must have been reserved for the faithful. My breath trailed behind me as I ran. Her red hair popped up from the pew, snarling. "Last chance."

The grey mass above her screamed, arms raised like King Kong.

I ran, jumped, and launched off the pew like it was the barrier at Max's Kansas City.

The idiot I ran into was thick as a goddamn fridge and moved back three steps as I bounced off him and the floor. I glared up as dawn's light gave away his appearance. Salt-and-pepper gray-haired priest, eyes wide, looked like Solomon Grundy about to crush Robin.

"Not again, Jody! Not again!"

He pinned my shoulders before I could raise a fist, then raised an elbow that could gouge my eye.

From behind, she slapped on a sleeper. Real. A blood choke. Cutting off his carotid artery.

"Jesus, Clancy," she said. "Sleep it off."

He clawed her arm, still in its coat sleeves, then stood. Mistake. She pulled back and the more he strained the quicker the fire died in his eyes. His back arced and her boots landed. Hands in the air, shaking … he suddenly fainted.

"Fwah," she said, releasing the hold and dropping him on his ass. "Swear to god he could have been a wrestler if he wanted." She turned to me and snarled at my fist of keys. "What the hell are you doing with those?"

I got up, keys dug into my hands. "Squaring the odds." I tossed them, and her cold hand snatched them midair.

"More like crippling your stupid hand. Lucky you never got a shot in."

"What was his damage?"

"Bastogne Forest, nineteen forty-four. Fella has more nightmares than Edgar Allan Poe." She grunted. "Forget I ever said that idiot's name."

"Nightmares about robbing his church?"

Spit frothed the priest's mouth. She kneeled. "He's not a thief, kid. He comes here to fight."

"God?"

She lifted his shoulders. "Among others." She glared. "I can't believe you thought keys in your fist made anything other than a trip to emergency for you. Do you even know how to fight?"

The iron of this moment should have been loud enough to wake the dead. I pulled myself into a pew. "You his sponsor?"

"He's my minister."

I smiled. "You're a practicing Lutheran?"

"Never stopped. Martin Luther said there shouldn't be anything between you and God but the bible."

"Yet we're in a church. With a minister who was shadowboxing the holy fuckin' ghost."

She smiled and the last time I'd seen it live was on TV at Red Wing. "Ask yourself this. Can you imagine another church that would have me?"

I stood.

"Where you going?"

I walked away. "Outside."

"Gimme a hand with him first."

You're the Black Widow Moscowitz, former lady wrestling champion, you can drag his sorry ass to the catacombs for all I fucking care, I thought.

But I just kept walking.

"Hey!"

"He's your priest, not mine."

I heard a jingle of metal, turned.

Keys were in midair, fastballing for my face.

Jagged edges bit my lip. They dropped.

"You're supposed to catch them. And good luck getting it started. I left it on because my battery is bananas." *Of course you did*, I thought. I picked them up as she dragged away the sleeping holy man. "Oof. C'mon Clancy. Let's find you greener pastures. And try losing a few pounds before our next match. Willya?"

Mom came out an hour later. The Pontiac was idling, sickly warm, and my hands thawed enough that I could twist the knob to the white noise left of the dial.

She slammed the door. "So you're no help at all. Is that a punk thing? I'm trying to save a holy man's life, get him propped up so he don't sick himself and choke and … " Her penciled eyebrow furled. "You got my bastard car started."

I spread my fingers so the heater warmed the sweat on my hands.

She tapped the keys in the ignition. They danced. "Care to share?"

I yawned. "Kinda been a long day, and now a long night."

She looked at me. Then outside. Then grinned. Her yellow-stained finger stabbed the cigarette lighter. "Which one?"

"Which what?"

"Which one of these cars did you break into, pull in front of this one, and use to jump start mine?"

"If you're so sure," I held my wrists out, "bring me in, officer."

She leaned in, gripping the steering wheel, veins flexed. "You've got a lot of balls to show up in my town, break into cars in front of my church, and not say shit when I ask."

My fingers coiled.

The lighter popped. She laughed. "Hell, maybe you are my kid after all."

We took off, pulling away from the main drag. Deeper into

the burbs.

"What about the Baby Ruth place?"

"That was two hours ago."

The sun was bleeding the sky into purple with pink stains. Shadows were becoming houses. Signs could be read.

I closed my eyes.

"Do you remember this street?"

It was like Godzilla giving a tour of Tokyo and I slid into silence.

"So many changes. Yet some stuff remains the same. Like the ghost signs. You ain't never had a Vernors or been to Art Materials but you they're still there in print. A piece of the past that held on. But fading."

Yeah. Fading.

Into a black hole...

"Rise and shine."

I snorted, woke, shook. Sweat chilled on my skin. The black hole gone. And adrenaline flared as—

I'm here. I'm really here. I keep waking up here. I'm here to do what—

I'm here to find out why Robbie died.

I need to find out why.

Why he died.

Shit …

I need to get to the AAW office. Or the gym.

Contact the photographer.

Contact Robbie's family.

Family.

Shit …

Penny. His sister. My pen pal. The black hole was getting stuffed.

She yanked the parking break. "I already hit my quota for dragging men around the city today. We're here."

Dawn covered everything in white and pink pastels. Dead ahead were a row of houses and parked cars dusted or buried. On my right, a chalet-style house. Compact. Driveway plowed. A really nice place to die of old age.

She opened the door, slammed down her lock, and slammed the door.

The key was still in the ignition.

Whatever.

She walked up the left side of the house, opposite the door.

Figured.

Following, the cold deepened. But the shock was gone. Expect to be numb and the balm of frost pushed into your face was almost comforting. Rat would scream whenever the temperature dropped to sixty degrees. "Colder than an ice cube's balls," he'd say. His lyrics were rarely that poetic.

She shoved open a metal gate covered with green mesh, with holes big enough to shove a Converse through. It closed. I flipped open the lock, kicked it as she rounded the back of the house.

She was down a small flight of stairs to a basement door, key in lock. She smiled. "Welcome to the Black Widow Motel." She shoved the door. "*Entrez-vous*."

I descended and entered the dark.

High windows at the base of the house allowed me enough light to make out the basics

A big main room. A new TV. An old couch. A kitchen with a two-burner stove and counter that divided the room. A hallway that led to a bathroom, I suspected, and the room where the Black Widow nested.

"Let there be light," she said.

With a flick of the switch, she revealed its true nature, bathed in soft yellow glow.

A shrine.

Covering the walls were framed pictures. Most were black and white. Some color. The black and white was more flattering. Each portrayed her choking out a variety of blondes. Face pure rage and black lip tar. Red hair midnight black in most. Her muscles were sharp. Peter once said he liked the older lady wrestlers, especially the heels. "They were tough. Fun. Looked scary like Elvira, which is sexy as hell."

Fresh vomit rose in my mouth.

Some of the frames held newspaper articles. "Black Widow Won't Submit to June Byers!" "Commie Wrestler Says She is Superior to Any American Man!"

Trophies filled a bookcase. Medals. Little statuettes.

And above the TV was a gold-and-red monstrosity. A lady's championship belt. Polished and shiny. Straps stretched out tighter than Christ's arms and each one tacked up hard as nails.

If there was a book in this room, it was hiding.

Every picture was a tribute to her strength, her viciousness, and her power.

"There's a roasted chicken in the fridge," she said, walking toward the short corridor. "I'm knocking out for at least six. Maybe eight since I went three rounds with Minister Clancy. You want to snoop around, be my guest. Keys are in the car, so don't you dare jack someone's vehicle here." She stepped into shadow.

"Can you really get me in to see the Swede?"

She kept walking into the dark. "Of course. I was his main attraction before you were born. Need proof? Read my walls. Don't steal my glory or I'll put you to sleep, too."

The bedroom door slammed.

I couldn't move.

Her face was everywhere.

Everywhere.

A dead woman's eyes, brought back to life, a goddamn zombie wrestler haunting me. Hunger ate my guts.

I opened the fridge.

A box of wine sat center stage.

FOURTEEN

ORPHANS AND WIDOWS

December 1978.

Pen,

Thanks. Your letter was like Christmas. Robbie is lucky to have you.

Things are crazy. My band got a gig. We're opening for CrampTramp. They're kinda big here. Sound like an angry Beach Boys if Brian Wilson was Screamin' Jay Hawkins. We're getting a cut of the door and three beers each.

School's awful, but kinda easy. Maybe I'll be like Lester Bangs, but not so old (idiot hated Big Star). We'll see.

No, I'm not mad at Robbie. He didn't hurt my feelings. I would have done the same thing. Sometimes folks have to lie about stuff to get it going. My dad told me that. Edgar Allan Poe lied about seeing a bunch of stuff, sold it as true, and then made better money with it as fiction.

So he lied about knowing my mom. Who gives a shit? If her death helps him, good. It hasn't done fuck all to me.

Hope you're doing well. If you ever, ever want to come to NYC you got a place to crash. You and Robbie are the only people in Minnesota I'd ever fucking care to see again. Hope working at Denny's is treating you well.

January 1979

Penny.

Got your letter a week ago and I am still so fucking mad I'm seeing everything in a pink blur, but I owe you the truth. And it's fucking ugly. Your brother is such a fucking coward that he can't write to me himself, can't ask me himself, and then when he lies he is so full of shit that I can smell his unwashed ass from here. I said it was fine if he lied about knowing my mom, fuck, he knows me ...but saying he's me?

I'm on an all-out offensive. I lied. I know tons of guys in the business. And each and every one of them is going to beat the horseshit out of his cocksucking face for lying about being a dead woman's son. Tell Judas the Obscure from Parts Unknown we're done. He wants help he can find a church. He is fucking dead to me. I'll hold a funeral in his honor so I can shit on his grave. Fuck him. And fuck you for helping him. I hope he dies in the ring.

Tell him the Demon says RIP.

S.A.

FIFTEEN

ICE AND SMILES

Unlike C. Ludstone, the world's most secretive photographer, Penny's address was in the White Pages. The thick book sat on a black table under the Black Widow's cover photo for *Pro Wrestling Spectacular* in 1973. She held some blonde in ripped tights and white boots, her face gripped by a scream, teeth strong as her black lipstick. "Black Widow: 'I Will Retire When I Cripple Valentine Twist!'"

2209 Bryant Avenue S. Great. Where the fuck was that?

I had no real memory of life here. Red Wing had burned a lot out. I remember our home had a wide driveway. Spring smelled like apples and I used to breathe too deep and sneeze like a shotgun that never ran out of shells. Lyndale. That was our neighborhood. But that meant nothing. Minneapolis was a feeling, not a place. And that feeling was ice and smiles.

The Pontiac's glove box was a treasure trove. Stale pack of Marlboros, no doubt for emergencies, that tasted okay in the cold. A bottle of Peach Schnapps I ended. And a yellowed city map singed, frayed, and with key spots burned out in Whittier. I found Bryant Street. Close to downtown. North of Lyndale. She had burned out the D. For dad.

Morning warmed with smoke and Schnapps. Light traffic for 5 AM. Crossed the Mississippi having missed it when we drove over to Dinkytown. City loomed like the first day of school. I still smelled of vomit.

The radio was a useless friend. Hit AM and felt old, but kinda comforted. The broadcaster sounded far away and lost in the 1950s. The 35 West spat me out and I rolled toward Lyndale Ave N, S, and Hennepin Ave. Radio man spat static and weather about "another sunny day" in the Twin Cities while Minneapolis looked like the frozen heart of hell.

I cut through the burbs, memories bubbling but nothing that popped out of the primordial ooze. Right on Franklin. Then up the hill to Bryant.

"Jesus."

ABC. NBC. CBS. Grey vans with KTCA, KTCI, and other K-Mart Brand News. National media and local losers plugging up the street and casting the morning in artificial glow of headlights and camera lights. I went two blocks up, parked, then left the car running. The cold slashed my body as I crunched back down, but by the time I hit Bryant I was numb.

Penny's place was two stories. Apartments. Journalists. Real ones. One hour behind NY, ready to go live to *Good Morning You Idiots* or *Today Is America*. A single Crown Vic was parked in front of the place. The cop was outside, smoking, the lone gun holding back the media stampede.

How to play him. Local boy coming home? Journalist? Nah, he's sick of journalists. Innocent. Not like all these vultures circling the sticks.

"Officer?"

I could tell he resented having to turn his face to look at me. "Ya?"

"I'm a friend of the family." One van's panel opened.

He focused on the vans. "Ya, okay." Two more doors slid aside.

"I went to school with Robbie," I said. Men in thick fur coats and earmuffs emerged from the passenger side. Others were setting up tripods.

"That so."

"Honest."

He yawned. The nicotine stain on his black glove the same tone as his moustache. "Prove it."

"How?"

"Where'd ya go to school?

"Red Wing." One of Penny's last letters said they expunged Robbie's records because of good behavior. You wouldn't know he'd gone unless you'd been there with him. Or a cop.

He closed his eyes, shook his head. "Go. But if you give them grief I'm dragging you out by the ear."

I nodded, then lurched under the tarp.

"Officer? Who is that?" said an annoying broadcast voice. A man in earmuffs with silver sideburns and brown hair. Looked like Reed Richards from the Fantastic Four was now with ABC News. His voice was a shit drop that brought all the rest of the flies swarming around the cop.

I lurched, listening, but they talked over each other and became a voice of a tiny crowd. Flashes hit my back. Like I was part of the story. I hoped this wouldn't screw up.

I didn't turn to see who shot my back.

The mailbox said the Varhoovens were 209.

The foyer was stained with slush from a dozen pairs of boots. Dirt and sweat stamped into old wood. Warm air from a burnt heater greeted me.

Fifteen creaky stairs later, I turned left and saw 209.

I breathed.

It smelled like vomit.

I knocked.

SIXTEEN

PENNY FOR YOUR THOUGHTS

Sully,

I received your last letter. I'm presuming it's the very last letter. Your pen strokes almost cut the paper, like engraving a tombstone. Which is a funny way to say I could feel your anger all the way here. And I agree. You have every right to be angry. Robbie never should have pretended to be you. But you know Robbie. He doesn't mean anything by it. He just wants to make it so bad in this sport, he couldn't find a way in to what I hope he'll call home. Lord knows it won't be here.

Please, try and understand him. He's just trying to make a dream come true. Just like you. Only for him it's not guitars and bars, but rings and ropes (gosh, I sound like Dr. Seuss). It doesn't excuse what he did. But you got out of Red Wing while he kept on alone and, well, he needs this lie more than you need the truth. I hope in time you can find it in your heart to forgive him. But I understand if it will take a long time.

I don't expect to see you until this wound is healed. Until then take care, Sully. You'll always be welcome at our place.

ROCK AND ROLL GHOST

At Red Wing, Robbie had one picture of Penny. She was dressed like a jester. Sixteen, chubby, hugging him against a tobacco sunburst sky. But fuck if that photo wasn't thirty years out of date.

Face desiccated. My mouth was dry just looking at her. I'd been around enough junkies, drunks, and speed freaks to know the difference in a line up.

"What the fuck do you want? I can't believe that fucker Norton let you past. Glorified mall cop I should kick his fucking ..."

Thankfully, I spoke amphetamine.

"Wait, I know you."

Dance uniform. Tights. Grey oversized sweater from an old boyfriend. Bra strap the color of Tahiti Treat. Ballet slippers and winter socks. Thin pony tail with dark roots and blonde tips.

"Penny."

She opened and closed the door to air out whatever she thought was plaguing her mind. "Holy fuck. Sully?" A red-nailed hand gripped my face, drew me close. "Jesus. You weren't even shaving the last time I saw you." Her nails dug in. "Why are you here?"

"Heard about Robbie," I said through a mushed mouth.

"How?"

I told her about the mag. About heading out here. About what I was going to do. I even showed Val's business card. Her nose crinkled with every detail. "What are the fucking odds? And why do you smell like puke?"

I shrugged. She dropped her talon.

"But what do you want here?"

"I want to find out what happened."

"He's dead. That's what happened. He's in the morgue and I've got to plan a funeral, contact all of our relatives, and not lose my job while doing it. For fucksake, he couldn't die after we performed *The 500 Hats of Bartholomew Cubbins*? Asshole. He is such a fucking asshole, but you know that, right? You knew better than most, goddamn that boy."

The front door cracked. Penny sneered. "Get in. I won't let those fuckers in here. Nope. Not on my watch."

She pulled me.

Speeders need control. And anything can set them off in different directions. You need patience.

I played boring. Dull. Simple. Safe.

Morning light turned the room into a Polaroid of a bohemian pad. A couch with thick and poofy cushions was covered in gym clothes and costumes. Vinegar and bleach bit my nose and tongue. Penny was a clean freak before she started pounding diet pills.

The door slammed. I sat on a recliner that was locked in a horizontal position. Waited.

"Vultures! It was bad enough when he had fans that figured out he crashed here, but holy fucking hell I will die before I tell these assholes a goddamn thing. Peeping Tom East Coast *assholes*!"

No photos of family, but lots of collages. Women. Parts of women. Faces. Legs. Thin. Dresses. Flowers. Penny was pretty creative in the parts she chose.

"So what do you want? A beer? Coffee? Jesus, I don't even know if you drink anymore."

Soon I had a mug in front of me. I heard about her theater. About how she was the reason they got Dr. Seuss to hand over rights to a play about hats. She ratted off stats about injustices. How Robbie stole the limelight. I waited while she talked, put on eyeliner using a strip of tinfoil as a mirror, and kept checking the door.

"And here I am, about to make history, and the big doofus falls down dead in the ring just when ..." She put the pencil to her lips. *Shh.*

I nodded.

The phone rang.

She grabbed it. "Yeah? Okay. It will get done. I'm still working on my brother's goddamn eulogy." The room hummed. Felt like I was a ghost trying to fill someone else's life.

Like he'd done with mine. Lying. Pretending to be the orphan of the Black Widow. That killed our friendship. But something else killed him.

"I swear! I can't go now. Cut me some goddamn slack."

Penny saw me flinch.

"I've got someone heading over now. His name is Sully. You can trust him."

Both of her hands scrambled inside a wicker basket full of thick fashion magazines with torn covers and frayed pages. "Don't worry." There was a jangle of pills in a bottle. "He's cool." She pulled out a vial and smiled. "... a friend of the family."

Fuck.

She slammed the receiver so hard my molars ached. "I'm so lucky you're here. I need you to bring this to a friend of mine. They need it. It's for weight loss." Talking this slow made her sound more full-of-shit, but I didn't care. "Can you do that for me? Please?"

Knocks at the door shattered the illusion. "Fuck off and die! You'll get nothing from me! Nothing!" Her one outlined eye glared... then moistened. "I just don't, I can't, what the hell, Robbie."

No hug. Better luck kissing a bobcat with a busted lip.

I stuck out my hand. The pills jingled in my palm. "Where?"

"My friend Mitzy. She works at Oarfolk."

I closed my fist. "Okay. But tell me what happened. What happened to him?"

She flinched. "Not here."

I shook my head. "Write it down." She'd have no memory of a promise, so this was my only chance.

I was one more nerve away from getting a black eye. But she tore into the clothes and pulled out a letter and then a blue ball point pen from her hair and scratched something down while more knocks came.

"Fine. You want it? Here it is."

She crumpled it into a ball. Then tossed the pen. I ducked. Two long strides and she was at the back window. Two moves and she opened it. One move and the ball was outside. "Go fetch it."

I ran so I could see the white orb. Like when you drop a penny, once it's out of sight you'll never see where it bounces.

The ball unfurled, tumbling through the air. It bounced on a large mound of snow piled into one corner of a back patio. Snow that didn't look soft. Ten-foot drop.

"Better hustle, Sully, because I am not opening that door for anyone."

I shoved my right foot out first, ankles bit by cold. A nail painted into the window sill hooked into my dad's jacket.

"Get out and get it done!"

Penny pushed. My jacket ripped. I fell.

And hell if Robbie's voice wasn't singing in my ear

"Spread your wings, Demon! Spread the pain across you like Christ on the cross!"

It was only after I landed on the jagged mound that I remembered Robbie's first rule—

Always land on your back.

I rolled away to laughter.

Upstairs in the next building to the right was a window full of four cackling faces. "Hey Hindenburg, nice crash!" said a goofy voice.

"Like they shoved a watermelon! Like on Letterman!"

I gave them the finger and they cheered. Fucking weirdos.

I rolled away, bruises growing across my skin. The letter was crumpled but too cold to get wet.

I plucked it.

"Air mail!" said one of the idiots, then they slammed the window shut.

Wind gusted. From the guts of my jacket white fluff fluttered like cloudy intestines.

I uncrumpled the letter. Penny's note was clear.

HE DIED OF A BROKEN HEART!

NOWHERE TO CALL HOME

Pen,

Hey. How are you? Good? How is dancing and acting? Remember when you were Cinderella? I think about that a lot.

Any word from Demon? If there's anyone he can listen to, it's you. You know, you meet people for a reason. I met my best friend in a hell hole. That's no accident. He needed me to save him. And here he is, the son of a wrestler. I mean, what are the odds? That's fate. Like finding a glass slipper.

Did you try his dad? He's a professor.

Pen, I need to make this right. I feel sick all the time. Because I know something. Something he needs to know. And it's important. But he hates me and now that stuff is getting good it's like I have acid in my blood.

Tell him. Tell him I want to be friends. That I need to talk. This is so big it's making me look small (HAHAHA!)

Hey, almost forgot. I'll be on TV this week. Not local. Still learning the ropes here in Georgia. But if I do what I'm doing I think I'm coming home. Real soon. Me on TV. Amazing, Like Cinderella.

Need to sleep. Please, tell Demon I'm sorry.

EIGHTEEN

WAKE UP CALL

"Nice ride."

I'd just gotten back to the Pontiac. Robbie's words churned. Silence. I needed it and a beer for breakfast.

"Does it drive itself, too?"

I thought I had walked casually away from the daisy chain of vans, holding the guts of my jacket in with my forearm. But a stringer followed me out of earshot of her cadre. I opened the car door, smelled old smoke and stale heat.

"Silent treatment? Fine." A loud cough. "Ahem! Sully Alexander, intrepid reporter for *Amazing Wrestling*. Val wants to know why you haven't contacted his photographer."

Five-foot-four and a bit. She wore the uniform of the Ramones if they'd been from the Minnie Apple. Blue jeans with rips. Red tights underneath. Salt-stained combat boots with duct tape on bottom, leather jacket with blue flannel up top. Around her neck was an old timey camera and big flash. A blue Maple Leafs hat sat like a target on her head.

"Ludstone."

She gasped. "I take it all back. You're Sherlock Holmes

from NYC."

"I didn't have your address."

"Wouldn't have mattered, I've been here all night. If you'd come here first, you would have seen some shit."

"Really? Who's in your pictures?"

"Everybody. Including you. One fucking guy gets inside Fort Atomic and it's an outsider." She dug into her zipper pocket and pulled out a cigarette. "Howdja pull off that trick? And can we talk inside your car? I'm freezing."

Ludstone sat shotgun, and lit up a tiny Bic with a huge flame. "You break in?"

"I know the family."

"Jesus, and Val told me you had no connections … yet you know the Atomic Kid?"

"Knew him."

She exhaled, misting the windshield. "Right, god. Condolences and all that jazz."

"No. I mean, sure. I knew him. Long time ago."

"Ah. You're a friend of the family."

Who just got shoved out a window. "I guess Val wants me to come home."

She took such a strong drag that half of what remained at the end of the filter was ash. "Ah, yeah … no." She fogged us up again. "You're his Man in Havana. Wants you to investigate everything."

I swallowed smoke. "Not much to investigate. He had a heart attack."

"You get that from Karen Carpenter up there?"

I shrugged. The closer Robbie's death got, the more I wanted to hit Greyhound for a ride back home. "He could just get Teddy."

Her eyes ballooned. "That fucking hack? No goddamn way. Listen, asshole, I'm sorry your friend is dead, but this is the biggest story in wrestling and, maybe for about ten Andy Warhol minutes, the country. And we're on it. You know a famous dead guy."

I sneered. "This won't matter in a year."

"In a year we could all be nuked out of existence. I live for today."
She had a point. "No one can tell this story like we can."

"We?"

"Print is dying. You need pictures to tell a horror story."

"Not sure that's what Val wants."

"Val? Christ, Sully, do all Big City assholes think this tiny? Val's paying us to investigate. You ever sign a contract with him?"

"No."

She banged the snow off her boot, then stomped on it. "So you don't owe him an exclusive."

Exclusive rights to the story? "No."

"And he pays you with a check that has no notes on it saying what you got paid for, right?"

"I get it. He can't claim he has rights to my work."

"Bingo! He'd have to spend money he doesn't have to sue you if we sell this fucker to a better mag. Time. Newsweek." She lit up. "Hell, maybe we make a picture book instead!"

I pinched my nose. This didn't matter. Yet it did. I needed sleep. I needed food. Robbie was dead. He was famous. Now's he's dead and even more famous. He lied to me. I killed our friendship. Now he's dead. He knew about the Black Widow, who isn't dead. I ignored him. Now he's dead.

"Dude?"

I turned the key to get the fuck out of there, mind still a black haze. The steering wheel shook. This fucking stupid Pontiac. At the cross street stood a snow man with hockey puck eyes that should have been stolen.

"Sully, get the fuck out of the car."

She shoved me.

I shoved back. "Fuck off."

"Dude, you're shaking."

"That's the fucking car."

"Then take your hands off the wheel."

I did. Everything rattled.

"The battery is dead."

She turned the key back, then left.

Snow obscured the skeletal trees that tangled with the wind. My face was wet and chilled.

Flakes. Each one an individual. None like any other. Crashing into each other as they fall from heaven. Landing on the hard earth, then there's a battle royale as they fight with each other, before being buried by a billion other competitors. A world made of white corpses, each one oh so very special.

For years he wasn't real, now he was dead. She was dead, and is now real. It's all a work, Life. It's all a work. Bullshit. Can't trust it. Can't trust anyone. Appearances are the first lie. Memory the worst flavor. It was easy on the page. You just took reality and turned it into what people wanted, or you used it to fuck with them. Because in the end we were all liars who chose to believe these guys were actually beating the fuck out of each other. We pretend that blood makes things more real. Robbie's blood was turning to formaldehyde. We accept a guy's leg being broken … and then the idiot is back on two legs throwing roundhouse kicks. We choose to ignore all the evidence we don't like. We deny the proof. We make our own reality out of easy answers and myths.

Until you can't push a dead friend's face out of your eyes.

Snow whistled by, then fell hard. So much for the forecast. The world vanished in a swirl of white.

The cold bit inches into my skin.

The world outside buried itself. The windshield a TV set to a UHF station at the end of its broadcasting day. I sniffed. My face cracked. In the rear view mirror my face stared back. Tear tracks were frozen from my eyes. Like a poor man's Alice Cooper. Little shiny tracks of frost beneath my face.

Bang-bang.

The snow from the driver side window fell against her mittens.

"Pop the hood," Ludstone said. I did. Then hit the wipers. They didn't move so I rolled down my window.

A green pick up blarred hard light at me. Hood popped. Like Jaws if the mechanical shark wore camouflage. Across the grill was a skull with googly eyes. A Cookie Monster Truck. My smile grew hard.

Robbie loved Cookie Monster. At feed time, he'd wait until the guards yawned then shoved in a muffin, an apple, anything into his giant mouth and say "Cooooookiiiie!", then sit down, normal as a snore in church, and not munch a bite.

I popped the hood, got out, and then watched Ludstone do a much better and more legal job bringing the Pontiac back from the dead.

"Jesus, you don't have these bolts tight. No wonder this thing dies all the time. Didn't anyone teach you about cars?"

"No. But I can write in the voice of five fake people, play most of the riffs from *Young, Loud and Snotty*, and, well, I can recite Edgar Allen Poe's 'The Raven.'"

She wiped her nose. "Bullshit."

"Once upon a midnight dreary, I pondered weak and weary, over many quaint—"

"Enough, thanks, I shouldn't have asked … who the fuck are you?"

My chin rose with pride. "Sully Alexander. The world's greatest wrestling journalist."

Not sure who started laughing first, but she stopped long enough to slam the hood. "Look," she said, "I got carried away. You got more blood in the ring than I do. You want to go home, fine. Leave it to these vultures." She spat in the snow. "You know they're going to say he was a junkie, that he OD'd like Bon Scott on his own vomit."

"I know. And you know what?"

She warmed her hand. "What?"

I scratched my stubble. "I want to know. I want to know everything. Because you're right, the bullshit is going to bury him. And he deserves better. And no one gives a fuck." Penny might care, but she was already far gone. And Robbie's mom … shit, was she even alive?

That was worth checking.

Because he wasn't the Atomic Kid to me. He wasn't a blip on pop culture's radar. He wasn't a dead wrestler. He wasn't six o'clock news. "Let's find out what killed Robbie."

I jingled the bottle of betties. The prescription said they were made out to Penny.

"Morning pick me up?" Ludstone said.

"Delivery."

"I don't judge."

"When it's done, we need to talk. And I need to eat. Coffee, too."

"There's a café at 36th and Lyndale. Opens in a half hour. You don't show, I'll assume everything you said is bullshit and go it on my own."

"The picture book?"

She snickered, walked back to Cookie Monster Truck, and flipped me the finger. "Stay awake, Sully. This train doesn't wait."

She drove off, leaving me in shredded snow and a car that worked.

I just wished I'd paid attention to how she fixed the battery.

Give a man a fish.

Whatever.

A short ride later I was parked in a snowstorm. Took ten minutes for me to be cool with turning the Pontiac off. "If it switches on again," I said to myself, "I stay awake for whatever bullshit Penny needs. If not, I hit the café now."

One twist of the ignition and it popped right back.

The record store's marquee had archaic lettering, the typeface for Bakshi's *Lord of the Rings* cartoon. Oar Folkjokeopus was closed. But Rat mentioned it during a night of hot knives after his last tour. "Every city has a place like this. The black heart of the revolution. The one place not tainted by corporate conformist bullshit. The dude who runs it owns a record label. Like *Dischord* and *Epitaph* but not so righteous. They were playing Big Star and all these kids who look like mill workers were wearing torn Ramones T-shirts and there was a fight between two local bands whose names I can't fucking remember. Like most assholes in the biz, they have good records."

Rat knew scenes like I knew wrestling territories. When I was still playing, I could keep up with every band: Black Flag in DC, the Minutemen out West, Meat Puppets in Arizona, Mission of Burma in Boston … but as soon as I pawned my guitar and started writing my brain could not hold it all in. Ric Flair kicked out Operation Ivy. Bruiser Brody crushed X. Nathaniel Princeton made the Misfits submit to the New England grapevine.

I wasn't sure which one of us was more pathetic.

Outside, I took in the corner like I was hustling smack. There was a bar across the street, neon quiet. Traffic was slushy and light. The cold felt good. And so did I.

"Hey, mark." High voice. Probably Mitzy.

I turned. "I'm a friend of Pen—"

A snowball mashed my face. Then a sucker punch to the guts stole my breath. I swung wild, eyes wet and freezing, but missed, spun, and landed on my face.

I swung an elbow backwards like a scythe. It cut air. But pro-vided distance.

"So Bruce Lee knows a little judo, uh?" The voice was frazzled, but controlled, and the words rolled out easy. He was hooded in gym clothes. Big. Wrestling big.

"Eat shit," I said, then spat.

He flinched, I rose, and threw a right but missed by a mile. Guy knew how to fight. "Guts without brains, my favorite combo."

The tackle mashed me against the Pontiac. I elbowed his back, but it was hard as a bathroom door. He tossed me over his shoulder. My landing this time was much better than the awkward drop from the window, but I had *nothing* inside. The hooded bastard loomed. "Last warning. There's a war on, mark. Fuck with the dead boy and his family and you're going to end up a casualty. Just like him."

I gave him the finger and a sneaker stomped my solar plexus. I choked on air.. Rolling to my side, I grunted. "Fuck you, rube."

Then I saw it. The vial of pills. Right by his sneaker.

I reached out, but he snatched it.

"Just 'cause you speak carny don't mean shit. Hurt the boy's family and I'll be back. Get on a Greyhound and get gone, mark. And thanks for the vitamins."

The sneakers ran off around the corner.

I shoved myself toward the store until there was snow in my underwear and my back was against the record store's wall. Dawn came.

I'd lost a lot of fights.

This felt different.

The Hooded Bastard. He'd been waiting. He saw me leave. Waited until I was alone.

Who did that?

A friend. No. A *real* friend.

The Hooded Bastard said this was a war. Robbie was a causality. I rolled to my knees. The Hooded Bastard's talk rolling in my head. Wars are fought by rich people who don't want to get their hand dirty. Regular people are causalities.

Pieces. I had pieces of an idea. But everything sucked, including breathing.

"Hey, you!"

A girl with big brown hair and workout tights walked up 36th.

Christ, I was making friends everywhere I go.

"Mitzy." I groaned.

"Yeah, where's Penny?"

I got to one knee. "Burying her brother."

"Then you have my medication?"

My knee braced as I stood. "Not anymore. Have to take it up with the guy who mugged me."

"What kind of faggot gets mugged outside Oarfolk? Fucking loser." She stormed off into the white shreds of snow. Where the hell was the Minnesota Nice?

I took out the envelop Penny had scrawled on. Robbie's

handwriting was blurred. Message degraded. Like recording a scratched record onto an old THX tape. If I hadn't already read it, I'd never make it out.

Pieces.

I folded it, shoved into my pocket, then got in the Pontiac.

NINETEEN

IT'S THE END OF THE WORLD AS WE KNOW IT

Amazing Wrestling is proud to present this exclusive interview with Sven "The Swede" Börne, one of the greatest pro wrestling champions of all time and president of All-American Wrestling (AAW), one of the most crucial wrestling promotions in the world. A man of few words, the Swede sat down with intrepid journalist Charles Clifford to explain why the world should fear the AAW.

Mr. Börne, thank you for taking time out of your busy schedule.

Get on with it, kid. I have to-do list bigger than your arm.

Since the 1950s, AAW has been the heart of wrestling in the Mid-West. What's the reason for your success?

We are innovators. We take chances.

Surely, so do other promotions.

Not like us.

Examples?

This is the last time I do your homework for you. Who gave the first-blood match before that idiot Stallone movie? Who did the steel cage battle royale? Who is bringing in most spectacular fighters from Japan, Canada, and Mexico to test our All-American best? Not New York. Not the hayseeds in the south.

How does being independent of the NWA promote innovation?

Look, I love the NWA. I was a member. But right now, they are a bunch of dinos, and I can say that because I'm only fifty and can still wrestle anyone. They can't see the future, just ape the past. And that's fine. More room for us.

What about the Global Wrestling Association? Like you, they are independent of the NWA. Are they rivals or partners for the future?

That depends on them. But they seem more interested in being Hollywood than wrestling. Like that retarded kid from Taxi.

That wasn't the GWA.

Yeah, but it could have been. AAW has the best wrestlers. We put on the best matches. Where do the best wrestle? Here. Everyone else is trying to emulate us because they know they can't beat us. And we're growing strong.

So, what does that mean for the future?

One word. WrestleFest.

We've heard rumors for years that this was in the works, but can you confirm what exactly fans can expect at WrestleFest?

Keep watching AAW and you'll see it for yourself. Now, if you don't mind, I have to take a call from Palm Springs.

TWENTY

CAFÉ RATIONICIATION

I hungered for speed, but drank the coffee slow. Hands thawing around the mug.

Album covers. Pics. Framed interviews. Café Route 66 was a blowjob to Dylan, the musical expeditionary from Minnesota. Like Jesus, he was a lot more popular because he wasn't around. New York is littered with Dylan stories, almost as boring as his music. But here? Worship started with Hurricane Coffee and Lay Lady Lay Pancakes.

Ludstone arrived with two plates. I didn't reach for my wallet.

"You get the next round," she said. "You fucking New York charity case. Now care to tell me why you look like hammered shit?" Her lone swears made the early birds grumble.

I told her.

"You got jumped by a wrestler?"

"Yeah."

"Shit, maybe you're tougher than I thought."

"Maybe."

"He was out there all night? I didn't see anyone."

"Guess he's a ninja, too."

"What the hell's a Neen-Ja?"

"Japanese assassins from Medieval Times. Come out of nowhere. Can do almost anything." When things were bad, Rat and I would sneak into Liberty Theater to eat stray popcorn and stay warm watching shit movies. The plot to all Ninja films was *ninjas are amazing*.

"And here I thought you were uncultured."

"Just an educated barbarian." I sipped. Apparently this coffee was water-flavored.

"Man, Sully," she said, forking eggs. "You look awful. You really want to keep poking at this corpse of a story?"

I smiled. "Look who's chickenshit now."

"Be glad I'm hungry, or I'd be jamming this up your nose." She chewed. Smile like the Cheshire Cat. "You recognize him from the roster?"

The oil-slicked coffee reflected my puffy face. "AAW wasn't really my beat. But no, wasn't Nathanial Princeton, Gentleman Slim, Samurai Nagasaki, or Blob Tanner or anyone who was getting TV time. High voice. Falsetto. Smooth talker. Probably two-thirty but billed as—"

"Two-fifty. Camera adds twenty." She chewed her Positively Forth Street bacon. "Think you could pick him out if you saw him?"

"Not unless they all wear hoods and sing like the Vienna Boys' Choir. But I'm not interested in who he is. It's what he said. That there's *a war*."

Her lips pouted as her bites slowed. "All wrestlers bullshit. Exaggerate."

"I know. They're full of shit and born to lie. But there was something …" But my sore head wouldn't play along. There was a connection. But it was … ah, fuck. It was disconnected.

"Does Sherlock have a migraine?"

"Not Sherlock. Auguste Dupin." No. Fuck. I didn't want to owe anything to Dad.

"That who clocked you? Some Mad Dog French-Canadian?"

"Huh? No. He's fake."

"Hate to break kayfabe for you, Sully. It's all fake. Uh … minus the injuries and, you know, your dead friend."

"Dupin's not a wrestler." Fuck, smart women were annoying. "He's a fictional character. He solves mysteries by using logic and body language and inference and deduction."

"I really think you mean Sherlock Holmes."

"Fuck Sherlock Holmes," I said a little too loudly, and everyone in the café stopped talking for a minute. "August Dupin was before Sherlock Holmes. That limey jackoff Doyle ripped off Edgar Allan Poe."

Mouth slack, Ludstone then smiled. "That is so lame. Go on, quoth the Raven."

"Shut up. The point is he did these tricks sometimes by looking at connections of all the elements of a crime, including people, psychology, other shit, to find out who killed the victim."

"How?"

"It was called ratiocination."

"Professor, I didn't ask what. I asked how?"

Coffee burned my mouth. "He held all the details in his head … used evidence like calculations." I shook my head. "But you have to be a genius to do it."

"Then we're both fucked."

I finished the coffee. "No. My … someone I knew once said Poe littered his room with the notes for the clues in the story."

"Like on Cagney and Lacey?"

"Then I'm Lacey."

"Screw you, Sully. Don't leave me at home with the kids!"

We cackled. Not laughed. Cackled.

"Fine. Let me go grab some shit from my place so we can razzamatazz your brain and find out what we already know." She got up, leaving half her food untouched. Not that I was staring. "Let's meet at your place. Where you crashing?"

My lips froze. "Dinkytown. Uh, could we meet late? Like

midnight? I'm with a roommate who works nights. Rather not annoy them with this stuff."

"So considerate," she said, eyes rolling. "Whatever the real reason is, fine. But if you get bored, you can find me at the Longhorne."

Annoyance bit my nerves. I didn't know how to act around Ludstone.

I was being myself.

Shit.

"Longhorne … is it a bar?"

"Yeah. Doing photos for a show. I know the Minnie Apple can't compete with the home of fucking Blondie, but our scene is cooler by a nautical mile." She yanked the last piece of bacon, shoved it in her mouth, then left.

Slowly, I finished the plate. Ate every crumb. Scraped all the egg. Drank three more cups until I felt like a facsimile of a human. Then bussed the plates, then made eye contact with the guy behind the counter. He smiled. Eyes dead.

I returned the favor.

"So," I said. "Where's the nearest library?"

TWENTY-ONE

ART AND HUMBUG

"To Remember Distinctly": The Hidden Hoax of the Rue Morgue, A Polemic by Damon Alexander, *Princeton University,* 1979.

In his 1943 textual analysis of "Murder in the Rue Morgue," Ernest Boll noted a series of shifts in wordage, tone, and grammar between what is believed to be the earliest manuscript of Poe's first tale or ratiocination and its debut in *Graham's Magazine.* While an able work of textual analysis, Boll failed to integrate as part of his reading the role of external research to create the final effect Poe desired: a tale whose ending was known to its creator but revealed itself as it were a mystery to all: in short, the birth of modern mystery fiction.

Poe's research methodology has been studied *ad nauseum* but only within the limited scope of contextual appreciation of criminal conduct available in "penny press" sources. The most famous of these is Edward T. Fagan's "Manufacturing Reality," which is most relevant though highly dated. I have dealt with this in my preceding article.

What all have missed is Poe's fascination with the fragmentation of life, the theme of his most gothic work, and secrets of other worlds hiding amidst the real world. How he conjured the plot of "Murder in the Rue Morgue" has not been viewed in this light in part because of lack of other external documentation, literary or verity. But I submit that most critiques have missed a golden opportunity in their dismissal of the so-called "Fanatical Letter."

In 1878, *The Baltimore Sun* published an anonymous reader's vehement defense of Poe's "The Mystery of Marie Rogêt," largely considered the weakest of the Dupin cycle. The "Fanatical Letter" alleged to reveal the shadow of Poe's writing by imitating the author's use of reverse logic and what we would call primitive psychoanalysis.

What all dismissals fail to recognize is the hand of Poe in the creation. This is due to the refusal of many within the study of his work to include his hoaxes and role in manipulating the public as part of his idiom. A detailed analysis of the text, when compared to the shifts in word choice noted in the work above, demonstrates a series of consistencies that give this claim credence. The French spellings of "Endevour," "Neighbour," and the recurrent misspelling of "clew," while intentional in the draft of the story, were in fact evidence of Poe's authorship of the letter (a full analysis was published in *The North American Review*).

It is only through the lens of humbug and hoax that we can appreciate the depth of the "Fanatical Letter." Poe was thwarted in his original masterpiece of hoaxing, "The Unparalleled Adventure of One Hans Pfaal," by the unfortunate coincidence of an earlier public fabrication about a lunar balloon journey. We know from his letters to Sherman Horsely that this failure to manipulate public opinion dogged him and compounded his interest in poetry and gothic literature. And the bridge between hoax and his development of craft was the tales of ratiocination, and the fanatical letter his last salvo.

The most compelling aspect of the Fanatical Letter are the author's "deduction" of Poe's methodology. The image created of a room filled with "clews" from cases, notes nailed to walls, of strings of many colors acting as causal "strands" between event, person, fact, and plot, as Poe takes the actual crime of the 1820 murder of Mary Cecilia Rogers in New York and her husband's later suicide into a the first Dupin tale, and employing a simplified version for the next story, and, finally, Poe's genius in "The Purloined Letter" resting on his ability to maintain the wealth of "clews" in his own mind, just like Dupin.

Thus, Poe had grasped his final straw as a master manipulator. Hiding in plain sight, he used a fictional character to tell us the truth about this methodology, writing in his natural vernacular and published as an amusement. By lying, he revealed the truth, and was dismissed. In this way, Poe had the last laugh as a master of humbug.

TWENTY-TWO

THE SWOON

"There better be a full tank," said the Black Widow.

"Nope." I sank into the couch. Old smoke embraced me like tomb dust. Fatigue ate hunger and got fat. "But your battery is fixed."

Rattling the fridge, you'd think she was strangling a skeleton. "That right? You didn't get that skill from your father. As mechanically apt as Helen Keller."

I shoved two books I'd brought from the Public Library's convenient mall location into a crevasse between cushions. The hole swallowed my hand and I pulled it out. Still had all my digits. "Nope."

"*Nope.* You sound like an extra on Hee-Haw." She walked out of the dark kitchen. "What are you doing?"

"Resting." Was hard to tell when last I slept. My guts ached.

She walked into the room, a denim nightmare wearing a green sweater. Light snapped on. She held the standing lamp in my direction. "Who roughed you up? That idiot from the bus?"

"More likely that psycho priest I saved you from."

"Saved? You would have been in the hospital with a broken hand if … look, I don't have time for macho man bullshit. Just get up and tell me all about your little investigation while I make my rounds."

"Rounds?"

"I can't just drop my life because you showed up."

I laughed. "Drop your life?"

"Everyone's a fucking George Carlin these days."

"You've been dead ten years. That's funny."

"You want access to the Swede? We need answers. Get in the car."

"Answers? You said you were his number one gal."

She took in a deep breath. "He's not taking my calls."

"Then I'm taking a nap." I yawned. "I need sleep or I'm going to start seeing shit that ain't there."

She strutted over. "Poor thing. Did you have a hard day? Find any clues?"

"A bunch. I've earned a nap."

She drew out another smoke. "If a friend of mine died, I wouldn't sit around reading books. I'd find out how he died before all the clues went cold."

"It's already cold. And he died of a heart attack."

"A twenty-three-year-old kid, built like a brick shit house, has a heart attack? God, you *are* a mark."

Mark.

There's a war on.

A Coke can rabbit punched my head.

"Ow."

"Wake up, kid. Enough time for sleep in the grave."

I opened the can. "Do you ever not talk like Gordon Solie is interviewing you?"

She laughed. "You're dry as toast. Finish that can, stand up, and get out some gas money."

I chugged. Burped. "Who we going to see?"

"Roberta."

"She an Angel that works for the Swede?"

The front door opened wide enough that the cold slapped me. "She's the dead kid's mom, you idiot."

Once more on this rollercoaster and night and day were

meaningless. Everything was blue, black, and white. I slipped in and out of it during the ride. Questions popped up.

"So," the Black Widow said, "the sister's a doper." How did she already know where Robbie's mom's place was? "Which means her opinion of medical procedures is as worthless as a three-dollar bill." A point, something meaningful, slid through the muck.

Then it stuck, like an eyelash beneath the lid.

I mashed my palms into my eyes. "You knew Robbie."

She checked her rear view. "What makes you say that?"

"You have no other reason to care."

Warm air bled through the heating vents, before a hard turn smacked me against the glass. We barreled over snow and curb and shot toward the tanks of a 76 Ball.

Her jaw jutted. "Get out."

I opened the door, snow going sideways. I was already warming my thumb to hitch a ride to the Longhorne to see Ludstone.

"Put in ten," she said. "And shut the damn door."

The cover for the gas tank popped as I walked into the station. A bell chimed as I entered.

76 was a wonderland. The light danced. Colors popped. The magic of consumerism sang to me in reds and blues, chips and pop, and the soft tones of Phil Collins on an unseen speaker that could have been anywhere. But the floor was an ice rink of black slush from a parade of winter boots.

Behind the counter, a fat old man in a crimson blazer read the *Star Tribune*.

"I need ten on pump one."

He sniffed, deep. Guy had a forehead like Frankenstein.

His ears were mashed.

Cauliflower.

"Hello?"

He folded his paper. "Cash first."

"Huh?"

"No cash, no gas."

"Ah, the friendly Midwest."

"Rip-offs come out of my check, chief. No green, no gas."

My guts watered at the sight and sound of this monster.

Sadistic Stan Rapowski. Alive and well and pumping gas in Minnesota. For an East Coast guy, that might as well be death. The ten was crumpled. I flattened it. "You look familiar."

"Flattery will get you nowheres."

"You beat the Red Sheik. One of your early tours of the Mid-South before you stuck around Jersey and worked New York. Word was you were a legit shooter."

Never saw his hand coming.

Iron. Each digit around my throat. I grabbed his wrists but he shook me so hard everything blurred until I saw the murder in his eyes. "Shooter? Who you think you talking to?"

"S…adistic …. Ssstan … Rapowski, the Polish Nightmare. I …"

"You *what*?"

"I … thought you were dead."

A bell chimed.

I slipped on the slush, landed ass first.

Two kids in orange and yellow snow pant outfits swished by. "Momma? Can we have Jiffy Pop?"

A tired mom trailed behind them, red ski outfit like the Canadian flag. "We have Jiffy Pop at home. Go to the bathroom." She looked at me like I'd crawled out of a hole in her wall. "You auditioning for a mop?"

Pain sizzled up my spine as I stood. "Can't all be Mom of the Year."

"Leave that lady alone," said Stan. My ten was gone. So was the Pontiac.

"What the hell…"

"She left you," Stan said, ringing up the cash. "Again."

Black slush soaked into my jeans, crawling up. "Again? How the hell would you—"

He slammed the cash drawer. "This time it'll be for good."

Down the aisle, the mother in red was shaking a Jiffy Pop. "My kids love this stuff so much."

The black slush rippled. My legs stuck like toothpicks in ice. "Stop this shit!"

"Trust me," Stan said. "I'm dead. I should know. Right, chief?"

"That was an accident!"

"Killing anyone is no accident," said the mom, slicing the air with the Jiffy Pop, foil about to burst. "She killed herself to stay away from you." At her side were her two boys. One smiled wide. The other was faceless. "At best, that's second-degree murder."

"Suicide," Stan said, then thumbed at himself as the black slush reached my neck. "Me? I got murdered."

Black slush filled my mouth.

"By you."

The Jiffy Pop burst.

"*Fuck!*"

I woke on the floor, surrounded by small bags of chips and a few stray Jiffy Pops. Everything hazy. The clerk leaned across the counter. He was black, thin, maybe twenty and wearing earmuffs. "Sir? Sir, you cannot sleep here."

I scrambled up. "Fuck, sorry. I'll put this stuff away."

"Just leave, okay?"

I must have looked like death fucked over.

My blood was iron. Sweating, I pulled out a ten from my pocket. "Wait, have I paid for gas yet?"

"No."

I smoothed out the ten. "Really sorry about the mess."

"It's not so bad," he said as he rang up the order, handed me a receipt. "Not like you killed anyone."

I smiled. Then left. Then laughed. Didn't stop until the Pontiac was ten bucks full.

As we drove away, another thing sunk.

Killing anyone is no accident.

"What took you so long?" said the Black Widow.

"Thought I saw a ghost."

"Well, exorcise that kinda language. Roberta is a two-fisted Catholic."

"How long?"

"Jesus, kid. I don't know when the old crow was baptized. Maybe sixty years ago?"

"How long did you know Robbie?"

Her lips pursed. "If we're going to find out who killed him we'll need to move fast. We've entered a chess game that's already in motion."

"No," I said. "It's a war. We're just chasing the first casualty."

She paused. Because she knew I was right, even if I didn't know why. "Now, when we see Roberta, a few things. Watch your language. Don't correct her. And don't say anything about ghosts. For god sake she just lost her son and, well, she … she hates wrestling."

"So you want me to do the talking?"

We pulled into a pale white parking lot lit by street lamps alone. Catholic Eldercare. "No way, *Jose*."

"Why the hell not?"

"Watch the hells."

"Why? I'm just a bullshit journalist. You're the bullshit wrestler."

She hit the brakes. We skidded to a stop and before I bounced back, she cuffed my left ear. "Ow!"

"Was that bullshit? Was my broken collar bone? My fifth metatarsal? The concussions that I lost count of? Don't you ever use that word again. You're not a mark, kid." I began to count to ten. "And the reason I'm doing the talking is that Roberta doesn't know I'm a wrestler. She thinks I was one of Robbie's college teachers."

College? Dude could barely write. "So this is a work, too?"

"Yes. Now, one last thing. You say nothing. Nothing. And your name is Jonah."

I counted to three. "Why."

"She can't know we're related."

"Why?"

"Well, that's a complicated story."

One. "Why?"

She flinched, closing her hands around the wheel, then turning to me. "She believes it was you, the real you, who got him into wrestling. Back at Red Wing."

Zero.

"Best bet is she believes you're the reason he's dead."

TWENTY-THREE

TANK YOU VERY MUCH

Dear Andy Kaufman,

I am writing to you out of fear and anger. You have a unique position on God's green earth. And instead of using it for good, you debase yourself by wrestling women, as if Sodom and Gomorrah were alive and well in New York City.

Can't you see that what you and other heathens call comedy is really nothing but fornication by another name? Our savior Jesus Christ did not die upon the cross so that an entire generation was corrupted by such debasing and wretched material. Trust me when I say I know what I am talking about.

My son has fallen in with the so-called wrestlers you claim to represent. Sodomites and thugs the every last one of them. Do not think for a minute that I am not wise to their antics. I am. They are heathens, as Leviticus instructs, and just more proof that this once great country is in full decline. I only pray that President Reagan can turn the tide of history once more to progress and Christian virtue and away from the lusty pagan seductions you and your ilk peddle to the feeble, the weak, and the troubled.

Robert, my son, is a fan. He watched you on the late night programs. I remembered your Jewish name. He is now out there in the wilds, conducting God knows what in the hopes of being like you, famous for wrestling, though I thank our Lord he has not degraded himself with women. Yet.

I am writing you to ask for your help. I want you to go on television and make a promise to all of your fans that you will never, ever wrestle again. Such an act of grace will surely purchase you the sympathy of our Lord and Savior Jesus Christ. You are one of two people responsible for his decline. The other, a reprobate from the juvenile system, has vanished and good riddance. But you, Mr. Kaufman, can influence millions. Do what you know is right. Your people have been stained with the blood of Christ on their hands for years. Please, take a step towards reconciliation. Help my boy. God bless you.

Roberta V.

TWENTY-FOUR

TAG TEAM

Cold cream and perfume. Both aromas made me think of pink. But Roberta's walls were white, minus the shadow of the cross above her TV. I sipped tea. Roberta's face was out of order. No tears. No grief. Just a little smile that made me itch.

"It's kind of you to visit," she said. Black hair dye, blouse and pants looking like a costume for mourning rather than the real thing. She also didn't look old enough for elder care. Unless fifty counted as elderly in Minnesota. "But he's home."

The China tea cup with blue swirl around the lip felt more precious than gold in this living tomb. I sipped, they chatted. My mind played with string: murder, prayers, war, casualty, mark, shooter … lions, tigers and bears-

Gah, it was gibberish.

"You're very strong, Roberta," said the Black Widow. "I only wish Robbie had been as strong."

"He was special. Not strong. But as sad as this day is, I feel a prayer I've been making for years has been answered. And this is your son?" She leaned forward from a royal blue chair that looked like it was built for agony. "Did you know my boy?"

"Just on TV," I said.

Her face pinched. "Then you did not know him at all," she said, leaning back. "He was going to be a chef. He had a palate, Katey. Like Juliet Child."

His favorite meal was hot dogs and his favorite drink was hot dog water.

"That he did. But he was so young, Roberta. It's so awful to think he's not here anymore, even if he's among the angels. Did he speak to you at all? Was he ill?"

"Robbie only called on my birthday, October 16. That was the last I heard from him."

"And what did he say?"

The parking lot at Catholic Eldercare had been half full. Unlike Penny's place. Those reporters weren't digging very deep. Or Roberta wasn't as easy to find.

"Well, he knew well not to talk about that wrestling business that killed him." Silence. Roberta took the bait. "I told him about everything in the family." I tried not to snooze while every goddamn cousin's birthday party and promotion was rattled off. Instead, I sipped. And listened.

And heard it.

Another sound on the edge of awareness. Breathing.

"Well, sounds like he got the family tree newsletter! Did he say anything to you?"

Roberta pressed out the wrinkle of her slacks. The silence confirmed it. Someone else was sleeping here. "He said the usual things."

"Like what?"

"Oh, that he was going to buy me a Cadillac, like Elvis did."

"You liked Elvis?"

"When I was a child," she said. "Then I grew up. Elvis is just a second-class Jesus."

I wondered if that was before she drank gin until she was a madwoman. At Red Wing, we showered as a group. Robbie had scars across both ass cheeks. Like jigsaw puzzle pieces mashed together.

Got him the kind of attention no kid wants. All of them Roberta's handiwork. "She'd heat up a coat hanger," he'd said. "And brand me. Holding that fucker with a dishrag that smelled worse than a dead dog." And yet until October he'd been promising this Christian trash a Cadillac.

"Excuse me," I said, placing the cup on the saucer, bringing it to the glass table. "May I use your bathroom?"

She smiled without joy. "Of course. Just leave it as you found it."

I stood and left as the talk continued.

"Anything odd about the way he spoke?"

"Robbie always spoke odd since he got back from Red Wing. You know that, Ms. Moscowitz."

Down the hall, the breathing grew louder. A snore. Steady, strong. Not like Rat, who would choke himself and wake up swinging. This was the snore of a bear.

"Stay to the left!" Roberta said, a tad loud. "Odd … well, there was one thing."

The bathroom was on the left. Another door on the right. Roberta's room.

Was it filled with crosses? Pictures of Elvis?

I gripped the handle and turned it slow.

"He promised me something."

"What was that, Roberta?"

The breathing belonged to a black mass.

"Well, that was it. He promised that he would make everything good this year. No more asking for money. That this was the year everything was going his way. Huh. Just goes to show how delusional these children can be when they're controlled by that idiot box."

The black mass wore a mask around his mouth and nose. Darth Vader meets Frankenstein. I walked in, eyes adjusting.

Eyes closed, the creature slept.

"Everyone took advantage of him, Ms. Moscowitz. Everyone turned him against me."

Face … oh god, it looked just like Robbie.

"All I ever did was help."

I inched closer.

The half-man, half-machine's chest rose and fell. The hospital bed. Get Well Cards on a small desk. The man was called Robert. He snorted. I froze.

"Judases. Every last one of them. Especially that Jew he met at Red Wing. No offense."

Silence, then: "You've had a hell of a day, Roberta."

I retreated to the bathroom. Did my business. Flushed. A stray pube hung off the white porcelain like an angry, frantic worm. Hands washed. Towel avoided. Lights off.

Resuming my place, I picked up my cup. It had not been refilled.

"Must be good to have a place to hide from those wrestling people," I said.

Roberta's jowls twitched. "I beg your pardon?"

"This is your father's room."

The Black Widow simmered and Roberta leaned forward. "I said to keep to the left."

"The door was open. I closed it, but heard him breathing. Must be under a different name. Not Varhooven. Keeps those TV and wrestling people away. Nice to have some place to hide. Where people won't get at you. Hound you. Hurt you like a red-hot coat hanger on a virgin ass."

Roberta did not shriek, retreat, or gasp. She turned to stone. "You talk too much when not spoken to."

I waited for the Black Widow to cuff my other ear. She put her cup down, drew herself up, and said, "He has a point, Roberta."

A flicker of worry deepened Roberta's creases.

"We want to respect your privacy. Especially now. And we agree with you. Something bad happened to Robbie in this no-good world of wrestling. But we are not the only ones. And they'll get here and find you, Roberta. Sooner or later." The Black Widow's red smile grew. "Let's keep it later if we can."

Roberta winced. "I think you both should go now."

"Of course." The Black Widow gripped the fine China tea pot and poured herself another cup, then Roberta, then me. "Just as soon as we find out if there was anything, just anything that stuck out with that last phone call. A name, a place." She put down the pot. "Something that just didn't sit well with you." She picked up a sugar cube, dropped it inside. "Something that made you feel weird." She stirred with a tiny spoon that looked like it belonged to a coke dealer. "Something strange."

Roberta crossed her arms. But she looked shrunken. "He lied to me."

"About what?"

"He said he had a new job. Who would hire a giant who dressed like a woman?" She actually lifted her nose as if the smell of that idea was rotten.

"What job?"

"Oh, he wouldn't say. But he was very proud. Too proud. That's how I knew it was a lie."

"Where?" I said. Roberta's face soured at my voice.

"Yes, Roberta. Where did he say he had a job? Was it here in town?"

"Oh, no. He was bragging. Said I'd be proud."

"Where?"

Her lips crinkled. The word as gross as a dead bug in her mouth. "New York."

*

Through the Pontiac's window, the night sky was bright. Everything glowed faintly blue as if covered in BooBerry cereal. Time held its breath until I uttered. "Why?"

"Care to be more specific?"

"Why did you bring me to see her?"

"I was curious to see if we could work together." She ashed her cigarette, gripped the wheel. "Wanted to get your two cents. Tag team her. And it worked like a charm."

Strings filled my head. One from the Black Widow's lair to

Roberta's hideaway. The latter didn't want to be seen. The former didn't want me around … until I got to her place. I huffed on the window and etched BS. "Who's coming over? Specifically, who is coming over to your place." I did my best to sound august, like Dupin. "The person you don't want me to see sleeping on the couch?"

"Everyone in New York as paranoid as you?"

Rat, Val, Teddy … okay, maybe. "Answering questions with questions means you're buying time for a lie. Don't bother. But don't think I buy this tag-team shit. Unless your partner ain't me." Velocity flushed my head back as she jammed the gas. We zoomed into the blue gloom. Smoke in her knuckles, she twisted the dial. "Islands in the Stream" blared as we rocketed through the streets, cutting red lights when they'd been a paler shade of orange.

We careened around corners, honks blaring as street gave way to an empty donut shop parking lot. She hit the brakes, fishtailing until my face mashed the window.

"Woo!" I said. "Slow down, Starsky!"

Breaks hit. She crushed the butt. Smoke puffed before it went out, then vanished. "Go on. Get it over with."

I wiped my face. "Care to be more specific?"

"Get it all out now, kid. All the cheap shots. All the hate. All the missed birthdays. All the lies. All the 'I hate you, Mommy' crap. Just unload it here because I do not have time to make it all up to you. I don't have a decade of Christmas gifts and hugs and kisses and other shit I was never, ever good at. Come on. Say it."

"Holy fuck. Are you making *me* feel bad for *you* playing dead for ten years? Now that is narcissistic, even for a world champ."

She closed her eyes, crow's feet tight, and shook her head from side to side. "Fuck if you aren't just like him, Living in the past. Two losers who never accomplished anything that wasn't just riding on other people's coattails. Your daddy with Poe, who's dead. You with the boys, but never going near a locker room. Always looking back, looking up." Her eyes snapped open. "Neither of you man enough

110

to *do* it. But there's something happening, kid. Something happening *right now*. And it's killing people. People I care about. So you want sympathy and crying, find a therapist. What I need is someone smart who I can trust. You may have your father's idiot tendencies but whatever brains you have for survival, rest assured, you got it from *me. Me.*" I opened my mouth to retort, but she barreled ahead, talking a mile a minute. "Your father wouldn't last ten seconds outside of the ivory tower and we both know it. So either get good with me being a shitty mama and help me find who did this to Robbie, or you can go this road alone, write your story for Val, and get the fuck out of my city."

Leave. Buy a donut. Fuck off. This is all beneath contempt. Pull a Poe and write your expose without doing jack shit. Get the fuck away from this dead woman. I gripped the door.

"Then stop bullshitting me," I said. The glove box's plastic visage was powdered blue with light. "I don't give a fuck why you abandoned us. That's on you. And you're right. I got on fine without you. And I'm the only one in this car who Kara doesn't hate. You'll go to your fucking grave knowing she wanted you around and if she ever, ever finds out that you chose to leave her in the fucking dumpster with Dad while I was in Red Wing she would be destroyed. So drop the bullshit or you'll lose any goddamn chance you will have in what's left of this life after death you've created in making good with the baby girl you tossed in the trash to be a mediocre wrestler in a world that doesn't give a shit." I turned. She seethed. I smiled. "I don't give a shit about you. You never gave a shit about me. So let's drop the tough mom wrestler and sullen son show. This is business. You have access. I have validation and unlike you I know how to write. We work together. We find out what happened. Because we both know there's more here than a heart attack. I have strands. Clues. Ideas. Intel. And I'll share, but you *will* tell me every fucking thing that happened to bring Robbie into your life. And what's going on at your apartment you don't want me to see. You will not fucking dodge, hide, lie, shoot, or kayfabe your way around me.

Tell me the truth, or you're no longer dead to your daughter. You're a piece of shit coward. If you agree, let's go to your place and get to work. Otherwise, I'll get out here."

I yanked the door, one leg out—

The engine rumbled as she stamped the gas. Controlled fury was her cruise control. I closed the door and she inhaled hard, which dropped her voice a half-octave. The words were slow, measured, and precise, just like her driving. "You are a miserable piece of trash and a no good shithook."

"I didn't get that from Dad. Now, how the fuck did you know Robbie?"

TWENTY-FIVE

FALLS COUNT ANYWHERE

Katey!

I know you said not to write, but you just needed to know.

I made it to Atlanta! You're right, Waffle House is the best, but I seem to be losing a lot of weight and water in this heat, yet I never feel dry. Always soaked. Mr. Watts is a tough cookie, but he says hello. I'm learning amazing things all the time. I can speak kayfabe pretty good and I'm minding my Ps and Qs. Just like you said.

It's rough, though. The old guys really like to give me grief. They sandbag me. My back is covered in potatoes. They say it's paying dues. Seeing if I come back. But I do. Every day. Smile on my face. It makes them so mad! I'm learning some of the psychology you mentioned. But I'm still ring crew. You keep saying pick my spots. I'm trying. But there's no room. I don't really get along with the young guys. There's one who seems nice. Funny. The guy talks so fast and so much it's like watching TV, and he just bounces all over the ring when the old dinos hit him. I call him Ping Pong and he hates it! I can be myself around him, you know? Big and dumb!

And I hate to ask, but if you could send me a little money I would be grateful. I'm sleeping in my car and I need to hide it from the cops.

Gas is cheaper than rent, as you said. But I'd like to chip in for a room with Ping Pong.

Also, how about this for a name: Bobby Nasty!

I promise I won't write again … until I am Mid-South Champion!

Katey: thank you for the Christmas card! I only have enough for a stamp so am using this old pad of paper. You said it. You said if I played smart I'd find my spot. Ping Pong and I are going to be a tag team. He's great. He's teaching me stuff like you.

Mr. Watts still hates me because I botched a match with this kid from Samoa, Tang. God, he's strong. He bet me I could not knock him down. But I remembered your advice. "Make friends with all Samoans." So I told him he couldn't knock me down, then had him push me across the ring! I sold it like I was hit by a cannonball. Tang laughed but Mr. Watts said I was still "Green as a cow's first turd." But Ping Pong is getting heat with the crowd. He gets color the hard way. I'm not scared to do it, but I'm not sure how to do it well. We opened a show in Shreveport because Brad Danger was in that car accident (do you know him?). We didn't stink up the joint! I'll take that as a win. And I took your advice and thought about all the wrestlers I loved, and other bands I loved, and it feels weird to say this because I promised not to bring him up.

I started acting like Sully did. At Red Wing. He loved Kiss, and the Demon. So, I started to bang my head, like I'm front row at Black Sabbath. But with Ozzy, not Dio.

Running out of space. Hopeyouarewellandthanksforthecheck.

Mama Kate,

Oh my god. The crowd pops. They love it. And I can't believe the heat I'm getting. It's like me and TV (that's Ping Pong's ring name) are real villains. We were chased by three guys after our match at the Coliseum. I'm still not blading but I popped a blood capsule for the Halloween show in Calgary and those Hosers went ape! We're so hated. It's great.

TV's been a true friend. We're hitting the gym. We're making the old guard look fat. They hate us, but they love that we draw. We're feeling like there's something special in the air. The money sucks, but it's better than when we started. But it's bigger than that. The fans. They're connecting with us. They like heavy metal and partying and, I know, I know I shouldn't say it. I miss Sully. He would make a great manager. But I know he won't talk to me. No matter how good it gets, I know he's still mad. I spoke to TV about it. Don't worry. I didn't say your name. He called it a "Faustian Bargain." A deal with the devil. Considering our gimmick, it seemed to fit.

TV talks a lot, and I realize I don't know as much, though I'm picking stuff up all the time. I wish I liked to read. Sully could read stuff and explain it so well it was like I read the book. I even read that poem he hated, "The Raven." I liked it. I think I could use some of it in interviews. I'm not good yet, so I just say one word in a spooky way. "Nevermore." TV says it sounds like I'm a ghost. What do you think?

Mama Kate. Holy shit. I got a call from the Swede. To audition. I'm driving back to Minneapolis now. Did you do this? Did you? I don't know what to say. It's big. But the Swede is saying I can't use my gimmick. Some kids in Schenectady killed themselves listening to Ozzy's "Suicide Solution." He says it's bad heat to be a heavy metal character. TV's heading to Calgary because he won't change his gimmick. I wish I had his guts. He said he'd get me an audition with Stu, even get to see the Hart Dungeon where he trains guys in shoot wrestling. But when do you get a chance to audition for the Swede?

I've been working on my character. A new one. Take what I've done and turn it around. I've been reading a lot more with TV gone. History and stuff. Gladiators and monster books, plus this one on Three-Mile Island.

Did I ever tell you about my dreams? I used to dream about nuclear war. Dad was convinced it was around the corner. Said it's why he drank. "Why not, if we're all corpses in the fire anyway?" But TV said something. If you run towards your fear, you make it your pet. So, I'm thinking of something like an atomic gladiator (TV calls me the atomic alligator!). Even a nuke can't stop him. Check out the photo I sent. The makeup plays on my old Demon gimmick. What do you think?

I'm terrified. The Swede's boot camp is legendary. TV said two wrestlers died trying to keep up with the old man. Ric Flair trained there, and the Iron Sheik. If you can't hack it, pack your boots. But like you said, if you let fear win you'll be a slave forever.

Next time you see me, Mama Kate, you better believe there's a bear hug coming. I would never have gotten this far without you. Any fame I get, it's coming back to you.

See you in the Fall.

TWENTY-SIX

SOUVENIR AND SCAVENGERS

By the time she parked, I was wide awake. "You were his mentor."

"For a while," said the Black Widow. "Then his friend. He had no one, Kid. You know his family. Coma, religious nuts, or—"

"He had Penny's—"

"Speed-Queen Drama-Freak? Sure. What a safety net. And now they're useless to talk to, it seems. That idiot actress knew me as his coach. So there was no way I could get close to her, or ever be in the same room as her and Roberta."

"You got more fake IDs than a local bar."

"Talk with her if you want. Waste your time. I don't give a shit." The words hit me wrong but I let it slide. Because there was more string now. Her and Robbie. Him getting famous. Like she had been. That could be it. She wanted a meal ticket. Fame she missed. Vicarious celebrity. The power behind the throne … cold leftovers to someone who had been a spotlight junkie.

"I want to find out who did this to him."

"You think he was murdered?" I asked.

"I don't think it was an accident. He was too young and too valuable."

"Who gains anything by cops and murder stinking up the AAW?"

She tapped the wheel. "Not the AAW."

"Face it, Val. The GWA played us. That's what I'd said. But I was bullshitting to save my job. I had no evidence that they set up the fake obit to make us look dumb. And that was a cherry bomb in the toilet compared to the nuke of killing the competition.

That Hooded bastard had said there was a war on. Strings braided in my head, but it was still goddamn fuzzy. I needed to study Poe, Dad's essays, before Ludstone came back ... and then I would have to explain the inclusion of The Black Widow Moscowitz. "Why are we waiting in your car?"

She drew out another Marlboro. "My apartment is usually cleaned while I'm out working. But given the stakes tonight I phoned in some favors so I could spend time on this case."

"Case? We're detectives now?"

"Just me. At best, you're a sidekick asking annoying questions like 'are we detectives now?'" Her falsetto was thin.

"Sure thing, Captain."

"Christ, you're annoying."

"And you're full of shit. No one has their house cleaned at 11 pm."

"Well, it's being cleaned, after a fashion." She dragged, but chewed on the filter.

Nervous. A tick. I opened the door.

"Don't do this, you jerk!"

"I said don't bullshit me."

I jogged through the bracing cold, quickly turning warm. Light flared from the door's window. The knob turned without a fight.

Five guys in wet boots and duct-taped shoes wandered around the main room. They were pawing Mom's stuff like mashers at a dirty theater off Times Square. My voice went riot. "What the *fuck* are you doing here?"

They squirmed. One was so fat he looked like an iceberg dressed as a lumberjack. "Sorry," he said, voice both high and low. "This is a private auction."

"Then the cops won't give a shit if I shoot your guts right here and now." I shoved my hand in the jacket. "Get out, motherfuckers!"

They did. "The Black Widow will hear about this," the fat one whined.

I slammed the door. It hit his ass, bounced back. I left it open and dug into the couch.

"Fuckers! Stop it right there!"

The iceberg froze, hands up like a cop show.

"I want the two books you stole."

"Books?"

"There were two books in this couch. Where are they?"

"The Black Widow didn't have any books for auction. While Richard Pike's Dirt Sheet claims she wrote a memoir during the filming of Black Widow's Curse, he never produced any evidence and I've asked on numerous consecutive occasions and she has always denied it. Thus it's more lore than reality, much like Mike Chapman's claim about Stranger Lewis' autobiography, narrated to Walter Gibson, creator of The Shadow—"

"Shut up." I approached the Iceberg's backside, hand back in my pocket. "This was an auction?"

"Of course. Completely legal. I'm the president of the Angel and Heels Memorabilia Club, Minnesota chapter. We do this every other month."

"One of you took books. My books. And I want them back."

"If they stole something, that's a matter for the police."

"Gimmie your wallet."

He did. It was tiny, brown, and smelled like it looked. "Douglas Arthur. You live on Harriet Ave. Now you will do everything in your power to get back the books your scavenger crew stole from me and bring it back in twenty-four hours. If not, I'm going to break your knees, have you eat a curb, and stomp your teeth out." I tossed the wallet outside. "Go."

He waddled after it. I shut the door. Fuck. I'd read everything. Each story. Dad's article. And damn if I didn't feel smart. But I was zombified. Reacting. Not thinking. Not building. Acting. Observing.

The books weren't the only thing missing.

The 1973 Pro Wrestling Spectacular above the White Pages? Gone.

There was also a gap in a bookshelf full of trophies.

Pieces of her past. Sold off.

To fans.

I turned the dial on the RCA. Thunked around for 23 channels until a test-pattern arrived and I found the time.

0:00

0:00

0:00

I blinked.

Was it 1 am? Or was this a failure of the Emergency Broadcast System? Was it only a test? The door closed with a click. "You scared off my fans worse than a bomb threat." She strutted into the kitchen.

"Fans? They were stealing your stuff."

The fridge backlit her hunchbacked form. "Buying my past."

Strands frayed in my head. But one seemed clearer. "So, why are you in the hole?"

The light shut off. Wine filled a highball glass. "Got any evidence of that?"

I shrugged. "Just your defensive stance."

She sipped. "If you must know, being the best mall detective in the Twin Cities does not allow me to buy my preferred box of wine."

"You must want Kara to know you're alive to lie so fast."

She sighed. "God, you are just like him. No sense of humor. Look, Freud, I resigned. Simple. Shitty. True. Boring."

"Tell me why you lost your job."

"I said 'resigned'. Stop the Torquemada act, kid "

"Give me a reason to."

She smiled with serrated malice. "Fine. The Triple Five Group did not care for my style."

"Who are they?"

"Seriously?"

"Do you think I read Day Jobs in the *Twin Cities Monthly*? No one cares about this place except those who are too scared to leave."

She sipped, shook her head. "Ever heard of the Mall of America?"

I went a little deeper. "You were head of security?"

"No. I was head of Mall Detection. Chasing junkies and teen-agers and geriatrics who use the food court as a bathroom. I did stings, detected a shoplifting ring, and was headed straight for head of security." She snorted. "But apparently having a woman in command of such things was a tad too progressive for a bunch of Canadians."

"Canada owns the Mall of America?"

"Didn't say that. Canadians. They designed it. Own it."

"That's why you didn't get the job. Why'd you get fired?"

She finished the glass. "Why do you think? C'mon, Poe little Detective. Yeah, I read those shitty stories. Dew-pin the blowhard. Tell me. Why would I lose the job?"

Drunk. But that was too easy. She wants me to say that. So I won't.

But she was told she couldn't do something.

By a bunch of guys. A string of deduction flailed in my mind. "You hit your boss."

She put the glass down on the kitchen counter. "Lucky guess. Tell me why."

"You felt ripped off."

"Close," she said, taking the pack of smokes from her purse. "But no bullseye."

"The actual guy was inferior."

"You are such a fucking man. You can't see it, can you?"

"Then tell me."

She considered the cigarette between her fingers. "My boss said there was a way I could qualify for the job."

I stepped back, ass hitting the TV.

She lifted up the cigarette like a doctor examining a needle. "I just had to start in a different position. On my knees."

"Oh gross-"

"So," she said, placing the butt between her teeth, "I agreed. Told him to drop his drawers. And when the belt hit the floor I drilled a punch straight into his liver." She ignited her lighter. "I potatoed his body. Broke his hand. Sprained an ankle. Got my chicken wing on him until he screamed Uncle and had him call himself Mommy's Little Sweety and then pissed himself. Fucking Marines think they're the cock of the walk. I did what the whole Jap army failed to do and walked out a champion." She lit the stick, puffed twice. "And became blacklisted in every strip mall in St. Paul."

Tiny words fell out of my mouth, scrambled over, and whispered. "I'm sorry."

"Yes. You are."

The string in my mind itched as I sank back into the couch. "When did it happen?"

"Last week. Asshole still hasn't sent my last check." Two threads tangled. "Why?"

"So, when was Robbie's big push was coming?"

"Big push?"

"You heard his mother. He was going to New York. And it wasn't to visit me."

She dragged in smoke, nice and slow. "The Mahones."

"They were poaching him from the Swede."

"Then who killed him?"

"There's no proof he was murdered. Not yet. Just strange circumstances."

"In *the business*, all circumstances are strange." She kept talking. But I slipped into the cracks of exhaustion. Falling was flying. And there was no bottom. Just the swoon of the pit.

TWENTY-SEVEN

GRUDGE MATCH

Amazing Wrestling Presents a Profile on … The Mahone Family! For three generations, the Mahones have been the engine of promotion in New York, New Jersey, and across the Eastern Seaboard. As one of only two independent promotions in the US of A, The Global Wrestling Alliance continues to grow. Now under the direction of Cassidy Mahone, Jr., the GWA is picking up steam with spectacular shows that are pushing the boundaries of just what can happen in the slam bang world of pro wrestling.

Mr. Mahone—

Please. Call me Cass. Mr. Mahone is my pa.

Okay! Cass, GWA's made national headlines with the first ever Chuck Norris Invitational Karate vs. Wrestling tournament at Madison Square Garden. What—

Chuck Norris is a great American. We met in the Forbidden City where my family holds a secret cosmopolitan summit on international fighting styles. Chuck said he was a fan of my father and of course the unbelievable talent of Mario Rogers, the most dominant heavyweight champion of all time. But he was worried about one of the competitors, a man known as the Scarlet Ninja. You likely don't know that ninjas are an ancient brotherhood of Japanese assassins with a reputation for dirty tricks. At the salt bath sauna, Chuck and I discussed strategy and I revealed one of Mario's most deadly nerve pinches. I bet Chuck that if he won the tournament with that nerve pinch, he'd owe me a favor. Let's just say that the Scarlet Ninja no longer has the nerve for combat!

You are one of two independent wrestling promotions, along with the AAW, charting your own course outside of the NWA territory system—

As my friend Liberace noted, I don't give the competition airtime. GWA has some amazing plans for the future and I'd love to tell you about.

Then by all means, tell us!

Well, most of it as confidential as the location of the Rolling Stones' practice space (I know where it is but will never tell). But as we demonstrate time and time again, GWA brings fans the most spectacular and unbelievable matches, with the greatest wrestlers from around the world. Who else but the GWA would bring in Chuck Norris, Muhammad Ali, and the All-American Stunt Man Evel Knievel to the best arenas in America!

Our intrepid photographer Teddy has snapped picks of you with Mick Jagger, Andy Warhol, and Diana Ross.

Only because they all love the GWA!

But some of your detractors say that you're too obsessed with celebrities and not enough—

That's ridiculous. I challenge anyone who says the GWA isn't keen on wrestling to come to our shows and tell that to Cobra Daniels, or Ron "The Marauder" Mace, or the Kentucky Nightmare. And there is no greater champion in this country or the world than Roman Daniels. None.

Is there any truth to the rumor that you're selling the GWA to MTV?

Ha! For three generations, the Mahones have created the best wrestling promotion in the world. If anything, MTV better watch out in the next year. We may buy it! Wrestling killed the Video Star! Now, if you don't mind, I have to catch a flight to LA! Wish I could say more, but keep your eye on GWA and you'll find out!

We thank Cassidy Mahone, Jr. for his time.

TWENTY-EIGHT

'82 TO DEAD

Coffee woke me.

Instant. Sharp. Ugly.

But my eyes were sandbagged.

Laughter rolled.

"I'm not kidding," said the Black Widow. "I was working security at The Heights."

"I love that theater," said a strange voice.

"That's where my career was born."

"You wrestled at The Heights?"

"Ha! I'm not that old! I saw the dying days of Vaudeville. My daddy would drop me off for hours while I worked at the hardware store. And they often had AT shows. Athletic contests and strongman stuff and there was a guy named Buffalo Roly who would take on all comers on the stage. He was a mountain of muscle and, as I'd find out later, as gay as a dozen balloons. The mustache should have been a clue. Anyhell, I'm working security incognito because lord no one suspects a woman can do this job. And there, lining up to see some goddam space movie, is Prince."

"Jesus, I must be the only one who doesn't have a Prince story."

"Not as good as mine, anyway. He was dressed in a purple velvet suit. In February. On each arm was some slut with wild hair and makeup straight out of the Grand Guignol. He bought his ticket, got a small popcorn, and carried on to the theater as if he was the king of the world hanging out with the peasants. But when he went to use the ladies' washroom, I had to follow."

"Ha! Holy shit."

"See, we'd had had complaints of men hiding out in the ladies' stalls. And most of the women wouldn't know there was a difference until they pulled down their panties to piss and then saw, next to them, some guy's stained loafers. But Prince? Hell, he wore higher heels than a Cabaret queen. No one would even think it was him!

"So I give him a two-minute lead, then storm in like I'm in the ring. He turns. And for a second, I think he has a gun."

"Fuck."

"I slap it out of his hand, and as it rattles I see it for what it is: a tiny purple bottle of cleanser."

"Prince was ... cleaning?"

"Yes. He apologized for the 'transgression,' voice firm and smooth as his songs. But one of his girls was something of a Princess, no pun intended, and needed things clean. So Prince, *Prince*, cleaned up the stall for her so that she'd be comfortable."

"So what did you do?"

"I've spent my life reading people, figuring out if they're full of themselves or full of shit. I scrutinized the Purple one and decided, he was just weird enough to be telling the truth. I watched as he finished his cleaning routine, washed his tiny hands for what seemed like hours, and then left the place cleaner than he found it."

Famous people stories. Close to fame.

Two strands that were fuzzy tied together while the Black Widow kept Ludstone entertained.

The part of me that felt bad for giving her shit rumbled while the braiding occurred.

She was abused, I thought. *She fought back. She's human. You're not a prized peach, either, Sully.*

But I was a cynic. She'd replaced me with Robbie. Helped him become famous. He was about to go nova the week before she lost her job.

She was banking on his success.

She was banking on a return on her investment

Now? It was dead. So, she was selling off her past to make ends meet.

Well, fuck her, the cynic said. *You didn't make these choices. She did. And she lost someone she knew. You lost someone you ran out on a decade ago.*

So, I was more like her than I wanted to admit.

Shit.

I stirred. Everything hurt. No wince. No grunt. Give her nothing to mock, complain, or critique.

On my feet.

"Frankenstein awakes," said the Black Widow.

"Frankenstein's the scientist," I said, stretching. "The one who makes the monster."

"And you say you're not a professor," said Ludstone. They stood at the kitchen counter. Her leather jacket was tossed on the corner of the couch. It had a glossy stain on one shoulder. "You missed a crazy show. Hüsker Dü cancelled last minute and were replaced by Morris Day and the Time. The fucking *Time!* I thought it would be a riot, as a lot of those Husker fans are skinhead shits … but it was soooo good. They blasted the audience for two hours. Stage diving to soul. Fucking phenomenal. And then Morris said that he brought a carton of eggs in case Prince showed up and asked if he could count on 'you punk ass white kids' to be his 'firing squad.' Oh god, it smelled so bad when they were done. Got some great shots, though."

I nodded, not caring. "Speaking of time—?"

"It's noon," said Ludstone.

Jesus. I hadn't slept that much since childhood. Felt okay but didn't trust it.

"I've caught up with your Aunt Kate. Seems like our dynamic duo is now a power trio."

I looked at the Black Widow. "That a fact, Auntie?"

She poured herself another cup of coffee, then filled Ludstone's glass. "Pooling information is as critical to asking better questions that lead to the truth. We'll all do better together."

I dragged myself toward them, sniffed. "*We* need paper. Pens. Paper clips. String."

"You starting an arts and craft center?"

"Testing your theory that there's something worse going on than a bad heart in a young guy."

"Humor him," Ludstone said. "He's the eccentric genius. We're the eye candy and muscle."

I hated my life.

Ten minutes later there was a card table. Then mangled index cards. Two Bics. Hairpins. Some loose-leaf paper. A pack of Chiclets, the gum that looks like baby teeth. Shoelaces. "Wow," Ludstone said, handing me her mug. "Agatha Christie has props."

"Okay, Dew-Pin," said the Black Widow. "Do your trick."

I put the mug in the center, steam long gone. "The coffee is Robbie. What else do we have?"

"The guy who attacked you," Ludstone said.

"I tell you he's a walking target," said the Black Widow. "Crazy smells the New York on him a mile away."

I scrawled *Hooded Wrestler* on an index card. Memory hit me again. I winced. What the fuck did he call me?

Mark. War. "Uh."

Ludstone leaned over the table while the Black Widow sat on the couch. "What's 'uh'?"

"Verbal tic. Probably some regional thing. Not here. Not New York."

"Forty-eight states to go." The Black Widow grabbed a paper and started reading.

I drank from the mug. "I think he's Canadian."

"They say 'eh?', champ" Ludstone said. "Don't you watch Bob and Doug Mackenzie?"

"Not if they're from Western Canada," said the Black Widow.

"Or the Maritimes," I added.

Canadian.

"Your nephew's well-traveled," Ludstone said.

"Takes after his mother," said the Black Widow, "god rest her soul."

Cheap shot. Getting me stuck in her web. Focus. I almost had a good idea.

Another card. *New York, GWA?*

"The Mahones?" Ludstone stretched her back and I avoided looking at her bosoms by sipping black coffee that tasted like pencils.

"What about them?" said the Black Widow.

"Roberta said Robbie had a job in New York. That means the GWA. Which means Little Junior made him an offer."

"Then why would he kill him?"

"He wouldn't," said the Black Widow. "His grandfather would. Not him. Even his daddy wasn't a true-blue monster."

"Sometimes it skips a generation," I said. The Black Widow flipped through the paper but didn't respond. I sipped from the Cup of Robbie and put it back. "If Robbie got an offer to go to New York, who would flip their wig?"

"The Swede," Ludstone said. "He's been building the Atomic Kid up for, what?"

"Not sure," said the Black Widow.

"When did you make the invite to him?" I said, while writing on more cards. *The Swede. Deal—*

The Black Widow shrugged. "Can't recall."

"Estimates are fine. Was it 1981?"

"Probably."

"Before or after your birthday?"

The glance was harsh but quickly diluted. "Before."

"After Christmas?"

"Yes."

"He entered the promotion strong. When did he go pro?"

Mid-South, 1979

Stampede, Canada 79-80

WCC, Texas, 80-81

CML, Mexico '81

AAW Deal December 26, '81-January 7th, '82.

AAW, '82-Dead.

Oct. '82, Offer to NYC?

"Fuck a duck," Ludstone said. "He was a cannonball. Three years to be a champion in waiting."

"That would piss off the old timers," I said, picking up the string. "You can verify that, can't you Aunt Kate?"

She shook her head. "Some old timers, sure. They hate green boys pushed fast. But the smart ones know a young buck can make everyone more money and they don't have to do anything. Plus, they tend to stroke the promoter to keep doing what they're doing no matter what the flavor of the month is with the fans. Reminds me of the time—"

"But Robbie was different," I said. "He wasn't a flash in the pan. He wasn't just a strongman. He had the goods. He could call it in the ring. He could connect with the crowd. He had a gimmick that worked. How was he liked by the boys?"

"No idea."

"But you trained him."

Her look was quizzical. "Guess you could call it that."

Ludstone's nose scrunched and I gave the Black Widow a hairy eyeball. "What the fuck does that mean?" I asked.

"Let's just say he … didn't come by much after he started with the Swede. Oh, he had reasons. His workouts took up much of the day. Then training for promos. Acting garbage." She closed her eyes. "Real workers make their own characters. They don't need to go to Julliard for Idiots." The animosity on her face matched the grind in her jaw.

Part of me shivered.

She was fed up. That look was prelude to a storming out. She held back whatever speech she'd been preparing and went back to the paper.

Slowly, Ludstone placed another Chiclet on the table. "But Princeton's the champ," Ludstone said. "And we all know he's on the way out. That was the whole point of building up AK."

"You know him?"

"Nathaniel the Prince?" The Black Widow snorted. "He's one of the few guys I never had to worry about. And before you ask, no, I was never good friends with him and you can better believe that the Swede has him on lock down and zipped that fancy dental work shut."

"So you don't think he'd kill Robbie."

She sighed even louder, folded the newspaper, and sat it on her lap. "You've spent years writing about my world and you're still not smart to the game. Wrestling isn't about wrestling. It's about politics. It's about playing poker while everyone else thinks it's chess."

"Wait," I said. "What did you say? Training for promos?"

Any other human wouldn't have seen what I saw on her face. The half-sec of frustration before she killed it. The Black Widow fucked up.

"Oh, you know," she said, "standing in front of his mirror and acting like that idiot who ripped a bat's head off."

"Ozzy," Ludstone said.

"Wherever he's from," said the Black Widow, "that heavy metal garbage he was practicing. That's what I mean by Julliard for Idiots."

But it was bullshit. Training. Not practicing. He had help. And she wouldn't say where. "I should probably check on Penny," I said. "Care to give me a ride?"

"That's it?" said the Black Widow. "A bunch of scribbles on paper and you're done?"

"I thought we'd give you some space," I said. "After all, you've lost someone you care about." She stiffened. "And I'm sure you'll want to go to the funeral. Pretty sure Penny will tell me where it is so we can prepare."

"For what?" Ludstone said, putting on her jacket.

I finished the cup. "For seeing our suspects in the wild. If the Swede has them all on lockdown, then the funeral is our only chance."

"Damn," Ludstone said. "He sounds like Columbo."

"Without the fashion sense," said the Black Widow. "Well, you do what you like. I have a lot of appointments, too."

"Then let's reconvene here at six," I said. "And compare notes. After all, pooling our brains, right?"

"Well said," said the Black Widow.

We'd never leave if I got the last word. I grabbed a stack of cards, a pen, and let her have that last barb. Ludstone and I took off into the wind and white. Cookie Monster Truck was two-wheeled on a snowbank. Out front of it were two snowmen about to be roadkill.

Once we were in the truck, and the engine was on, I turned to Ludstone. "Hey, you ever hear of wrestlers who *train* to do promos?"

"Someone doesn't believe their Aunt Kate is telling the truth," she said. She launched over a mound, turning hard, and avoided snowman slaughter.

"Robbie had a lot of talent. So much it screwed him up for a regular life. And he was always loud, but the guy I saw on screen yesterday, the one everyone talks about, that's a guy who was good with the mic. Most guys practice this stuff for years while driving from one shit gig to another. The road is their grad school. But Robbie didn't have time. He was shoved up before that skill could naturally develop. So where did he go to get so good?"

She shrugged. "You're talking about performance. That's theater. Isn't his sister—"

"He'd *never* go where she would. She was a legitimate actress. What he did was carny shit. Where do people with no talent for theater go to get trained?"

Ludstone smiled, full joker, then laughed. "Oh, I know. Shit. You're not bad at this stuff."

That was only true if it led to the truth, with Aunt Katey spinning lies faster than I could cut them down. "Where?"

She sighed, then shook her head. "Have you ever heard of improv?"

TWENTY-EIGHT

THEATER OF THE ABSURD

Excerpts from Jack Ripe, *THE HIGH-WIRE MAN: CONFESSIONS OF A CARNY COMEDIAN.*

There are two truths to remember with improvisation. First, it's American, and second, whoever its parents are they sure as heck ain't New York or LA!

Because it is a child of many parents. And its own children are heralded. John Belushi and the other Saturday Night people are all children of something I helped create. But if you dig around the bones of the art form, most people associate it with one place: Chicago. And that's where the mother of improv came from.

Viola Spolin was a gem. Genius. Teacher. She is owed the kudos and desserts for taking her theater games for immigrants and children in the 1920s, games that helped people communicate without competition and focus on feeling and connection, and turn it into a performance. Her kid, Paulie Sills, was the first to see the potential in Chicago. But let me tell you,lightning struck twice in the 1950s Midwest.

I had just returned from the Barnum Circus tour in the

Philippines and Japan and was suffering a case of malaria that lost me work in grease paint and wire. But my friend Marianne Clemins and her boyfriend at the time, Joel Hershberg, were working steady nights performing jazz in Minneapolis. They needed an opening act. Lungs full of gunk, I took the family jalopy into what would be the final destination for a road kid.

The gag was this. Joel and I used to fill hours in the car by doing a gag. Just a story built from one word at a time. Marianne acted as the conductor, shouting out dramatic terms like "conflict!" or "secret" and we'd have to trust and challenge each other to make the story hold mustard. Joe's had seen Negro comics and band leaders do this on the road with such style and dash. It felt like an act, but there were no lines, no set up, just a suggestion from the audience.

Ours was pathetic and sophomoric, a fun, frivolous, and a free way to kill time. Perfect for an opening bit! We called it "Cool Play," riffing on the beatniks who came to shows. We'd ask the audience to "give us something really cool."

It's hard to convince anyone how bad it was when it began. But all great things are born in awful fits and starts. "Cool Play" was strange, antic, and frustrating for us and a spectacle of strange for the audience. But Marianne was clear. "There's something here. Like jazz, folks want to see the high wire act without a net." Now she was speaking my language! "But you talk over each other. You're trying to be the hep cat of the heap. Try playing as friends, not adversaries. Remember, a band isn't at war with each other when the singer or the saxophonist is soloing or taking us somewhere new. We're all on board. We're all helping." If it were not for Marianne, "Cool Play" would have been "Doomsday."

As our troupe's theatrical run ended at *The Tropics*, I had the opportunity to finish my degree in education at a local college and "Cool Play" would not let my mind go! My professor was a disciple of Stanislavski and more uptight than the Stalin's nanny. He referred to me as "Mr. Circus" in class. He had no idea that for me that was a badge of honor, and was disappointed that I had no shame! While everyone was gearing up to be the next Butler or Brecht, I was studying the Comedia Del Arte and the Grand Guignole and seeing a pattern that would shape my ideas. I would need a new troupe. But they couldn't be normal. They needed to be the freaks and misfits. So I had an open audition call for a theater troupe. But our first class was at the professional wrestling show.

I had known The Swede, back when he was a carny wrestler in Iowa. Quiet, smart, charismatic … and merciful fates he read a lot and not just in English and Swedish. German. French. Samoan. He could recite poetry from Baudelaire in Swahili! He briefly worked for my parents and we struck up a friendship because, like me, he had an antic mind, loved cribbage, and was always asking questions. I taught him sleight of hand, how to juggle, and other tricks of my trade. He told me road stories of real fights where men lost eyes, of when Strangler Lewis taught him a hold that no man can break, and how to get out of a grapevine and wrist lock. We were fast friends, and I was sad to see him go. While "Cool Play" percolated like coffee in a samovar, I recognized that there was something in it that reminded me of the Swede and how wrestlers do their shows.

Now this is when the smart set chime in. "Jack, we all know that wrestling stuff is fake!" Tell that to a wrestler and you'll see just how fake it *really* is! And the truth is, it's real. What you see in the ring doesn't get any more authentic. They are trained athletes and combat experts. So when the bell rings, it gets real, very quick. But in exhibition bouts, men like Lou Thesz and others make sure that they don't kill their junior opponents so much as demonstrate their skill. Almost like a performance. How to show off without hurting each other.

When I told the Swede about Cool Play, and how Joel and I got in each other's way, he agreed to have my little troupe of freaks and misfits watch an exhibition.

Little did I know this would be the birth of what we called "Jazz Plays." and what all you fans of Belushi and Chevy Chase call "improv."

TWENTY-NINE

OPEN MIC

"Jack is a kook," Ludstone said, turning onto Hennepin. "And a dirty old bastard. But a legend. And he's got deep roots with wrestling during the golden age of the Swede's break from the NWA."

"How did *you* hear of him?"

She cackled. "Shit. You *are* from New York. It's like saying 'how did you hear of P. T. Barnum.' Everyone grew up with the Galactic Circus Theater. It was kinda punk, actually. The bad boys of theater went there. And a handful of dykes. Some were even cute." She smiled.

"So you've been?"

"Fuck, Sully. If you date anyone not boring in this town they're either on stage at the Longhorn, The Entry, or at Galactic Circus. And for my sins I've dated a few folks who thought they could train at Galactic Circus, get a job at Second City, Chicago, and then fill Belushi's dead boots. One thought improv was the greatest thing since oral sex."

"Is it?"

"Only if you blow the wrong way."

"But what the fuck does it have to do with wrestling? *Besides* this old man Jack stuff?"

"Think of it like a game show, where people have to make stuff up quick. Put on skits and shows."

"Christ, this sounds awful."

"Yup! Ninety percent of it is garbage. But when it's good, it's kinda wild."

"Fucking lousy ratio for anything."

She shrugged, turning right. "Right. Like every show the Pistols did was magic. Or Dee Dee Ramone is always on the beat. From what little I know of it, improv is the punk rock of theater. It produces a couple big acts, but the crazy shit is why you do it. It's like when you go to a show, and one band is awesome, one band is shit, and one band doesn't show up … but it's all the same band."

"I guess I'll have to see how much it sucks to make a fair comment."

"Har."

"But there's … something here that makes sense. This shitty theater stuff—"

"Improv."

"—is probably good for a guy studying promos. It's theater. It's audiences. It's guys who know how to get a reaction from the crowd. Like you said, if Robbie was being fast-tracked he had no time to learn this stuff on his own. Galactic Circus might have been his cheat sheet."

She turned left and we bounced a curb before righting ourselves.

"Sorry. Trying to avoid black ice."

The patchwork of wounds across my body flexed. Ow. Fuck. Ow. "So you know where this Jack lives?"

"Nope. Carny guy. He's a control freak and privacy nut. Plus, like wrestlers, he loves two things: strippers and slinging bullshit. He may have opened the door to Robbie, but someone else would have trained him."

"So we're going to a strip joint."

"You wish. Who's the improv asshole in this town who loves wrestling?"

"Only one way to find out."

I jolted forward, shoulder taking the worst of the hit on the dash. I really needed my own car.

She rolled her eyes. "Seatbelts aren't just ornaments, Stunt Man Sully."

"That nickname sucks."

"I know."

"We're here!"

She parked beside a brownstone theater with an awful yellow and white marquee flaked with snow, old school circus lettering declaring *GALACTIC CIRCUS THEATER: COMEDY WITHOUT A NET*. In a window surrounded by glass and unlit bulbs was a poster for a show called *IBManiac: The Show that Does Not Compute*. And on the brown doors with saloon windows was a sign. "Drop-In Class Today!"

I whined like a teen. "Do we have to?"

"Got a better lead with all your strings?"

Nope. This stupid theater might house the last person to see Robbie before his big match.

Ludstone led the way.

Popcorn. Waxy chocolate. Old paint. Day-old sour beer. A smell evoking the magic of childhood and the sadness of isolation. The concession stand was yellow, afternoon shade gloomy and dull on its husk. On the right was a wall of black and white head shots. SNL people, I presumed. The thin guys with big smiles. The fat guys being cute or playing with their eyebrows. One black guy and one Chicano, each trying to look cool and non-threatening with starched colors. The women were last. Each trying to look beautiful. And controlled. The wall was completely allergic to Asians.

I had seen a lot of standup in New York. Rat booked us gigs anywhere, and often anywhere would have anyone who called themselves a comic. My judgment after three nights of their stuff was thus: There are three kinds of standup. Desperate assholes who want the world to love them. Pure assholes who think being angry is funny. And actual talented people. Like Kaufman with his unfunny puppets and fucking with the audience. Or groovy Joel Hodgson, a prop guy I saw on Letterman, whose big move was failing at card tricks. Shit, I think he was from Minnesota. But 99% of comics are Type One. Being around their desperate neediness was no good for me.

"Everyone say *whoooo!*"

The voice came from inside

Woo! came a chorus. But not like Ric Flair. It was goofy. Awkward. Like kids at camp learning some stupid game. Groups. I hated groups as much as comics.

Ludstone looked at the ten feet between us. I'd stopped at the wall of desperate clowns and had not budged. "Uh, you aren't scared of comedy types, are you?"

"Just reverse psychology." Marching, I pushed past Ludstone.

It had been a bar once. Folding chairs were pushed to the side. Nightclub lighting. A hodgepodge of teens and twenty-somethings and a handful of oldies stood in a circle. The clown in the center was wearing a black t-shirt and yellow and pink Hawaiian shirt. Sweat hung off him as he jittered, making eye contact with his "students." His nose was hooked and his hair long in the back, short in front. As if a punk and a metalhead were fighting for his skull.

"Great job, everybody! Did you feel how things work better when you agree? You build ideas. You build worlds. You make characters come alive and you get away from the blah blah blah of arguments. There's a famous story about Joan Rivers, you know, my mom?"

Laughter. They laughed at this idiot's bad joke. Like fresh cult members who hadn't realized they drank the Kool-Aid.

"She was in a scene with Del Close, the godfather of improv in Chicago who stole all his good ideas from our founder, Jack. *Anyway!* They were in a scene and Del said "You can't leave me, Martha. What about our kids?' And Joan Rivers said. "*We don't have any kids!*'"

I snorted.

And the Twin Cities' answer to Robin Williams looked at me. "Yes, it was funny. But it killed the scene. It's a blackout. If she had said "Fuck the kids, they're not yours anyway!" they could have *gone somewhere*. Things could have *worsened*. There'd be more *story*. Right? Instead, she denied his reality. And when you do that, you might as well kick the audience in the face because if *we* can't agree on reality why should they *believe* in our reality. Right?"

I shrugged.

He shrugged. "Ah shrugging! It's awesome. Everyone, no matter what I say, let's try a shrug."

"Wanna go to the dance with me?" he said.

They shrugged.

"Team, did you finish the Johnson account?"

They shrugged, then laughed.

"Mr. President, did you launch the nukes?"

They shrugged.

"Great suggestion, new guy," said the fucking clown. "C'mon and bring your genius closer and join the circle."

My fist coiled. We locked eyes. Then it relaxed. "Davey Nichols," I said.

"The one and only!" he responded.

The one and only kid who sent me to Red Wing.

THIRTY

BEAT THE JESTER

Dear Dr. Jack Palate,

I've completed the initial assessment of Sully Alexander regarding the incident at Fitzgerald Public School, and given Sully's reaction I am obligated to warn you of something that may make his time at Red Wing problematic. You have the reports concerning Davey Nichols and his family, as well as the school's administration. Sully was highly resistant to answering the questions. He spoke in single word dismissals or refused to answer for the initial five minutes. You suggested I lead with questions about the incident. When that failed to generate responses, I decided to ask about what happened before the fight.

His body language changed. He restrained himself with crossed arms, legs pressed together. In the report from the English teacher, Mrs. D. Taylor, there was evidence of Davey "teasing" Sully. No specifics were given.

I asked Sully about the teasing. Having read his file, I recognized the name of his mother, who was a professional wrestler. I asked if the teasing involved people mentioning his mother.

He became vocally hostile. He indicated he didn't "give a

[expletive]"about his mother.

Reviewing the dossier, I discovered that his younger sister, Kara, was now at the school. She had previously been at a special school for people with physical retardation and other deficiencies (though she is mentally normal). I asked if the teasing was about her.

He gave me an order. "Don't talk about her. Ever."

Sully's behavior had been resistant but was now threatening and I decided to reassert command. I asked if Davey had talked about his sister Kara.

Sully leapt across the table, grabbing me by the collarbone and engaged in a short melee before he was restrained while screaming threats, which included ripping out my eyes and defecating into my skull.

It is my professional opinion that Sully has the potential for self-harm and harming of others while at Red Wing. He should not start with group work but be teamed with one individual, preferably one diagnosed with introvert behavior, until he has become adjusted to life at the facility.

That said, I must say that it is encouraging that Sully offered a warning. Many of our inmates have chosen violence before establishing boundaries. I suspect he will do better in an environment of clear rules and obligations.

Dr. Charles Womack, P.D., M.D.

THIRTY-ONE

CONSEQUENCE ALLEY

The nose.

It was the new one.

I'd given him that nose.

"Stunned by my famous face, huh?" Davey said. "Well, I promise I don't bite … *much.*" More sheep laughed. He waved me in. "C'mon! All you need is you!"

"Great!" Ludstone said, dragging me into the circle. "Sorry we're late. Parking was awful."

Davey's accent switched to Southern yokel. "Always is, dis close to da mighty Mississippi." Then back to clown. "So, let's introduce the newcomers to the friend circle."

Kill me.

"I'm Charm," said Ludstone.

Everyone shoved their fist in the air and said "*Charm!*"

"Now that's a magic name!" Davey said, likely the one-billionth time she'd heard that line. But what the hell was Charm a nickname for, Charmaine?

"And who is the man in the green jacket?" asked Davey.

"Alex," I said, figuring it was a close enough truth that I'd remember. Good liars needed much better memories.

"*Alex!*"

Davey clapped. "Great! What we are going to do now is a game called Scary Face."

Please, please kill me.

"Someone will initiate a face to the partner on their left. That's your other left, Mona!"

The sheep laughed.

He walked toward me. The sheep moved. He stood to my left. "That's the 'offer.' Then the next person tries to imitate that face as much as they can and pass it to the next one. And what's going to happen is magic. A story will be told. The face will change. We will change because of this face. And remember to mimic *everything they do*. And everything includes—"

"Volume, body language, facial expressions, and attitude," said a razor-thin kid with wide eyes and a smug smile. "You say this every week."

"And one day you'll get it right every week, *Franklin*. It's attitude, expression, body language, and volume!"

Fucker always had a good memory. Could read you. Read when the words he was using as weapons hit or missed. Words like sick. Freak. Retard.

"Relax," Davey said. "This is improv! There are no mistakes, and no one gets hurt! Now, here we go!"

He twisted back to me. "Bip!" he said, body rigid. Like a robot. Then a sheep turned to their left and said "bip!" a bit louder, teetering from one side to the next.

"Beep," said another, moving their arms stiff.

"Blurp!"

The fuse of stupid was lit, racing down, each time I heard a word. Not a robot.

Freak. Cripple. Retard.

I unclenched my fist, but no blood dropped from the tip. The stupid face got passed around as each person added their own shitty idea.

Freak. Crip. 'Tard.

Volume grew as it drew close. Then it hit Ludstone. She turned. Contortions snarled her face. She screamed, "Tard!"

Clockwork. I swung.

The face I made. Eyes starved for attention. Nose busted. My Frankenclown.

I never saw my punch coming.

Clockwork, I punched him. Fist shot through the air, but the monster pivoted. Clockwork, my arm tangled in some judo shit. Airborne, I slid on the ground. Somehow his hand gripped my wrist as if he'd let me down easy. But there was nothing inside me but shock.

"And that's scene!" Davey said. He looked up at everyone. Ludstone was pulling back a haymaker. "Don't worry folks, Alex here is a stuntman who teaches stage combat. Say hi, Alex!" He squeezed me to play along. Like a wrestler cueing a reversal. He wanted to make me look good.

Wind long out of my chest, I waved. "Hello from Hollywood."

"Let's take five minutes and then we'll start doing some mini shows!" The students grabbed jackets and smokes and headed for the outside. Davey winked at Ludstone, then down at me as the last kid left. "You want a hand, Alex?"

I nodded.

He heaved, I rose, then I poked his eyes like Moe from the Three Stooges.

Ludstone shoved me. "What the hell is wrong with you?"

"It's fine!" Davey said, covering his face, then hissed. "It's actually hilarious. Because I know I deserve it." He blinked. Tears welled. "Don't I, Sully?

"Yes," I said. "You do."

He sniffed, big honker half-congested. "Well, go on. You waited, what, a decade to get in a cheap shot? I'd hate for you to have wasted plane fare just to get one lick in and miss by a mile. Or was it bus fare? Either way." He dropped his hands by his sides. "Come on."

Set up. It had to be. He had some serious judo training. A fair fight would kill me. But I could taste the venom in me like white lightning.

Ludstone flicked my ear.

"Ow."

"Is this old shit?" she said.

"Yes," Davey said.

"Then I don't *give* a shit. Davey? We need to talk to you."

But his eyes were on me. "You were never much for talking, Sully."

"Why bother," I replied. "You never shut up." But the sting in my ear broke the spell. I didn't come here to fight the one guy who might help us find how Robbie died. Instead I shoved anger into the icebox, then lifted my chin. "Including about my sister."

The smirk sagged. "Look, I was a miserable twit back then. It's before I found improv." I laughed, and he did too. He made it sound like AA. Or a cult. "I know, I make it sound like a religion. But it saved me. I'm trying to use my powers for good. Not like when I was a kid."

"So," Ludstone said, walking between us. "We'd like to talk—"

"Asshole," I said. "Fuck your come to Jesus moment."

Ludstone closed her eyes.

"You got off easy," I said. "I got Red Wing."

Ludstone muttered. "Fucking shit."

He took a step back, but leaned forward. "You got juvie and a clean record. And trust me, I was pushing for you to be tried as an adult." Ludstone looked at me as if I'd just murdered a basket of newborn kittens. Davey pointed at his nose. "But this? Four surgeries and I'm still a busted nose clown."

"Wrong turn if you're looking for an apology."

He closed his eyes, mouth twisted. "You're right. I don't need one, Sully." His eyes opened. "You do. I'm sorry for what I did." The hand that had flipped me extended itself.

Ludstone glared.

"Wanna make things square?" I said. "Tell me. Who at the Galactic Circus trained the Atomic Kid?"

The hand retreated.

"I'm guessing it was you by the judo you tossed at me," I said. "It was his favorite martial art because it was about falling and not getting hurt."

Davey softened his grimace. "You knew him?" He glanced at his giant watch around his tiny wrist. "Look, I need to finish this class. You should go."

"The fuck I am," I said. "And if you think you'll get lucky with tossing me again, brother, please buy a lottery ticket. I'm going to be on you like napalm. The more you pull, the more I'll stick, until you burn and talk. I went to Red Wing for whipping your ass." I ground my teeth, moved forward. "Imagine what I'll do now with a clean record and a dead friend."

His back hit the folding chairs that rattled like cheap thunder. "Fine, okay, great, but can you wait outside? I need to keep this class happy and fun and you're like kryptonite to both."

Ludstone pulled me back. "We'll just watch. Tell them we're from a local film company, looking for talent along with our stuntman." She mimicked shooting her camera at me. "Just say we aren't doing interviews. You'll look like a hot shot and then we'll get to talk."

"You're clearly the brains of the operation, Charm," He said "And the beauty." I raised an eyebrow and he put his hands up in submission. "Fine. Fine. Sorry to leave you out. Sully? You're the *beast*. Now please, let me get through this class and I'll be happy to answer all the questions you may have."

The acolytes returned. We hung back and watched the spectacle as Davey did his Inspiration Clown Cult shtick. The room was tenser. He'd make a joke about us. They'd laugh. Ludstone would smile. I did, too.

"Huh?" she said.

"He used to be pretty," I said. "And rich. And fast. Lungs like a new engine. He was hard to catch."

"How did you catch him?"

I chewed my thumb nail, which was rapidly turning black. "Took months. I punched a sock I hung from my window. Fast. Accurate. Did it every day while he called my sister a retard. He got bolder. He came closer. Thinking me meek and beaten. Trying to get me to do what he wanted. Didn't budge me. Kept punching. And he kept getting closer. Always with dudes that cheered him on. Jocks, freaks, everyone. I was the most unpopular thing since calculus exams. Then he *pushed* me. Laid his hands on me and shoved. I did nothing. School was getting out for summer. Pushed me with a crowd following him half the way home. They got bored just watching. They all tagged me. Potatoed my back. My legs. My stomach. I did nothing."

While we talked in the corner, Davey directed the improv sheep. Shitty comedy. Bad sketch. And they laughed and slapped each other's backs.

My jaw relaxed. "But I knew where he lived. And he was going to summer camp, like all rich kids. I figured I had one day to strike or else he'd vanish forever."

Davey helped two guys learn to agree instead of fight.

"So, I got up at six. Walked an hour. Everything fucking hurt. Knocked on his door at 8 a.m."

They re-do the scene. They say they are on the moon, building a base to save America from the Russians.

"His mom opened the door. She wore high heels at home. White ones. Don't remember her face."

The Russians attack, but the two men build a Pun Cannon and fire.

"I say I'm a friend from school. That he has my copy of *Cue for Treason*. I need to return it to the library or they won't give me my report card. I say we were study buddies and I give the name of some other kid in class. The one who kicked my shins."

The Russians start saying "Join the Revlon Revolution" and putting make-up on everyone on the moon.

"She gets Davey."

Everyone is so beautiful they forget about the war.

"He comes to the door."

They start making love.

"Before he can speak, I punch his throat."

It becomes ugly on stage. The dudes get grabby.

"While he chokes, hands holding his throat, I punch his nose."

They become a monster.

"He cries. Can't see. But he can't make a sound. I yank him by his shirt outside."

Davey waved his hands.

"Didn't stop punching until his mother pulls me off."

Davey took the stage.

"My fists bled on her white heels."

Dave yelled "Scene! Great job, everybody. I'd like to thank Charm and Alex for being such good sports." Applause rained. I nodded. Charm took a dramatic bow, whipping her hair back. Dave dug into his pocket. "Rachel Messing will be here in five for those doing the character workshop. Now, don't forget, everyone gets two bucks off our hilarious new show, *IBManiac*. If you've seen it once—"

"*You've seen it once*," they said, all chuckling.

Davey smiles, looks at me, then said, "And now for my next trick. A vanishing act!"

"No!" I said.

He darted for the backstage door faster than I could punch.

THIRTY-TWO

LESSONS FROM QUICKDRAW

From *Curse of the Black Widow: Confessions of a Lady Heel and former Queen of the Ring,* unpublished biography of Katerina Moscowitz, as told to C. N., 1977.

I have never been a good mother. But I did one thing right. I taught my kid how to punch. I throw a mean left hook, not that I ever get to use it. I keep it in the trunk of tricks and have practiced hands since Billy Wolfe hired me, green as a grass, when I was still roller-skating burgers to dirty old bastards.

Protect yourself. God, that should be a woman's first commandment. Because this world is littered with ways to kill you. Most of them wearing stained underwear. I watched fights. Studied them. PhD in pugilism and know more judo holds than a sack full of Japs (sorry, Japanese, though I admit I still have nightmares about my daddy at New Guinea). See, my memory is what you would call photographic. But not for names and dates and useless shit like books. For action. I learn quick by watching and quicker when in the thick of it. So I got in fights with people better than me. They always won the first round, which was fine. Learned all about psychology. Lull my prey into a false sense of their own greatness and, wham, Good Night, Sweet Princess.

But about the kid. He was scrawny. Quiet. Useless with his hands. But he adored me. So I'd send him letters on how to mix it up when he would get picked on, which was always, and told him I'd learned it from Cowboy Bob West. Real Canadian cowboy who ran away from the Great White North to the USA. Was Golden Gloves at one time. Rat-ass poor, so he couldn't afford a gym, but his uncle was a featherweight who boxed in the army. Taught him this trick.

Hang a sock up in your room. Take an orthodox stance. Straight right. Practice form, accuracy, speed, in that order. Learn to land your punch. Do it one hundred times a day for a year. And you'll have a knock out in your fist. Only his uncle was full of shit. Being good with a single punch meant you only ever had one shot. Rare is that fight, let me tell you.

But I'll be damned if the little bastard believed what I'd said. When he got tossed off to juvie, the cops asked *me* if I'd beat up the ankle biter my kid had trashed. Me! I was stuck being a mother and now I'm getting accused of assault and battery?

Why did I share this lie? It wasn't to hurt him. Not to make fun. The kid just needed something. A security blanket. A gimmick. Anything to feel safe because I was gone and his dad was a brainiac who'd get scared jaywalking in daylight. The little monster wanted to be like me. Who could blame him? But learning to fight takes guts, talent, discipline. You couldn't be soft and the kid cried when his favorite cartoon, the one about the rich boy with the Indian friend, was canceled. I knew the real world would eat him alive. So, a little kayfabe was sprinkled on his mind. Like Santa Claus or the Easter Bunny (and god how he cried when he found out the Bunny was also fake) or an idiot uncle handing bad advice to his poor nephew. I had no idea the little monster would actually do it, like a damned fool, and actually turn one hand into a weapon.

I should have known better. I could see it in him. The hunger. The anger. It comes from weakness. He wasn't good at anything, really. Just imitations. He could watch a cartoon and have the voices down pat. Why? It kills me to say it, but I don't think he had much there to begin with. That's why people imitate. They don't have any originality, or individualism. Carbon copies of better people. And I didn't want that for him. All I ever wanted to do was help him. And what did he do? Get sent out to the sticks because he damn near beat a kid half to death for calling my baby girl names.

If it had been me, no cops would have come. There would have been no charges. And I wouldn't have been sent to that hole. Because that kid would have *stayed down* and *shut up*.

THIRTY-THREE

IRISH WHIP

Pummeling through the improv sheep, I hit the backstage door.

A hallway. Red walls. Cheap light. Mirrors and clown art. Davey at the end. T-section. He hits the wall, guns it to the left. He's still so fucking fast.

Didn't care if Ludstone was behind me. I ran. Hit the wall, turn left.

Ten feet away, Davey pushed the back door. Avalanche of daylight.

I ran into the cold white, furious.

He knows something. He's running because I'm right. He's connected. I made the connection. He's the trailing thread of string. He's a black skeleton in the white of the outside world. Lungs gasping, I chugged on into the cold as my breath becomes visible. Hands freezing, fist tight, nose hair frosty.

The black skeleton turned right.

We're outside. Parking lot. Plowed, but filthy. He's jacketless, sneakers kicking up dirty snow. Aiming for a motorcycle.

I keep going, but he's already on the bike. Digging in his pocket. Keys.

Lungs blown, I run anyway.

No tricks, No fancy. Only one mode. Ramming speed.

He kicks down. The engine lights up. He spins around, stares.

"Die," I scream, but he peels away, aiming for the street entrance.

Hopeless, I run as he reaches the sidewalk—

A horn blares and the Cookie Monster Truck fills the exit.

Davey endos his bike, front wheel stuck in the earth while the back one goes ass-over-tit, bounces off the truck, and lands on the sidewalk—

Davey shoots out his arms, like I did falling from Penny's window. He scrambles up, slow.

Smiling, I dive. Drive him into the Cookie Monster, lift him up and toss him behind me.

Just like the Hooded Bastard did to me. Felt so good I got hard. Folks walking the sidewalk gawk as I pull myself up, one hand on the bike's handlebars, and I do my best Davey Nichols. "Don't worry, folks! This is all just stunt work for tonight's show! See?" I kicked him in the liver and he shuddered. "No one is hurt! Do you want free tickets?"

They did not.

I killed the engine on the bike, tossed the keys into the parking lot, then kneeled. "Let's go for a ride, Davey. It's cold outside."

Davey's sweat was turning to ice. "You can't. I can't break my word. I promised."

I gripped his ugly nose. He shut up. "Cut the tough guy routine. Get in the car. Or I'll do something that'll send me back to Red Wing." I twisted.

"No! Fine! Fuck!"

Once I shoved him inside the Cookie Monster we rolled down Hennepin, toward the bridge. Davey sat between us. Ludstone kept stoic with the heat cranked up. The radio wheezed with static as we picked up a college station somewhere left of the dial. It faded in and out as we crossed the Mississippi.

"We got a quarter tank," I said. "When we stop for gas, I'm going to start breaking your fingers unless you talk."

He shook, shoulders hunched. "I promised."

"We just want to know who trained Robbie," Charm said. "We know it was someone at the Galactic Circus." We didn't, but it was a good lie.

"Saw you take a bump," I said. "Like a pro. Did Robbie teach you? Some kind of work exchange? Microphone work for self-defense and prat falls?"

"We know Jack is plugged in with the Swede," Charm said.

"Old school buddies," I said.

"And there's no way AK got so good on the mic all by himself. So the Swede called Jack. And Jack called you to teach him to work the mic and crowd."

Davey closed his eyes. "I can't."

"Can't what?" I said.

"I swore I'd never tell anyone. And I won't. My word is my honor."

My open palm slapped his nose. Red trails came from each wide nostril. "Your word? You lie for a living. On stage. To students. How many of those folks are going to fill Belushi's shoes or even get on a bus to New York and not starve to death? You sell bullshit. That wall of funny faces is selling an illusion. Take this class, you'll get famous like them. But those folks aren't bound for NBC. They're bound to take classes with you until they run out of dough or get tired of your shtick. You're a con man selling unattainable fame under the guise of running a school. And you got in with the AAW. Why? Cash?" He shook his head, arms in his lap, then in his armpits, then back to his lap. The string in my head connecting him to Robbie hummed. "You were going to jump out of improv for wrestling. That's what they promised." Davey pinched his nose, then snapped his fingers away. "Because you ain't Belushi, either. You're not in New York, are you? Hell, you're not even in Chicago. You're still here, the hometown hero of this idiot factory. Then you went to the colosseum to see AAW and you heard the crowd. You saw stands filled with fans. And then Kaufmann gets on Letterman and now every two-bit comedian wants a piece of wrestling. Guess it beats playing to the barflies and students who won't fuck you."

He shook his head.

"Makes sense," Charm said. The truck skidded; the river of ice below us was thick and cracked. "You go from arenas to the bar, must be a hell of a let down."

"Who connected you two?" I said.

Davey closed his eyes.

I flicked his ear and they opened. "A friend of mine is dead. He was twenty-three. No way this was an accident. If you helped push him to the grave, I will fucking tear out your eyes."

Silence. Rat had made this threat to more than one promoter and barkeep, and it worked two times out of three. I chewed off a hangnail. "You got until three."

"We still have gas," Charm said.

"I got no patience." I spat the nail at my feet. "One." I clawed my fingers above his wide eye like the pincers in A Clockwork Orange. "Two." I tore his hair back and the blood ran down his face. "Three—"

Davey screamed as I dove my hand.

The brakes screeched. Flung into the seatbelt straps, I bounced around. Davey covered his face. We'd stopped in a McDonald's parking lot. "Ease off, Dr. Claw," Charm said. "You may dig jail, but I don't. Davey, please. Just tell us and we'll let you go."

He sniffed. "You don't get it. If I tell you, they'll get me."

"Who?" I said.

"Trust me, I didn't know this would get bad. I just wanted to help."

"Help what?"

"He was a natural. He didn't need that much coaching. Fuck, he probably didn't even need me."

"Who connected you two?"

He, relaxed, deflated. "If I say, they'll do worse than rip out my eyes. Fuck, if anyone saw me with you guys they're going to think I spoke already." Scared. He sounded scared. Like he was living

with a death sentence. Bravado? Gone. Just looked sick and tired.
"I liked the guy, truly. He was funny. He took improv seriously."
He sneered at me. "Pun *intended*. I was so glad he got the push. He
worked so hard. But … someone thought like you did. That I was
fucking with him. Or making him look like a fool. He jumped me.
Told me to stay away. Told me to leave Robbie alone, that he didn't
need anyone outside the business telling him what to do. Then he
tossed me around like you did. Fucking strong."

Davey had a run in with my guardian angel, the Hooded Bastard.

"Another wrestler," I said.

He nodded.

"But not the one who connected you guys."

"No. Look, I was sworn to secrecy. The guys who hired me, this
matters to them."

I sucked blood from my finger, then a strand in my head tightened. "Wait a minute." I faced him. "You mean kayfabe."

The word punched him in the face. "What?"

Charm's eyes met mine. We laughed. Someone honked. "Let's
get some drive thru," I said, cackling. "This mark thinks we don't
know that wrestling ain't real."

THIRTY-FOUR

SMARKS

Tootz will tell you different. Sandow will have bragged it was he himself who created the term. But none of them will reveal the truth. They refuse to break it. They will enter the grave and the great darkness telling you everything your eyes have seen is a shoot. But there is something else at play here. Unlike them, I am not afraid.

It came out of the carnivals, like so much else. When you'd be traveling with an AT show, and you had to pick a stick from the roustabouts and peg mashers or clowns, you had to maintain the illusion and you couldn't trust these two-bits to keep the smoke rolling. We needed a language for the confidence trick. Marks littered the midway, poking and prodding for a reason to call the bluff.

We lived in two worlds. Gods among the marks, and mortals among each other. And if we did our jobs well, to all those concerned, there was only one world that mattered. Which one they saw depended on how well we kept kayfabe.

Pig Latin? Foolishness. Carnivals were laced with a thousand dialects of lies. We were haven to foreigners from Eastern Europe, from Russia to Turkey to the Orient and all posts in between. What unified them all is real Latin, for even the Russians we had were

Christian and the Asiatics were quick learners. "Be cavey," "look out." The term was lost in the noise of crowds, heard only by those who spoke it. A cultured word from the orphans of Europe. Just in case you thought we were all sub-literate attractions.

More terms followed. Work was what we did with Sticks, planting them in the audience and feeding the marks the idea he had a chance. But outside, for money, marbles, or chalk, we could all shoot. You start by shooting. You must. Too many times I've seen men walk into the ring and call us clowns and jesters. Athletes. Actors. Comedians. All think they can do what we do. But the secret is out as soon as the bell sounds. There is nothing more real than a man screaming in a grapevine, or drowned to sleep in the arms of a someone he considered a fool and pretender.

All wrestlers are killers who chose to let their prey live.

I ask you, mark, when I have a man at my mercy and allow him to live to work another day, how phony am I?

Strangler: Memoir of a Champion, self-published in 1969, based on interviews by Chris Chapman, discredited as a forgery by the NWA, AAW, GWA and other promotions in 1969.

THIRTY-FIVE

RING MASTERS

The Happy Meal box in my lap was empty, but I smiled. The toy hamburger container that sat in my hand had been transformed into a brown robot. "See, Davey?" I chewed the last sweet bit of my cheeseburger, then sucked on my straw. "Just like this toy, we know about the secret world of wrestling. I've been writing about it for years. Charm has been backstage more than me. We've held kayfabe longer than you."

The Happy Meal in Davey's lap remained closed.

"The way I see it," I said, pontificating like my dad, "you're going to need friends. If Jack finds out you broke kayfabe, your career as a loudmouth is over."

"Asshole," he said, hands on his knees.

"I'm just getting started," I said. "But if you bring us to Jack, we can talk kayfabe. Clear you of any wrong doing."

"I take it back," he said. "You're a *first-class* asshole."

I put the toy on the dash. "And you're no Dave Letterman. But I'm not wrong. Would you like to know how I know?"

He sniffed.

"If I was wrong, you'd say so. But you don't."

He shook his head.

"You're smart. And fast. Your mouth is a machine gun. Instead, you're silent. Because you know I'm right. So bring us to Jack and we'll clear your name." I opened his Happy Meal. "We'll say that you said nothing. You kept your word." I took out a fry. "You are an honorable member of the fraternity of gladiators—"

"Or else you'll bury me," he said, cutting me off.

I shoved the fry in my mouth. "Yup."

Sliding his hand into the box, he removed the burger. "Take me back to Galactic Circus. No, really. Jack lives there. Upstairs."

"So he witnessed that little display?" Charm said.

"He's a carny. He sleeps through car crashes and wakes up for show time. But it's home. Can't be far from the spotlight."

"Creepy," Charm said, pulling an illegal U and gunning it back the way we came. The robot burger slid off the dash. I snatched it.

Davey flinched.

I smiled.

We took the backstage door. Charm led. Davey in the center. Me in the back.

Now I enjoyed the posters. Ripe and Vance Jumbo Circus. Sun-bleached art. Melting clowns. Sad lions. Starved acrobats with street make-up. Big tops and spotlights in dusty yellow and drained blues. Racist caricatures of Chinamen and Turks. A ringmaster armed with bullhorn and whip. A wrestler with cowboy mustache and toga. Tarzan with dumbbells, big compared to the clown standing next to him. And then a picture of a strongman clown. KISS meets the Hulk.

"Sully?" Charm said.

I bumped Davey, deliberately.

"Woo!" came the cries of the bar as we headed past the door toward a flight of stairs. Up. Up. And to the left.

A long hallway. Office and storage doors. On the far left, a sign upon a door: "No One of Consequence." I was sick of Jack Ripe already and we hadn't even spoke. We flanked Davey.

He knocked. "Jack?"

Nothing.

We didn't budge.

Another round of knocks. "Hey, Jack?" Davey dug into his pockets. "He's a damn vampire." Keys jangled. My hands itched. The lock turned. The door swung open.

"Hey, Jack! Sorry to disturb you."

Davey stepped inside.

But the stink shoved us back.

Charm covered her nose. "What the fuck is it?"

Shit. Barf. Voided stuff. Like a dog beat to death. Wheezing worse than asthma and asbestos.

Something moved in the fetid dark.

Stained glass dusted the white light of winter in the room.

An old man was bent over an old wooden throne. Naked. Bruises collaged his body. Above him stood a shirtless masked man, powerlifter belt in his giant hand. Arm raised for a coup de grace.

THIRTY-SIX

FIRST OF MAY

Excerpted from FUNTOP: THE ENCYCLOPEDIA OF THE AMERICAN CIRCUS

Ripe, Jack, (b. March 15, 1929—)

Jack "Red" Ripe was known in the industry as a "little big top," a career performer and jack of all trades. Despite success in the wake of the Depression as a child performer working with his parents in camps of WPA workers, his star never reached the zenith of the Barnums and Baileys. A colleague noted that he was at his best when a clown, working in the tradition of Grimaldi. Ripe had an almost unreal tolerance for physical pain and exertion, attributed to surviving a childhood bout of polio that crippled some of his nerves. His endurance for agony allowed him to do pratfalls, slapstick, and physical stunts where others of the grease paint trade focused on magic and props. Thus his act as the "Amazing Bumpo" became a much-desired attraction with Hendricks Bros., Ricketts, and a brief stint with Barnum and Bailey (though a family dispute led to his demise with the venerable institution, see *Popcorn Incident*). But it was the adrenaline of the high wire that called him most. Perhaps as a result of his need to rise above the fray, he developed a high-wire stunt known as the "atomic cannonball" in 1949. Rumors abound on the malfunction that led to Ripe's demise, but a witness reported to the *Dubuque Telegraph-Herald* that the cannon "tossed the man out with a grand explosion." The stands caught fire and Ripe broke his leg, ending his career. He later resurfaced in Minneapolis, Minnesota, where he built a theater based on Vaudeville traditions and improvisational comedy (now made famous thanks to Second City in Chicago and *Saturday Night Live*). He remains an avid collector of circus memorabilia.

THIRTY-SEVEN

ENDURANCE ARTIST

I ran into the shit stink. The old man waved me away. "Don't!"

But all I saw was the Hooded Bastard, now wearing a mask. Swinging wild, my forearm slapped his as he blocked my blow, but I kept at it.

"Stop!" cried the old man.

A palm strike to the face stunned the massive guy, but he grabbed a fistful of my puffy green jacket. The belt dropped between us. Then the guy tossed me into the dark. For a moment, I flew. Smacking the book case, the floor raced to kiss my face. Shit and liquid touched my lips.

Vomit left my mouth. A fist clutched me and pulled me from the floor. The density of his strength was as palpable as the acid on my tongue.

"Drop him!" Ludstone yelled.

"Fucking don't!" I said, swinging an elbow that ate air.

"Hey, Rube!" It came from the old man.

The monster tossed me. I landed hard beneath the muted sunlight, choking on my own spit. But the ground was dry.

The old man, legs extended, was balancing on his palm, his

body aloft in the air. "Mung," said the old man, legs dropping with the slow grace of a ballerina. Naked, bruised, and as muscled as a Depression-era photo of a street fighter. But his face was goofy. Wide, buck teeth. "We're done. Just clean up. And get this poor man a towel." Voice was gravely, but high, like a Gnome who smoked tobacco out of a busted hash pipe. He turned so I no longer had to stare at his ass. Instead, his giant thatch of grey pubes clouded whatever cock he had. "But you must admit you deserved what you got, breaking into a man's inner sanctum." Then he looked at Davey. "I look forward to hearing why you decided to invite total strangers into my private life, Davey. Consider it the last act of your time with the Galactic Circus."

And good god, the man's face was a drape of tears, running without him crying as if it were poison sucked from a wound. Charm walked toward me, then retreated. A white shape cut the dark. I caught it like Ozzy snatching a bat, then wiped the shit from my face. "Tell him, Davey," I said, trying not to impersonate a claymation dog.

"Jack, I'm so sorry, but these folks knew Robbie. They know he was here. They're reporters."

Jack's eyes flashed. "You brought paper people here?"

"I work for Val Weston," I said. That brought his dagger stare to me. "*Amazing Wrestling.*"

"Which makes you even worse. Val's a self-righteous two-bit no account. A pretender. So tell me why I don't have Mung toss you through this window?"

"If he does, we'll report that a dead man trained at Galactic Circus."

He smirked. "Blackmail, is it? What makes me fear a guy from out of town with my shit on his face? Tell me that?"

"Mr. Ripe, we're just trying to find out what happened to Robbie." Charm's eyes were quivering.

"For the top dollar, no doubt," he said, arching his back. Mung arrived with a bucket and a five-liter bottle of Clorox.

"No," I said. "For the truth. Otherwise, he's going to die a joke. I won't let that happen."

He kneeled down, fuzzy balls swinging. "And who are you?"

"Sully Alexander. Son of the Black Widow Moscowitz. And Robbie's only friend in Red Wing."

His nose crinkled. "Alexander." Cheek turned. "The Demon?"

Cringing, I nodded. "That's what he called me."

"Davey? Close the door." He stood, then offered me my hand. "Mr. Alexander, I apologize."

"My hand is covered in shit," I said.

"I know. It's mine."

Bleach has a funny flavor. Bright. Electricity through barbed wire. Clowns surrounded me from portrait frames as I rinsed out all of my facial cracks and crevices. One of the clowns was crinkled, brown and grey, as if soot was the secret ingredient for sadness. Slumped on the busted wheel of a wagon, this sad fuck looked down at me. "You think *you* got troubles," said the caption underneath this king on a junk throne. His pants had been chewed by a combine, shredded like tissue paper.

"Fuck you, Willie," I said. The green jacket sat on the toilet. The rip in the guts was now matched by Mung's death grip. Murmurs from outside the clown bathroom caused me to silence the faucet's gurgle.

"I understand it must be distressing to have found me in my birthday suit, but we all grieve our own way."

"Hey, I like V. C. Andrews novels," Ludstone said, "I have no right to judge, but how was this grieving?"

"I'm what the old barkers call a physical attraction. My nerves, you see, don't operate like others and thus I don't *feel* the way others feel. This is a physical ailment, one that has, sadly, cocooned some of my emotional life. I need certain conditions in order to activate my feelings. If I don't, I get terribly ill. Rather a big problem with comedy, and, in this case, grief. Mung helps in this regard."

"Doesn't it hurt?"

I slung my jacket over my shoulder, gave King Clown the finger, and hit the light.

"Of course. That's the point. The trick, as my old mentor said, is not minding."

The orange and brown robe hung off his body like overripe skin. The ascot twice as big as his neck needed. The glasses gave him a weak tone. Jack Ripe sat, legs crossed like a woman. Charm sat on the floor with Davey, who was cross-legged and staring at nothing. Kids at kindergarten. Mung was at the door. Everyone smelled like Clorox. The bottle was comforting in my hand.

"Ah, the Demon returns," Ripe said. "Feel better?"

Bleach lightning still flickered. "Sure. Another shitface day. Listen, Davey did not break kayfabe."

He sighed. "I never like hearing that term from marks." He waved away my imminent objection. "Yes, you were born into our world, but only the periphery. That said, I am glad to hear my most recent initiate has maintained honor among thieves." He gave Davey a nod. "Do not worry, David. You will still have your job. I hear you knew each other?"

"He gave me three years in juvie for me giving him his nose," I said.

Ripe laughed, then clapped. "Smart! I like you, Demon."

"Stop calling me that."

"Of course, of course. We're all upset. But the way he spoke about you—"

"I don't care. I just want to know what Robbie did here at the Galactic Circus. And *why.*"

"But you already know," he said. "He came here for stage training. To help his career."

"Yeah, but why now?" I said, walking closer. "You can take years building a wrestler into a sensation. Sure, he had heat, and clearly was a superstar in the making. But why the rush?" I kept what I knew about New York on ice because I could tell the old man liked to talk. Idiot older people often tell you anything you want, if you can suck up the patience to listen through their bullshit stories.

"Do you read Tolstoy?" he said.

Perfect. Play dumb. "No, you train with him?"

He snorted. "For fun and giggles, could you tell me the last book you read?"

"I had a copy of *Carrie* I found in the Port Authority bathroom."

"Trash," he said. This from a man with a clown boner. "Tolstoy was the greatest novelist of the past two hundred years. *War and Peace*?"

Charm smiled. "Afraid my partner is only into old horror guys."

He turned to Charm. "Then let me address the brains and beauty of the duo." He leaned forward. "Tolstoy was infatuated with Napoleon. He believed Bonapart was selected by history to lead us into the next phase of the human story. And that he was only able to emerge because of the chaos, horror, and mania of the French Revolution. Strife and change produced Napoleon and allowed him to change Europe by the sword."

"I skipped history," I said. "Get to the part where you reveal the goddamn point."

Mung stepped forward. "Quiet," he said.

"Nice accent," I said. "Tongan? Given how well you tossed me I'd say you know more Sumo and Judo than a real ninja."

He snorted. "Big mouth, little man."

And that was all I needed to hear: this wasn't the Hooded Bastard.

"You got lucky."

He laughed. "Next time, I'll make it fair. I'll give you a gun and twenty feet."

"Mung, please," Ripe said. "You've more than earned your keep. I'll call you for our next appointment." Mung nodded, turned to the door, and left. Ninjas leaving improv theaters being normal in Minneapolis. "The point, Demon," Ripe continued, "is that moments come where conditions allow for revolution to produce its heroes."

"Robbie was the Napoleon of wrestling?"

He grinned. "He was going to be. He could learn just about

anything taught to him."

"He was a natural," Davey said, still glaring at the floor. "Fast wit, but wasn't too verbose. We had to work on that. He had the timing, but he needed the words."

"And we helped him find them," Jack said. "Robbie wasn't going to make green. He was going to make gold and lead his Merry Band of Muscle into the next decade. There was Gotch. There was Strangler Lewis. There was Gorgeous George. There was Buddy Rodgers. There is Rick Flair and Bruno Marino. There would be The Atomic Kid."

"And?" I said, stepping closer. "What happened?"

"Well, you know what happened."

"He was only twenty-four years old," Charm said. "It wasn't natural."

He leaned back. "I fear I've known too many strongmen and shooters. The smart ones lived into old age. But the ambitious often took shortcuts."

"How does a wrestler take shortcuts that kill?" I said.

"Depends on what you know of the alchemy of the human body." He raised an eyebrow. "What do you know of AAS?"

"Is that a wrestling promotion?"

He closed his eyes, growing more frustrated. "Allow me to spell it out for you. Anabolic-androgenic steroids?"

THIRTY-EIGHT

VITAMINS

"On June 1, 1889, Charles Édouard Brown-Séquard, a prominent French physiologist, announced at the Société de Biologie in Paris that he had devised a rejuvenating therapy for the body and mind. The 72-year-old professor reported that he had drastically reversed his own decline by injecting himself with a liquid extract derived from the testicles of dogs and guinea pigs. These injections, he told his audience, had increased his physical strength and intellectual energy, relieved his constipation and even lengthened the arc of his urine."

John M. Hoberman and Charles E. Yesalis, "The History of Synthetic Testosterone," *Scientific American* (February 1975), 76.

THIRTY-NINE

NIGHT FOR ITS OWN SAKE

New strands in my head began to wrap around a needle. Rat crossed my mind. Talk of injections like inflating bliss.

"The steroids make it so you don't feel the shitstains in your Fruit of the Looms," Jack said.

"So … like Popeye with spinach?"

"A crude comparison," Ripe said, "but apt. I have been around strongmen long enough to know they are vain, fearful of being weak, and willing to sacrifice their old age for a glorious young life. Like Achilles."

"Or junkies," I said. Charm glared at me. Davey sank lower in his crossed legs.

"More apt," Ripe said, motioning to a seat on the floor beside Davey. "Could you imagine your old ally from Red Wing being a Colossus of the ring?"

I shrugged. "He was a fucking teenager. I just figured he got a growth spurt, hit the gym. He was dedicated."

"And impressionable," Ripe said.

"Wild claim, any goddamn evidence?"

Jack nodded. "Davey?"

The runt lifted his head as if it were a bowling ball. "He …
learned quick. Because he was always imitating others. He tried to
be me for like two weeks. I mean socially," Davey said. "He wanted
to please everyone, be friends with everyone—and that meant
doing anything and everything. He liked being a spectacle and that
led him to people who saw him as … a clown. One willing to try
anything." His lips puckered.

Jack took two steps closer and glared at me. "Ain't going to narc
on you," I said, "just tell me. What shit was he doing?

Davey looked at Ripe, who winked, and then the little shit
opened up like a trench coat. "Oh god, everything. Any kind of
booze he was good with, but he'd take pills if they were around and
… he'd get high with us. Just grass, man, we're not Aerosmith. And
then he'd bring stuff to make friends."

"With who?"

Davey looked at Ripe, who nodded. "The mainstage troupe. He'd
train with me, then hang backstage or in the wings to watch. We'd
party afterwards and he had great stuff. Uppers. Speed, mostly.
But," he shook his head. "Well, we were out all night at Marlow's
and he was going to the gym. He always brought his gym bag. And,
well, this is weird."

"Get on with it," Charm said.

"Alright, okay, he said he needed a favor." The favor, Davey said,
was taking a two-inch needle and injecting it in his ass. "There were
lots of holes. Old ones. I guess he was doing it himself. Keeping it
secret. He said it was to help his knee heal. Which made no sense,
since I was shooting that junk into his ass. And the acne, god, was
like a pizza face … on his ass." I stepped closer. I kicked his face. He
rolled back but not before I tackled him, scrambled, and raised my
hand up high.

"Sully!" Charm said. "Don't!"

"Back the fuck off," I growled, all eyes on Davey. "You killed him!"

"What? No! That was two months ago!"

"Why should I believe you?"

"Because it's the truth," Ripe said, unmoving. "And you won't blind a man in my presence without going to prison. Put the bleach down, Demon."

The bottle bounced off the wall, spilling across the floor. Charm got up to avoid the liquid approach. Davey's shirt was tight in my fists. "Lie to me," I said, slow, and quiet, "and I will go to prison. Not Red Wing." I stood, glancing at Ripe, then released Davey. "So drugs made his heart pop?"

"I wish it were more epic," Jack said. "Robbie became a narcotic degenerate. The heart, you see, is also a muscle. The drug does not target one area, but all muscle growth. I suspect that his heart grew too big. Hence, the heart attack. Robbie killed Robbie."

I lurched forward. "I want to talk to the Swede."

His eyes relaxed. "I bet you do. But you'll never get the chance."

"Where is he?"

Jack's head lurched to one side. "My boy, I pay a Tongan death fighter to beat me so that I can cry. What good do you think you can do with those tiny little fists?"

Glass broke against my knuckle as I drilled his eye. Spectacle remnants dropped like angry snow. "Where?"

The mussed-up glasses and crooked smile made Ripe into a dummy. "I understand your anger, but unless you are prepared to murder me—"

"Sully!" Charm, on her feet, waved her hand in front of my face and for a half-second I backed down. "This isn't helping."

The old man smiled, glasses still crooked like Jerry Lewis. "Come now, I got the impression from our mutual deceased friend that your bite was worse than your—"

The coat fell to the floor, stuffing like clouds bleeding out, as my hand clutched his pencil neck. "Don't need to hurt you to choke your bark."

"Sully," Charm said, striding toward me. "We're leaving."

I released the old man. "Fuck you. He meant shit all to you people. Just another carnival attraction to use for fame."

He coughed into his fist. "One who died under the needle."

Charm hooked my arm and dragged me back. "Davey?"

"Oh, Davey will be staying," Ripe said. "He is a child of the the-ater. And this is home."

Davey, the live-wire, was broken on the floor next to my coat. "You're a fucking puppet," I said. "If you killed him, if you put the needle in his hand, I'm coming for you, Davey." Charm pulled open the door. "Hell can't save you. Or a perverted carny."

Male laughter trailed me as I stormed away from Ripe, then the workshop, and then the fucking world. Opening the stage door, a dozen of the improv idiots were walking like ducks while a thir-ty-year old woman with wide hips from whiskey chased by Little Debbies screamed "Find the leader duck! Who will follow? Just don't dry hump each other, okay? Our insurance doesn't cover mallard STDs." Beneath her bangs were green eyes. "You here for the drop-in?"

"Just needed the shitter," Charm said. "Thanks!" We strolled through the lobby, out of earshot. "Jesus Christ, what the fuck was that?" Charm muttered beneath her breath.

The popcorn smelled rancid. "He had it coming."

"Who fucking doesn't? How does killing him make sense?"

The door to the outside bit my palm with cold. "Time will do that. I just needed—"

"To hit him?"

White light burned as the door opened. Two steps out, and I was alone.

Charm stood in the dark lobby.

"What?"

"Know what?" Charm said. "I think I might take that drop-in class after all."

The cold hurt. "What? What about the story? We need to find the Swede. He's the only one who has any of these answers."

Her face was blank as an unbaked pie crust. "Maybe it's best we do some digging on our own. We can compare the strings and cards later." She took a step back. She twisted on the balls of her boot heels. "Try not to kill anyone on the way back home, Demon." The door closed.

Out on Hennepin, the wind cut across the Mississippi like a dull, thick butter knife. Cookie Monster Truck was locked. And there was better money on a wrestler becoming governor than in my groveling back to that carny prick for my jacket.

A gaggle of kids passed me, coughing grass smoke and avoiding eye contact. Two feet past me, they started laughing.

"Smells like the janitor's closet."

"Dude is a human TP stain."

Plumes of grass thickened as they strolled on toward the bridge. I held still.

What the fuck was I doing.

Playing detective. August Dupin, Jr. Edition.

My friend was dead. He pretended to be me. Took my place when I thought my mom was dead. Led a life that could have been mine. Now some carny fag said he was spiking his veins. He did it. He fucked up. He killed himself just when the spotlight was on him.

And I was hitting people. Again. Scaring people. Again.

This is why you imitate other people. Why you take their voices. Write imaginary interviews with real people. Control. No red button about to go nuclear in your eyes. But everyone is pushing yours. Shouldn't have had that drink with the alky on the bus. Should have slept. Should have stayed home. Instead I came to this city for answers and all I got are lies. Bullshit. It's all a work. Not a shoot. *Go back*, I told myself, *to New York. Forget this place. Forget your friend. Forget your promise to Kara. Make up some story for Val. Go back to washing dishes when he trashes you in the business.*

Go back to the hole, Demon.

"Sully?"

Ice fell from my eyes with a blink.

The clouds of stuffing from my jacket's wounds flittered in the breeze. Davey held the green armor before him.

"Take it."

I did. "Your master is wrong," I said. "And you're full of shit." The jacket's de-stuffed arms were as lifeless as fiberglass. "He didn't kill himself."

"I agree." He sniffed.

I slid my arms into the sleeves. "Why?"

He tapped his outside pocket. "So long, Sully. Maybe one day we can … maybe one day you'll forgive me. I'm not a bad guy."

"You injected his ass. That don't make you a saint, either."

He smiled. "Jews don't have saints, moron," he said, then laughed. He pushed the door inside and I shoved my hand into the pockets.

A paper boulder sat in the left one.

I walked away from the river until I hit a gas station. A crumpled one-dollar bill bought me a Snickers and coffee. While the coffee warmed my right hand, I plucked the blue paper boulder with my left, shook it between two ghost-white fingers. One side was an ad for *IBManiac*, the other held Sharpie scrawl.

"Russell Muldoon. 3614 Harriet Avenue."

Jesus fucking Christ.

Muldoon. God of the Dirt Sheet and the most feared journalist in wrestling.

The only one of us shitbags who told the truth.

FORTY

SHADOW IN THE SPOTLIGHT

Wrestle Dirt: They Tell It Like It Is, We Tell the Truth.
RIP Billy Jean DeCurso (1943-1980).

This one hurts. "Jeannie" was where it all started. *Diary of the Squared Circle* started out as a Lou Thesz fan club newsletter. She loved Lou and George and even Sven the Swede and Shooter Mahone. She always said that Tootz Mondt gave her the title of "The Only Woman in Wrestling Nobody Hates." She earned it because she loved this business, its people, and its confidentiality. But she also pushed the envelope forward a half-inch or so, sharing details that earned her a fandom all her own.

Diary of the Squared Circle offered small amounts of truth alongside the world of *kayfabe* (Pig Latin for "keep fake"). It started innocently, with birthdates and the real hometowns of some of the biggest stars of yesteryear (you would be surprised how many of them come from Wisconsin). She also became the center of a web of newsletters, fanzines, and fan clubs across the world. She even had the personal mailing address of Antonio Inoki in Japan (and his vacation home in South Korea). They trusted her. She trusted them. In exchange for this information she kept what she really knew secret. "She knows more secrets about the business than Strangler Lewis and Cassidy Mahone combined," one source told me. Until she dared to tell the truth.

Jeannie was set to start a brand-new newsletter. She said she'd noticed something going on in the business she didn't like. She said it was "like a shadow in the spotlight." She wouldn't tell me what it was, but gave me two words that have stayed with me ever since.

"PAY ATTENTION."

Which is why *Wrestling Dirt* exists. Because when Jeannie died in Tacoma, Washington, I attended her funeral. Based on the cards and letters I inherited from Jeannie, the following promoters, bookers, and wrestlers were contacted to attend. The following chose to stay home.

Cassidy Mahone, Sr.
Cassidy Mahone, Jr.
Ron Mace
Sven Börne
Sam Munchick
Lou Thesz
Buddy Cruze
Eddie Campbell
Bill Watts
Dusty Rhodes
Ric Flair

She died keeping your secrets. I live to tell the truth. Prepare for the shadow to meet the light.

This is Wrestle Dirt.

FORTY-ONE

GAME OVER

I slid the phone booth door shut. Too cold for the smell of urine and shit to waft up from the yellow, iced floor.

"Operator."

"I'd like to make a collect call."

"For what city?"

"New York."

"Do you have your party's number?"

I did.

"Your name?"

"Sully Alexander."

The Demon.

"Hold please."

Holding.

Not thinking about Charm's scared eyes. Pain in my fist. Jack Ripe's stupid grin. Davey's nose. Job balanced upon the top rope, but with its boots unlaced.

"Mr. Weston, will you agree to a collect call from Sully Alexander?"

Silence.

"Hold please."

Click.

"You cheap mook," he said, then laughed. "You better be exhausted from all the material you've been gathering. I send you on a profile and you end up with the biggest story in wrestling since the birth off TV! What have you got and how soon can I get it?"

Wind whipped the booth, Val's voice like a shitty metal band's singer.

"Rumors. Mostly. Tons of different stories."

"But there's only one that matters. Everyone in the country wants to know how the Atomic Kid died. No one gives a shit about titles or if Andy Kaufmann is really a woman. The big lug broke the biggest rule in wrestling. He died in the ring. Which means we need to make our investigation top drawer, sell as many copies as we can while the world is watching. Because sales will drop once he's in the dirt. So, what are those assholes in Minnesota saying? Was it Princeton? Black Adder? Katana Hiroshima, the dirty Jap with a similar atomic shtick?"

"Well, one source—"

Val laughed. "Great, great! Talking like a real journalist! That will sell this so hard we'll both have pools this Christmas. Okay, Woodward and Bernstein, what are all your Deep Throats yakking about?"

My red and raw right hands stuffed the clouds of fluff back in their wounds. I clamped down the first rip. "One thought he might be a drug addict."

"No fucking way."

"I know. I don't buy it. I'm going to dig deeper and get to the—"

"You're not reading me, Sully. We don't print drug stories. Not even this one. "

I pressed the wound close. "Right."

"We won't sell copies telling about the boys shooting, snorting, smoking, and drinking. Can't even allude to it like we do with the ring rats they fuck. Drugs? That will bring the heat on them from real cops. We need the best story about The Atomic Kid. Which means taking the truth and inflating it just enough that we keep kayfabe and wink at reality, as Tully Bones put it. Printing a drug story is death."

My hand shook. "Right. Totally." Beeps in the distance. Garbage trucks?

"What else you got?"

Sucking the last piece of nougat from my molar, I swallowed. "Had a lead on the Swede. But the guy wouldn't give up his house address. Do you have it?"

"Fuck. Doesn't matter now, kid. Even if I did, he'd be surrounded by lawyers and say nothing. Forget about the Swede. What about the roster?"

I'd been attacked by two wrestlers in twenty-four hours. "Anonymous tips, mostly." I relaxed my grip. "One said that Robbie was a casualty. Like in a war."

The word bred abnormal silence. Then a deep swallow and a clearing of throat, finally. "Really?"

My voice took on a pleading tone. Weak. Pathetic. Almost Teddy-like. "What does he mean, Val?"

Grunts. The receiver distorted what I translated as Val pounding back a Coke. "Kid, you're off the garden path. We need a sensational story. We need reality dressed in kayfabe. I'm starting to think you're a little too young to be doing what we need. Maybe Teddy would do better. Everyone loves Teddy."

I pinched my nose. "No, Val. I got this. My mother," I said, lips grimacing "is lining up interviews. It's just taken a day or so because of the chaos. She knows people here. They trust her." I sneered. "More than Teddy."

"Playing your ace, huh?" he chuckled. "You bought yourself a reprieve, Sully. When's the funeral?"

"A couple days. I'm in with the family."

"So you'll be there? With my photographer?"

Everything puckered. "Yup."

"Well why the hell didn't you start with that instead of bleedin' my money and time on useless bullshit?"

"Okay, boss," I said.

"Three days. I want the whole issue. One feature. Usual columns. Ten photos. Get as many at the funeral as possible. And just in case you think I don't respect you, you're making double time and a half. That's a mint to you, Sully. A mint."

Each digit of my hand relaxed. "Done."

"That's my boy. Use the telex address I gave you and make the copy clean. And if you want a bonus feature, we can do a retrospective on your mom. Hell, even I thought she was dead!" He laughed, then the phone clicked. He was gone in my hand.

After checking a map at the Husky gas station, I walked.

No snow in the air. Just clouds.

The streets were wider than New York, but smaller than I remembered. Everything smelled like ice cubes and TV dinners shoved deep in Rat's freezer cooler. He had a thing about ice. Stole it from anywhere he could. Rat grew up in Atlanta, and there, ice was like currency. "You'd see this at Dairy Queen," he'd say, gnawing his nails. "Didn't matter if you were the King of Savanah or Lord of the Ghetto, everyone worshipped Dairy Queen because it's got A/C. Fuck the melting pot. The Dairy Queen is the Cooler of America."

Maybe Rat was still alive.

In the absence of facts, do I get to choose? A Rat in a box. A Rat playing a bar.

Does it matter which one sticks in my skull? Is one more real?

Death was supposed to be the one definite thing. And breaking death was fantasy.

Poe called it the swoon. That space between. Closest thing to Oz in real life. Where dreams felt real. Dead came back.

But they didn't. They just never fucking died in the first place.

The Black Widow never died. Just like Sadistic Stan, it had been a con. A work.

Robbie was dead. A shoot.

The strings tied to lies or dead ends in my skull.

Jesus, I felt like a dumbass student in dad's first year literature class. The shit who read Descartes or Nietzsche and figured, well, I know one quote so I know it all. I think therefore I am. That which does not kill us makes us stronger. I was never kinder to the old man than during the whole week before I killed him…

"Fuck you, Poe!" I yelled.

A Dodge Ares honked.

The sun sunk behind me, and shadows grew. The city was a muffled scream, buried in clothes, suffocating in snow, trapped in all the little itty bitty pieces of life.

Harriet Street. The same color of suburban desperation. Houses. Families. Cars. Snowmen. Bullshit.

Another worm of strings flapped around my grey matter.

Fine. *You're on your own*, I told myself. So what else is new? Just answer the question. Like it's the SATs, but this time you went. Who the fuck *would* kill Robbie? That question made more sense than the answer of a needle in the ass and an exploding heart. There had to be a reason. Not an accident. Not being a drughead for muscle injections.

Breathing heavy, I started a jog down Harriet. The street was like the giant ribcage of some monstrous dinosaur. Skeletal trees bent their limbs overhead to rake me. Nose running, I slowed down.

Russell Muldoon's house. Fuck. Two stories. Big. Probably a backyard. If he ever wanted to sell, some real estate agent could make a lot of cash. Up front there was a glass bubble where I think an indoor garden lay off of an enclosed porch. An orange light hung in there, turning the air wavy.

Muldoon's home was death. Of my career, anyway. Val didn't have a lot of rules about fans and outsiders. "But if you talk to a dirt sheet," he'd said, draining a Coke grasped in his swollen hand, "I'll burn your reputation to the ground. You won't be able to take a piss within a hundred feet of any wrestler."

Only wrestler I cared about was past pissing.

Only person who cared about truth in wrestling was in this house.

What the fuck did *I* care about?

Val's promise of riches? I'd be broke in six months and back to cranking out wrestling reviews in my apartment until the next calamity that turned heads and put seats in asses. Val … he was a dead end, too. Only he'd never tell you that.

I shoved the cloudy remains of my jacket back in the hole. Three steps, then a little stone path. Three steps, then a white, metallic door that held out the wind.

Banged three times.

Nothing.

Three more times, nothing.

I turned. Nothing but snow-stained streets and a cold walk back. *Davey*, I thought, *I'm going to kill you.*

A rustle from inside. Eyes closed. I was hoping this might be the end.

Open.

I turned.

The inner door opened.

Through the screen of the outer door it was hard to see her. But it was a her.

"Yes?"

"I'm here to see Russell Muldoon."

A second passed. "I'm afraid you have the wrong address. Are you okay?"

"Why?"

"You're shaking."

"I'm fine. Are you sure? This is important. I need … I need Russell's help. I'm a friend of Robbie Varhooven."

"I don't know who that is and you should probably run along."

"He died. Yesterday."

"I'm sorry to hear that but—"

"There are people who are going to lie about him. Say he killed himself. Or that it was an accident. I don't think they're right. But I need help. Everyone lies." Tears raced down my cheeks, then froze. "But Muldoon, he's the only one who tells the truth. He could tell me if my friend died for no reason. Or if he's a casualty of a war no one is talking about." I coughed, laughed, and wiped my face. "Forget it. I'm wasting your time. Sorry to disturb you."

Each of my three steps down the path were as heavy as Misfits basslines.

Time to hack my friend's body for Val. Bury my friend in bullshit. Because I was out of moves. Make a payday. Stay in the world of kayfabe. Penny would think I killed him. The world would think he had a bad heart. The boys would think he was a junkie for muscle drugs. Everyone would pick their poison.

Snap. I turned around.

Ice broke off the outer door as it opened. Her breath clouded, face distorted. "Who gave you this address?"

"Davey Nichols. I presumed he was a friend of Russell."

The cloud cleared. At first glance, she looked like a nun. Long thick dress. Formal blouse. Both dull green. Round face. Brown hair done up in braids. Religious outfit that looked warm and neutered. "Come on. You'll die in this cold." She walked back inside. The door shut quick but didn't clang.

No argument here.

The outer room was humid. Smelled like dirt. A big orange light on the right was playing the part of the sun to an indoor greenhouse. Who the fuck had a greenhouse going in winter in Minnesota? There was a single pair of flat, black boots on the ground. The air smelled wet and sweet, but not salty like sweat.

Grass?

"Take your shoes off," she called from deep inside the house. "And please watch where you step. I've just finished cleaning."

If this was a horror movie, I'd be slashed to ribbons by a chainsaw or a machete in the next five minutes. But at least I'd die warm. The house ached with the tone of formality. Every picture was an antique. The wallpaper looked dull. It was like standing in a set from a made-for-TV movie called <u>Cure for Insomnia</u>.

A light snapped on at the end of the hallway. "Would you like something warm to drink?"

"Please," I said. Formality seemed to matter and I could play the role. "Thank you."

"Coffee or tea?"

"Whatever is easiest for you."

"Believe it or not I'm capable of both, as well as harder tasks."

She sounded like a school teacher. Maybe this was Russell's mother. Fuck, did the guy still live at home? What kind of loser was he? A year after Red Wing and I'd had enough of Dad's shit for a lifetime and then it was a Greyhound and New York and that was all she wrote. But I was willing to bet my pawned SG that some of the guys who pawned the Black Widow's career inventory were also couch surfing their primordial home. *Et tu*, Muldoon?

The light felt hot as I approached the next room. I rubbed my face on my sleeves. A faucet flashed on. The kitchen was large. Smelled of Chinese spices I associated with Wang's restaurant. Was she Chinese? The string in my head just formed a question mark. "I've just made some dumplings if you're hungry." She'd pulled out a wooden stool that sat at a small, round kitchen table in a breakfast nook. Her back to me, she was setting a kettle on a big stove that looked like a science fiction gadget.

"Thank you, yes."

The gas hissed, then a flick of her hand and a match lit the blue flame. "How long were you walking?"

"Don't have a watch," I said, taking the seat. Relief flooded my thighs. "Started out at the Galactic Circus."

She looked at her fridge, as if a calculator. "That's almost an hour on foot."

"I'm fine." But her mind was still running sums. "Is Russell here?"

She poured out a pot that steamed up her face, dumplings tumbling into a sieve. "What is your name?"

"Sully. Yours?"

"Sasha." She lifted the sieve. "You know Davey."

I crossed my arms. "Went to school together." How the hell old was Russell if this was his mom? She was, what, thirty? Or maybe she was his wife. Hell, Val was married. But most guys who loved this shit were doomed for bachelorhood and back alley blowjobs they bought with their bar mitzvah money. Or … Christ. I was fucking stupid. And now I had to play even dumber. She deftly poured the dumplings into a ceramic bowl with a blue-ribbon design. "How do you know Russell? You his roommate?"

"He stays here sometimes," Sasha said, then walked over. "To be honest, I'm not sure if he'll be back." She placed the dumplings before me. The steam was a mix of sesame oil, white pepper, and Asian five-spice. "Him and Davey are also old friends."

"Cool. What do they have in common?"

She sat. "Theater."

I laughed. "Is that what you call what Davey does? Seems more like clown stuff."

The thinnest of smiles came across her moon face. "He *is* a clown. One of the oldest forms of entertainment."

Fuck. We were dueling. And I didn't know the rules. Or how many men did I have to waste before it was Game Over. The dumplings steamed between us. "So you do improv?"

"I've gone to a show."

I laughed. "So bad you'd never want to do it yourself, huh?"

The smile cracked a little more. Her age was hard to dig. Face so white with makeup she could have been twenty or forty-five. "It has a spirit I respect. It is one of the few forms of art where failure is championed. In other arts, failure means death."

I leaned back. "Kinda the opposite of wrestling."

She betrayed no sign of acknowledgement.

"In wrestling, failure means people die."

"I thought wrestlers hurt each other."

"Only by accident. But if you like theater, consider this. Wrestling is a form of theater. The actors sell violence, but no one gets hurt. In that way it's the most—"

"American art form of all," she finished. And her smile was taut, small, like gunshot wound. "Sully Alexander," she said. "The man who replaced Kardassopoulos at *Amazing Wrestling*. Son of the Black Widow Moscowitz. Former cellmate at Red Wing of the late Robert Varhooven, who wrestled under the name The Demon before joining the Swede's promotion as the Atomic Kid." She lifted the bowl. "And you need my help. Dumpling?"

FORTY-TWO

UNBELIEVABLE TRUTH

Horace Griffin, Champions of Bunk: The Tricksters of the Squared Circle (1937)

It will seem ridiculous to the modern reader with a modicum of intelligence that what is witnessed at the fairgrounds and arenas is an actual sporting event instead of spectacle. And yet, test that theory in practice through the means of journalism and one finds oneself alone with death threats and physical altercations. In unpacking this investigation, I have been assaulted no less than five times in five states. When violence wasn't available, doors were slammed. Phone calls at midnight suggested I had less than a day to live unless I left their hometown and stopped asking questions that would seem banal and ordinary to any cub reporter. Having served in the Argonne with the D-Battery of the 129th Field Artillery while many of these actors and confidence men were idling at home to take advantage of the nest of widows left behind by better stock, I had made my deal with God before my first battle. I was not to be intimidated by anyone less than the Grim Reaper itself.

And yet it is one of the paradoxes of this investigation that actors and con men can indeed be deadly. One only needs to hear about the use of "policemen": shooters and hookers whose real knowledge of Greco-Roman, Turkish, and Oriental combat holds and vicious attitudes helped keep this mix of fighters, pretenders, and more in line. Each promotion had its own hit-squads of policemen who they would use against rivals from other territories. Behind the wall of muscled clay colossi sat a small army of nasty little gremlins of grappling who could be used like a sharpshooter's bullet to take out the competition. Such men hid in the shadows of saloons, restaurants, and motels as I traversed the territories for the truth. That I lived for this work to see light attests to not only my fortitude, but the strength of the greatest shield of all: the power of the truth.

Wrestling is not just spectacle. It is a world bound by a covenant of secrecy and violence that makes money for promoters while leaving carnage in the form of wrestlers' bodies. Complicit in this are gaming commissions, radio, and newspapers. All have promoted the illusion of wrestling's legitimacy as it has become even more of a spectacle. Silent in the papers are the growing obituaries of old wrestlers. Many die blinded by trachoma. Others have their hearts give out. Others, I fear, will end like Mike Romano.

And it was here, in his match against Jack Donovan in Washington in 1926, that the two worlds of spectacle and truth collided. When Romano was pronounced dead in the ring, the crowd refused to believe the doctor's call. The chant began: "Fixed." And yet, a week after his obituary in the *Times*, the colosseum was at full attendance.

What happened in the week Romano died remains instructive. As an old magician once told me after the death of a wrestler in a hangman's drop, "The audience wants to be fooled. Especially when the truth is death."

FORTY-THREE

THE DUNGEON

The last dumpling entered my mouth. "Why the alter ego?"

"You use five." Sasha sipped her coffee. "Why do *you* do it?"

"Kayfabe," I said. "No choice. The readers either believe or want to believe we're like the Mighty Marvel Bullpen, full of characters as interesting as the wrestlers. It's part of the fantasy. But dirt sheets are about truth."

She tilted her head. "No, Sully. They're not. Rumor, fantasy, lies. I've discovered at least seven that were created to discredit me."

"Over what?"

She smiled. "Billing."

"Fuck that, really?"

"Last year, when Ron Mace was in a contract dispute with Stu Hart in Calgary, he was set to drop his light-heavyweight title. Instead, he just left town with the belt. Stu sent a couple of policemen to fix Ron and get the belt back. Ron ended up in a Canadian hospital—my source sent a picture—and missed his debut in Mid-South. But Bill Watts assumed he'd make the show because one of the policemen called him, impersonated Ron, and confirmed his deadline. First lesson, treat Stu Hart like garbage and you will be reminded that he survived the Depression fighting for his life in street fights in subzero temperature."

"So you're from Canada," I said.

She leaned back. "What's your evidence?"

"No one gives a shit about Stu Hart and Stampede Wrestling but Canadians. Plus, you say 'show' and 'zero' like a Minnesotan on valium."

"You're the first Minnesotan to recognize it."

I'd said I was from New York, but I ignored the jab. "It helped that you didn't say 'eh?' at the end of your sentence." It itched my shit that she knew I was from here. Needed to focus. "So Watts gave you grief for what? Pictures of Mace in a brace?"

She sipped. "No. I reported that Mace would not be fighting against Stagger Lee. But Watts had hired some bodybuilding jobber to wear a mask and had started a story through *your* magazine that Mace had been scarred by acid and now wore a mask. I'd mailed out the latest issue with Mace's picture a week before the jobber's debut as the masked Mace at the Sam Houston Colosseum. Watts was furious. He put a hit out in the fan magazines. I can't verify how much. But dirt sheets showed up with the sole purpose of debasing me."

"That didn't work," I said.

"Disinformation needs mass. He couldn't convince your boss or other kayfabe mags to go near me. Because they feared what I sold."

"The truth. Which is why I'm here."

The coffee hovered right below her lips. "You understand, Sully, your career died the moment you stepped inside my home. And you've given me the power to ruin you."

The tiny mug before me was still chugging heat. My hand rested above it. "You can't ruin what has no value. I don't care about my career. I got one hundred bucks and a handful of days to find out what happened to Robbie before he's either turned into a joke or forgotten altogether. And the strangeness of what's happening in the wake of his death, … I just want to know the truth. I want it to make sense. I want to cut through the straightjacket of lies and bullshit that are getting stacked and locked on my friend. I want to know what happened for real. His death is going to be turned into a work. His death will become a cash grab by the Swede, or Val, or others. And I need you to tie off some of the stranger ends."

"And what do I get out of it?"

Pushing my palms into my eyes. "Here I thought you'd just want to do the right thing."

"You are one of three people who know the truth about Russell Muldoon."

"Who's the third?"

She put down the card. "Here is what I want. Dirt on Val."

Sweat was turning me into a stink machine. "What kind of dirt?"

Her voice became playful. "All of it. Including his contacts in the NWA, GWA, AAW, and other territories. Who hands him the locker room data. I want everything. And remember who you're talking to. I'll smell a work like shit on your shoes."

Ugh. Val kept that shit in a vault. But *Peter* would crack the vault's code after a few drinks. I had stories for days about Val's days in the boxing mags, being friends with other wrestlers, working backstage and earning their trust by having a good eye for talent that would go nova. Talent like Robbie. "Plus," Peter had said, "every other wrestler is a secret homo."

Sasha raised her eyebrow. "I have a deadline, Sully. Dirt for truth on the death of the Atomic Kid. And, a promise. If we find a smoke-filled room with a cadre of wrestlers around a gun, you can write it for *Wrestle Dirt*." She put down the cup. "I've never offered this to anyone. We can both ruin or support each other, Sully." She stood, cup in hand. "Show yourself out if you want, and I'll say nothing. But if you want to know what's *really* happening, I am the only one who can help you." She walked out of the kitchen and further down the hall where a door had lain in darkness. The hinges squeaked.

I stood. Downed the cup. "Here's what I know."

I spoke my piece.

"Follow me," she said.
She led me into the dark.

FORTY-FOUR

FANDOM

Shooters, Issue 2, December (1980)
EDITORIAL: CHEST-POUNDING MAD!

I want to talk about Giant Baba and his heart condition. I want to talk about how Harley Race may be retiring. I want to talk about Abdullah the Butcher's busted ear drum. But I can't, Shoot Nation. Because of what a no-good bastard did to our business.

Russell Muldoon is a no-good faggot who lies to make himself feel good about all the havoc he's causing with his little newspaper. I've spent more than a little time in trying to deduce where in the territories he's working. But he's cagey. He must have a network of worms who feed him stuff on the territories. Given the focus of the last few issues, I can say without much doubt that he is not in the South. He's an East Coast Guy. Academic. Righteous. A fucking dilettante and pretender.

The self-hating homosexual is the scourge of our sport. They are spoilers who take the magic away and replace it with lies and conjecture and call themselves journalists. I've been a real journalist. I know a fake real from real real. I speak kayfabe like a Red speaks Bolshevism. And I can say without a shadow of a doubt that Muldoon's rag is poison to our fandom.

Not to sound paranoid, but there is clear indication that Muldoon is in our ranks. He is likely using a false name. Be cautious about who you share with, Shooter Nation. Trust the inner rings. Keep your kayfabe tight as a nun's asshole.

We need your help, Shooter Nation. We need to find this punk and put him out of business. I want to call on all of you to share your leads. Mail them in to the address below. I've enlisted the aid of *Iron Ring* and *Kayfabian* and dozens of other sheets who want the great Muldoon wiped from our earth. Our joint membership is over a thousand strong. If you love our work, join us and help us gather the details on Muldoon so we can rid fandom of his stink.

We'll also be looking for recommendations on who to do the job. We have a lot of old policemen in mind who would love to hook Muldoon until his eyes bled. If you know of an old Hooker or Shooter up for the task, by all means, include their particulars and we'll get in contact on our own. Then, Shooter Nation, we'll see how tough Muldoon will talk about our business.

Lastly, those who wish to send The Marauder Ron Mace get well soon cards can also do so at the address below.

Stay strong

THE MASKED GORILLA,
PRIMATE-IN-CHIEF

PO BOX 1990
Pueblo, Colorado
81008

FORTY-FIVE

INSULT TO INJURY

A cavern of bookshelves lined Sasha's dungeon, but there wasn't a book to be found. Video cassettes were packed tight into every inch of the wooden shelves. Etched on their yellow and white paper were a thousand different examples of American handwriting and code titles.

Colone in Germany, 1979.
Dynov. T. Mask
Last Match of D. Von Erich
All Japan
Swede, Thesz.
Stampede Bootleg

Three large tables also displayed a map of recorded and stolen matches. Before me was a bootleg paradise. But all I could think of was jizz.

Peter had a thing for porno. Hunting it. Owning it. Like that Mad Magazine cartoon about the "wolf" who freezes all the women he seduced so they are on stand-by when he needs them. Al Goldstein told him where the "Good Stuff" hid in the cellars and warehouses of the Bronx and Queens. He'd drag me along.

Educating his protégé. Wasn't a hard sell.

Until the smell. Sawdust. Particle board covered in plastic. VHS cassettes in white and dark sleeves. All of it soaked in the dirty clove stink of old, hard, yellow-gray jizz.

Lemon and saffron. That's what Sasha used to clean her place. But the filth of my memories sprinkled on the present.

"The Heart of Darkness," I said.

She stood before a large RCA with a VCR. "How so?"

"Sorry. That's what Val called bootleg warehouses. He thought they sucked away fans from his bag. Should have called it a black hole. Suspect he hasn't read Joseph Conrad."

"And you have?"

I shrugged. "My dad's a professor."

"Princeton, correct?"

"Every time you do that, I feel like taking a shit."

"I hope you don't. I keep this place cleaner than most five-star kitchens."

"So, you can rate five-star matches?" Russell Muldoon was infamous as a "rater"; developing a rating system for wrestling like Leonard Maltin movie reviews. Infamous was his turkey rating for a match that stunk. Which was most of them. Russell Muldoon was the Dorothy Parker of taste when it came to wrestling. I'd read *Wrestle Dirt* in the shitter, knowing Val would never dare to go where Rat shot up to find my shame. Near as I remember, there were only two five-star matches. One was Dynamite Kid vs. Tiger Mask. The other? Swede vs. Lou Thesz, heir of Strangler Lewis, and the man some say refused to lose to the Scandinavian Nightmare.

"You watched all of these?" I said.

"More than once. Tell me, Sully, why did your friend die?"

I unzipped my jacket. "You didn't ask me how."

"No."

"Do you know?"

"My question first. Do you know *why* your friend died?"

Surrounded by dirty tapes, jacket slung over my arm, I kept one hand in my pocket. *Remain calm*, I thought. *She's still testing you.* Testing if she can trust me. And see what I know. "Yes."

In the dim light her movements were hard to catch. The screen flickered, filled with static. "So why did he die?"

Chest out. "He was a casualty."

She nodded.

"You know how he died?" I asked.

She tapped the top of her TV. "I believe so."

"I didn't ask what you believe. You're Russell Muldoon. What the fuck do you *know*?"

Her jaw turned sharp at me. "Pass me the cassette. You know which one."

The string of my mind had two ends. I tied one to the past.

Holding my breath, I picked up the cassette, brought it to her.

She removed it from the sleeve. "You need to see this." Another button pressed. A cassette holder emerged from the top of the VCR like a sideways toaster. She put in the tape, then pressed it back down. The words "Swede, Lou Thesz," vanishing inside the little magic robot. "Pay attention," she said.

Static became men.

They emerged as black and white elephants. They prowled, laying hands, locks and holds and counter moves in a snowstorm. Soundless. The hum of Sasha's furnace the ambient tone as two old men in their prime moved with jaguar reflexes and slaps.

Boring as fuck.

"Pay attention," she said again, watching my eyes glaze over.

Five minutes later, the worst of the static eased. Thesz was the taller, rangier. The Swede tighter, rougher. Peter said a good wrestling match was better than any short story in *Esquire*, which seemed a shit-low bar.

"Pay attention."

A half-hour of wristlocks, grapevines, and a stand-up grapple—

-a series of quick switches, a forearm, and then the Swede exploded with a flying head-scissors and pulled Thesz over the ropes and spilled him on the floor before following down himself.

"Stop it for a sec," I said.

Sasha pressed a fat button with a quotation sign on it.

"Can you go back? Like a minute?"

She pressed arrow buttons and the Swede flew back in the ring, Thesz between his legs.

"Fucking headache machine," I said, pinching my nose.

"You get used to it."

"Maybe you. I like going forward. Not back."

"And yet here you are."

"Could you hit play again?"

And I saw it clearer. Before the head scissors. Before the flurry.

There had been a lock up. This is when wrestlers talk so the fans can't hear. In this era, men scripted endings but much of the action was "called" in the ring.

In a Greco-Roman stance, something was said.

"Stop it again."

She did. "What do you see?"

Her poker face was perfect. I hated being tested. But I had the answer.

"Whatever was said in the lock up pissed off the Swede and he tossed Thesz out on his ass. He made him look weak. In Texas. NWA territory."

She nodded. "This is when the AAW was born."

"Sure, everyone knows the 'story' of this match." Peter said it was the match where the Swede got tired of losing to a man who he thought he could legit beat and become an even bigger champion. But the NWA commission, the bosses who ruled the territories, said he didn't have the charisma of Thesz. So the best he could be was a noted rival, who was the Superman of his era and a legit tough guy and hooker. Few, if anyone, dared to "take liberties" with Thesz. I'd just watched the Swede dump him like garbage out a six-story walkup. "This was a work that became a shoot."

She smiled. "I'd agree."

"Now what the fuck does this have to do with my friend's death?"

"Everything." She pressed play.

The cameras of the era were the size of tanks. All they could do was sit in one place and zoom. Through the ropes, the Swede and Thesz raked each other with fists and forearms until the Swede got close enough to drag Thesz's head down.

"He's got him locked in Strangler Lewis's own blood choke," I said. "Shit. That's adding insult to injury."

The Ref stayed in the ring. He counted to ten.

Double disqualification.

But when the Swede dropped the hold, Thesz fell to the floor. Static blizzards filled the screen then everything went dark. "He knocked him out in the choke," I said. "That's rare. But what's this got to do with the Atomic Kid?"

"Then you don't see everything. But few of you do." The TV snapped off and she crossed her arms. "You say your friend was a casualty."

"Yes."

"That means there *is* a war."

Strands danced in my head like worms in rain. "The NWA have been at war with the AAW since what, 1960? And the Swede's stronger than ever. Yay, capitalism."

"You're right. So who is actually at war with the AAW."

"Jesus, you mean Cassidy Jr. and the GWA?"

"The war is eternal. It was created the minute wrestling became fake in the twenties, Sully. But the war is always prefaced by revolution. First, it was the Gold Dust Trio. The inventors of modern wrestling."

"Sure, Strangler Lewis and Tootz Mondst and Billy Sandow. I know this story. They created Slam Bang Wrestling, like a vaudeville show, packaged. Got wrestling to be exciting with timed matches, dynamic moves, and scripted endings. Turned it into a play. But they kept their champs actual hookers so no one could screw with them. Guys like Thesz and the Swede. I'm getting tired of the Oracle of the Squared Circle routine. If there's a war, and Robbie is a casualty, fuck the history lesson. Who ordered him dead?"

She hit eject. "The same man who conned you and Val that Stan Rapowski was dead."

I felt like my clothes had been ripped off. I covered my balls. "Cassidy Jr. ordered a hit?"

"That is what I believe."

"Why? And tell me shit I don't know."

She removed the cartridge. "He's attempting to destroy all the territories. His goal is to become the *only* promotion in the United States. A national dictatorship."

"So is the Swede, and neither one has knocked out the NWA in fifty years. They all have a non-aggression pact. Little fiefdoms the NWA lets them have. What's changed?"

"Time," she said. "The Swede is old. Cassidy is young. And more daring. And strange. And he will win because he's not interested in appeasing the NWA. He is interested in revolution, not compromise. The future, for him, was the Atomic Kid. And the Kid wouldn't leave the AAW."

I grinned. "Bullshit. Cassidy had poached him."

The poker face dropped. "Pardon?"

Relishing the moment, my words fell out slow and steady. "He *was* headed to New York."

She shook her head. "I think you are mistaken."

"Nope."

"Who told you this?"

"Sorry, I protect my sources. What's your proof that Cassidy put out the hit?"

"Listen," she said, patience muted. "There have been two revolutions in this business. The first was led by the Gold Dust Trio. The second was a result of TV. And the next is upon us. The old guard is not evolving. The NWA is becoming irrelevant. There are two parties who can make the future and both wanted The Atomic Kid to lead the revolution. He had the charisma. He had the look. He could work. And he was simple enough to be led."

"Hey," I said … then backed off. "Okay, that's fair."

"Cassidy wanted him. But he swore his loyalty to the Swede."

"Why?"

She seemed exasperated. "The Swede had something on him."

"What?"

She smirked. "Tit for tat, Sully."

"Not even close. You've told me nothing I didn't know. I've told you more than Russell Muldoon knew. I'm starting to think Russell Muldoon is full of shit. You say Cassidy wanted him and couldn't get him. I'm saying Cassidy had him and someone else must have killed him. He had a ticket to New York. He was out of here. Maybe as soon as he got the belt off of Princeton."

She ticked her head to the side. "Stanislaus Zybyszko."

The name quietly rolled off her tongue.

Not quietly enough.

Adrenaline raced thanks to a small ignition of paranoia.

The Slavic name had rolled out of her mouth with the slippery cadence of a mother tongue. Not the neutral tone of her measured lectures.

"Fuck, I'm going to regret this but, who is Stanislaus Zybyszko? Any relation to Eddie Zybyszko in the AAW?"

"Only by their inauthentic name," she said, her tone back to normal. "Zybyszko," she said, imitating me, "is the Benedict Arnold of the 1920s. Or George Washington."

Fear kept me awake through the last history lesson.

The Gold Dust Trio ran a tight crew and Zybyszko was among the deadliest real fighters of the era. But he was a lousy champ. Real wrestling was boring, even when scripted, so some promoters started to experiment with dudes who had celebrity and were tough guys. One was ex-football player Wayne Munn. Lewis dropped the belt to Munn, who had next to nothing in his arsenal against a real wrestler. The Trio told Zybyszko to fight Munn and lose, to continue to solidify his reputation as a legit wrestler. He agreed. And then fucked them over.

The Trio's main rival was a former employ named Jo Stetcher. "All revolutions are followed by Civil War," Sasha said. "Wrestling was no different." Stetcher paid off Zybyszko. So, when the two men met, everyone thought it was a work that would make a grand payday. A forty-seven-year-old Polish strongman, and the young All-American hero.

The match started out a work. Going through the motions. Then, Zybyszko turned it into a real shoot. Munn was overwhelmed, looked like a chump, and then was pinned against his will. The Ref was forced to count 1, 2, 3 … and the big bad Pole left with the belt for another league. "The birth of the territories was a double cross." She lay her hands down on the tapes like a blind kid reading Braille. "But who double-crossed who? Who does this serve?"

"I'm done." I turned my back.

"Patience," she said.

"Fuck you," I said. "Unless you got something to share." Her eyes rose from the tapes, but she remained bent, a general before a war map. "I've helped you more than you've helped me," I said. "You thought he was hit from NYC. Either you tell me why or else you can finger these tapes all you want. I'll find the Swede another way and get an answer."

"You mean your mother."

"I mean I'm done, Comrade Kayfabe. You ain't getting shit about my contacts. You ain't getting shit from me. Unless you tell me, in bold terms, clear as a fucking prescription for vitamins, why you think NYC killed him. Who told you. Who was it. Why?"

She pulled herself up, hands behind her back. All emotion dropped from her countenance. Eyes empty of humanity. A predator on pause. Fuck. If she was a Commie, I'd just signed my death warrant.

"Fair," she said. She turned, walked towards a red door. Once she was inside, the door closed. A light flashed on.

She could be grabbing an AK-47

Or a blade taken from a dead Afghan soldier

Or one of the knives that stabbed Rasputin.

Maybe there were Spetznaz in the attic, fresh from their hunter killer missions in Afghanistan, waiting to seize me, cut my throat, and drain my blood on the floor.

Maybe the body of Lenin was frozen outside, awaiting a bolt of lightning to bring him to live and crush me.

But if I split, she'd lock that red door forever.

The light vanished.

She walked in from the dark maw, carrying a small metal box, about the size of a six pack of Bud cans. "Here." She handed it to me.

It was heavy. Probably could stop a bullet. The combination lock was set to triple zeroes. I pressed the release and lifted the top.

Inside sat an inky fanzine.

The cover read *Zola's Wrestling Sheet!*

The cover was a crudely drawn wrestler with big makeup and arms. Across his chest were the letters AK.

"Zola," Sasha said, "was the penname of Harold Watchorn, a wrestling fan in Queens. He was a professional friend." Emotion tugged her face. "His dirt sheet was brand new. He was inspired by my work. He also worked ring crew for the GWA. This was the first issue. And the last." She stepped closer. "He was murdered last week, days after I received my copy. Killed in his own home." The dumplings on her breath had hints of old smoke. "Strangled to death."

FORTY-SIX

CASUALTY OF WAR

Zola's Wrestling Sheet!
October 1983
The AK Revolution: A Play by Play, Blow by Blow Account of How
an Angle Is Born and Killed.

Warning: It is my sincere belief that this story will end in murder.
All facts here were supported by at least one other corroborating
piece of evidence. Following in the tradition of the great Russell
Muldoon, I cannot in good conscience not share this with the leading dirt editors who are the true policemen of our business. I'm
hoping that maybe, just maybe, this can send a shock through the
system to stop a tragedy, one I'm too cowardly to do on my own.

Over the past year, the GWA has been slowly dropping its old-
guard talent. Veteran workers over 30 without a strong fan base
are finding less and less time on the roster. Roman Daniels is the
exception. The current champ, though he has been pushing hard
against growing pressure to play up his "Greek" heritage (forget
that he's a half Cherokee from Daytona, and that his first name

isn't Greek but Roman). One outburst, witnessed by a ref, was that he wouldn't "wear Gladiator garb" to the ring (for more on how much Cassidy Junior likes to Play Dress Up, see the next article, "Wrestling or Central Casting?").

But wrestlers with far less stroke have been let go. None of the old guard feel safe. And over the past six months, most talk has been about new arrivals from all over the territories: Owen Arrow; Rufus "Tiger" Salinger; Blob Huckabee, and the one who brought the most fear and elation: TV Psycho.

TV had been slated to go with the Atomic Kid to AAW, but instead did a short tour of Stampede Wrestling while his partner headed to Minnesota. But the detour had little to do with money (as Russell Muldoon has reported, Stu Hart may have filed for bankruptcy in Canada). TVP was keeping himself out of the Swede's reach, as Stu was still made at the AAW for poaching Nathaniel Prince five years ago and making a mint (Princeton is actually a Calgary native, see *Wrestler Dirt* Issue 49, Secret Origins). On a short contract, TV was set to arrive in NYC in November. But he was supposed to spend that time convincing the Atomic Kid to leave his contract and come to New York. These were the words of Main Booker Tony Marsella, who was released from his contract this week.

Marsella had been tasked with cleaning up the roster after the Culture Watch incident, when Killer Joe assaulted a member of the outside media. The fall out of that open-hand slap was vicious. Killer Joe was fined to fill the bank for the reporter's lawsuit and fired in front of the boys in the locker room as an example.

Killer Joe's response was to tangle with Marsella. He missed with a straight right and Marsella tangled him in a double chicken wing, dislocating his arm before breaking his wrist. This was witnessed by the author and the entire roster at the end of a house show in Newark. But also in the room was a man called Finch. He's called the second-booker. But by the look of his knuckles, nose, ears, and shoulders, he's an old policeman: sixty, fit, mild gut. There are only rumors about Finch. He says nothing. Flanks Marsella, and never leaves the locker room, where he's usually found reading thick novels.

With the firings, and Finch's presence, no one feels safe in the locker room except for the ignorant new faces and heels, and all of them are awaiting the arrival of TV and AK. All of this was happening in the span of two months. Speculation has been wild. There is a belief by the old guard that Cassidy Jr. is now ready for a war. His goal is national domination. He will poach, cripple, and destroy the NWA and the AAW and all who stand in his way. And the two who will lead the charge will be TV as a heel, and AK as a babyface.

Most of the talk in the locker room is about how the revolution will change things. So much of the GWA's past ten years under Cassidy Sr. has been about the old faces crushing young heels. Much of this is due to investment in names like Brunowski, Scheller, and other champions who could still draw the ethnic crowds in the Eastern Seaboard. For Cassidy's National Revolution, as a Quebecker on ring crew calls it, he needs All-American heroes. White. Young. Big. Contrasting. And guys who can connect with the crowd.

Roman's gate numbers have decreased steadily over the past year. And he is spending less time in the gym. But he's still one of the last hookers on staff. He won't leave unless there's a big pay day. According to the rumors, TV Psycho was set to squash Daniels, ruining his last golden reign. And the old guard would fail to upset the loud-mouth TV champ, and the need for a hero would generate the road to bigger gates and the build of the Atomic Kid, with Daniels in his corner. Passing of the torch, like Lewis did with Strangler. This was to be the catalyst for Cassidy's move into other territories. TV and AK had fans in Canada, the Midwest, and with those secure Cassidy would then devour the South. The West would fall shortly after.

But the lynchpin was The Atomic Kid.

This was told to me by an old shooter who was retired, a guy close to Marsella and the Cassidy family. While this could be sour grapes, something happened in the past week that makes me worry it's true.

Allegedly, AK was supposed to meet Cassidy at his villa in Montauk. He didn't make it. My source says that this is common. Folks don't show so they can ask for more money. Make the deadline feel deadlier. There was no one on the roster who could take AK's place, he noted. Now the build was screwed. Roman Daniels started a useless feud with a new hire, Chip Boulder, best known as Savage Steve Strong in the now defunct WCWT out of Hawaii. He has no presence besides his physique and his gimmick of being a silent monster is hard to sell. So TV's push to be champion was reset for early December.

Once SSS showed up, one person in the locker room went missing. Finch. It's been decades since one league sent their own policeman into another territory to "smarten" up the talent. But if you saw Finch, you'd know why I worry. If he worked over The Atomic Kid, maybe that would be enough to convince him to honor his contract.

FORTY-SEVEN

BROADWAY

I tossed the dead guy's zine back into the box. "This just proves he missed a meeting."

"You claim he said yes," Sasha noted, hands still scaling her tapes. "But when?"

"Mid-October."

"Source? I gave up mine."

"You gave up a dead guy." Her eyes hardened. "Fine. His mother."

"You have access to his family."

"Sorta."

"That's more than me. And useful."

"Finch went and fixed Robbie somehow? Had some kind of wrestler mojo that makes other guys die in the ring?"

"Shhh," she whispered, scouring her tapes.

The tapes shuddered when my fist thumped the table. She stood up straight, like a knife fresh out of its sheath.

"Pay attention," she said.

Her fingers flexed. I took a step back, hit a shelf, and shuddered. "I am. Are you? We are at a contradiction. Two permutations lead us out. Name them."

She pressed closer. The strands tightened. "Either he was bound for NYC, breaking the Swede's trust. Or he was staying in the AAW and reneging on Cassidy's deal. Depending on what he wanted, each promoter had a good reason to be mad. But who would be mad enough to kill?"

"Two questions need answers to create links in this chain. Was he really going to New York? If yes, who in the AAW would kill him? If he was staying in Minnesota—"

"Then did Cassidy send this guy Finch to … do something to him?"

"We need more information," she said, breath like tobacco and old food. "And each of us has access to different sources."

My lip snarled. "You mean the Black Widow."

"She knew wrestlers who match the vintage of Finch."

"Which means you don't know who he is."

She lifted her chin. It was sharper in the weak light. "I will travel through these tapes faster on my own. Come back after your funeral. Bring what you know. We will complete the chain. And tell no one of what you saw here. Forty-eight hours."

She turned her back to me.

"What's it like?"

She ignored me.

"Being a Red agent?"

A musical flutter of notes came from Sasha before she hummed to herself. "Oh, Sully. You are such a mark. Run along, now. Your mother is waiting for you."

That word hit harder than a boot to the balls.

And her insult was many things, just not a denial.

I went upstairs quietly, the Russian Bear Ivan Molotov's voice singing "The Internationale" inside my head. In the hallway was a phone. A cab was en route as I sat in what I saw as the safehouse for Agent Sasha Soviet, the fake name for her alias "Russell Muldoon."

Muldoon. A blob of memory popped. *William* Muldoon was a true Greco-Roman champ who would later police fake wrestling as chairman of the New York State Athletic Commission at the turn of the century. He kept the illusion going and hurt those who threatened it.

Our Muldoon was a revolutionary.

And probably a no-good Commie.

That no one suspected because she was a woman.

All roads were leading back to the Black Widow.

Two honks outside. I left Sasha. The cabbie played the news.

"Local wrestler and rising star Robert Varhooven, who died yesterday during a match, will be buried tomorrow at Lakewood Cemetery. The public has been asked to respect the privacy of the family, and AAW promoter and local celebrity Sven "The Swede" Börne has promised a public celebration of Varhooven's life this coming weekend at the Coliseum. The event will be free and feature many of the local wrestlers and celebrities who knew him." Rumbling north, a weak snow fell. Things stayed blurry. The wipers skittered across the windshield. Clarity came, then fell, then vanished, then returned. Fucking headache.

A hit. A causality. A war. A revolution. A commie plot?

It was all preposterous. And yet the aftermath was riddled with strings that were tied. The worms were fucking each other in the back of my skull.

The Black Widow's lair came into view an hour later. But the Pontiac was gone.

Fuck.

Paid the cab, went around the fancy abode, through the gate, and down the steps.

I still didn't have a key.

I grabbed the knob. Turned.

Open sesame.

I tapped the door with my foot. Snow drifted inside and vanished into the dark.

A large black iceberg sat in the center.

No, not again, Fuck the Hooded Bastard or Mung or anyone—

—I charged.

A squeal.

Flab, not muscle, sucked in the blow of my shoulder like jelly as we toppled over the couch and on the floor. Thuds followed us down. I climbed up mount Jello while he whimpered until I had a thick throat in one hand and a fist in the other. I dropped a punch, then grabbed one of the things that thudded. I yanked it up and prepared to drop like an anvil.

"No!" it said "Stop! It's me! Douglas!"

The anvil in my hand was a book.

Poe.

Dad.

The curator of the Black Widow's shit. Fuck. "Douglas," I said, then took three deep breaths. "Right."

"You said to come back."

"And you did."

"I said I would!" He coughed.

I released my grip. The finger marks were buried deep in his neck. "Sorry."

"I didn't lie."

"I know. I'm sorry." I pulled my ass off him, took a step back. My heel slapped another book's cover and I fell back on my own ass. We lay on our backs, huffing.

"You okay, Douglas?"

"I think so. Are you okay?"

No. "Man. I … over reacted."

"I mean, I get it. You thought I was a burglar or worse. I'd do the same thing."

The image of this fleshmountain of a fan crashing into a masked guy with a striped shirt and dollar-sign-bag made me smile. "I bet you would. And you'd crush him like Mike Monolith."

He sighed, nose whistling. "That's my dad."

"Huh."

"I even have his whisky jug,"

"Wow." I sat up like Frankenstein. "Custodian of legends.'

His mess of hair and thin porkchop sideburns remained at slug's eye view. "Someone has to remember. The real death is being forgotten. Edgar Allan Poe knew this."

"You read those books?"

"I like literature that stays with you. Poe is sticky."

Clasping the couch edge, I yanked myself up. Needed to play nice with a guy I just assaulted. A guy who could send me to jail with a phone call. Time to be like Teddy. "Fascinating. Why do you think he'll endure?"

His hands steepled above his chest, he wheezed. "People aren't happy," Douglas said. "The end of the world is normal. And we're all going to die. You either ignore these truths, or embrace them." I stuck out my hand. He took it. Sweaty, it enveloped mine like an oven mitt. I leaned back. Dude was made of soft rocks. My shoulder damn near popped as I tugged and he rolled until he could get a knee up to launch into a standing position. "Poe embraced death and sadness. Wrestling helps us ignore it."

I sucked in air while sweat dropped from his brow. "Deep. Say, you know where the Black Widow is?"

"Of course. It's Thursday."

"What's Thursday?"

It took fifteen minutes in Douglas's Plymouth Reliant with the wood paneling to make me believe. Fifteen minutes in a car so clean you could simultaneously fuck and eat soup off the seats, the air 9/10ths Mr. Clean, 1/10th bleach. Fifteen minutes later I was fighting the urge to run the fuck away from where we were headed. Fifteen minutes after that we are off the 35 and on Portland, and the streets were like corduroy roads made of snow. Douglas' girth was the only thing anchoring us from being shot into a ditch.

We pulled into a smoothly plowed parking lot. A dark building sat at the center. Trucks and big cars, chains on their tires, clustered near the entrance with a fistful of lights. Richfield American Legion.

Right up front was the Black Widow's Pontiac. Parked in a

handicap space. "Christ."

Douglas pulled in next to her. Grunting, he shoved his hands between his legs. "Might want to get a seat. It takes me a while to get my handicap sign."

The more cleaning-agent air I sucked into my lungs, the more I felt like an acid trip was about to burst. "See you inside."

He huffed. "Eventually. Nice talking to you, Sully. Always good to meet a nephew of the Black Widow."

I smiled, then split.

The Legion itself was a brick building the size of a school. Reminded me of an M80. Or the world's biggest Jiffy Pop. Inside was gentle thunder. I pulled open the large wooden door. Ten feet away a row of curtains tried to keep out the noise. Men screaming. Chanting. Clapping.

"Widow! Widow! Widow!"

To my right, a three-chinned man with long hair under his stupid Holden Caulfield hat sat manning a lectern. Snail-faced, he looked down his nose. "Show's started."

"I can hear that," I said.

"Five bucks."

"I'm with the talent."

"Well then you should have been here for warm up and drill," he said.

My wallet cracked.

Four ones.

The rotten part in the basement of my guts said, *"Fuck this guy, you can take him."*

The crowd "Oooh'd!"

"Now why don't you break your piggy bank," he said, "and rustle up the quarters to hang with the grown-ups?"

I swallowed. Think, Sully. Then act. Literally, *act.*

"Fine, I didn't want to say this. Val Easton sent me."

The chins jiggled. "Right. To a Legion show."

"No, to do a profile on the Atomic Kid. But the fucker died. All

AAW shows are cancelled until that memorial gig. So you, sir, get a feature in a national syndication. And if you tell me your name, I'll make sure it gets highlighted." I shoved the wallet in my pocket. "Or you can brag to everyone on the roster about how you turned down the opportunity for national exposure. For five bucks. I'm sure the promoter won't hold a grudge."

His face was a melting sundae under his stupid hat.

I raised my hands, palms out. "Fine, I tried, buddy. Enjoy the four dollars you didn't make."

I turned, hand on the door.

"Fuck, hurry up," he said, box under his arm. "And my name is Wayne Pritchard."

I smiled big. "Who could forget a name like that. Thanks, Blaine."

"Asshole," he said at my backside as I yanked aside the curtains.

Sawdust and sweat filled my nose. Bar lighting and one big disk of fluorescent light. Dust motes poked dark holes in the illumination and shook the world as a body was slammed in a USA decorated ring in exhausted red, white, and blue.

Could not have been more than one hundred people in fold up chairs, the gaps between them like blotted out bingo numbers. Whisky and five-cent cigars permeated my senses. It could have been 1920, 1950, or 1984; fucking ancient Greece had started it all and here we were with factory workers and steel millers, construction guys doing lumber work for Christmas, a couple of dorky teens with shades to hide their bloodshot eyes; a fistful of grannies screaming obscenities they'd beg forgiveness for on Sunday. Some wore wrestling masks too big for their tiny faces. The church of wrestling was in session.

"*Whooo!*" the voices yelled in unison. I turned to the ring.

The Black Widow stood upon the second rope in the corner. Red hair sticking out as if Ronald McDonald had been electrocuted. Black lines around her eyes. Black lipstick. A one-piece singlet and boots that bare a white hammer and sickle. Underneath fishnet tights, her flesh was pale, chubby, but firm. A tough athlete turned old broad. Her mouth a perpetual scowl.

Scary.

Her opponent lay on the blue mat, convulsing. Canary-yellow tights in two pieces. Brown leggings. Big and long blond hair. Probably America Jones by the stars and stripes on her thick, flat ass.

The Black Widow slapped her elbow.

Everyone clapped but me.

She screamed "*Dasvidaniya!*" and leapt into the air.

Something sharp poked my back.

"Stay still, " a husky voice curdled in my ear. "Or you'll be splattered like a watermelon from the tenth floor."

FORTY-EIGHT

AND NOW, A WORD FROM OUR SPONSORS

1975: KTMA

Announcer: And Now A Word from the Heavyweight Wrestling Champion of the World, Sven "The Swede" Börne!

The Swede: Hey Kids! This is the Swede. And before any match, I train hard, fight harder, and always take Dr. Kessler's Vit-Omix pills. They give me the energy I need to take on any and all threats to my championship gold!

Kids run to the Swede.

Kids: Hey, Swede! Where do we get them?

The Swede kneels, big arms around the kids.

The Swede: Vit-Omix is made by the best sports scientists money can buy! Imagine all the best food groups, minerals and vitamins slammed together into one swallow, helping your body grow!

The Swede stands and lifts all of the kids up.

Kids: Wow!

The Swede: Vit-Omix is so special it's not available in stores. Order it now and have it brought to your home! Just send five dollars care of this station, and I'll send Vit-Omix to you!

Kids thrust their arms up.

Kids: Alright!"

Freeze frame.

Be like the Swede, Order Vit-Omix today!

Vit-Omix is for recreational and entertainment use only and is not considered medicine by the Federal Drug Administration or the Bureau of Consumer Reporting.

FORTY-NINE

JOBBERS

The Black Widow was horizontal, six feet in the air, elbow thrust out as if she was on the phone and legs crossed as if she didn't give a shit. Flashes snapped off around the ring.

"Stay frosty, guy," said the voice behind the poke in my back.

The "Hammer and Sickle" elbow crashed. Dust filled the air like pollen, turning the match into a third-generation video tape like the ones in Sasha's basement tomb.

When the bouncing stopped, the Black Widow was on top of her foe, arms crossed.

"Gotta say," said the Hooded Bastard, "the old heel still has it. Most her age are rusty as a bathroom sink at a Motel Six." He poked harder, the Jim Bean on his breath dripped. "I told you to stay away."

"Shoot me," I said.

The poke sharpened. "You think I'm bluffing?"

The ref dropped to the floor.

"I think I don't give a shit."

One, two, three!

The crowd roared and I turned around.

Hands in the pocket of a giant grey University of Michigan

sweatshirt stood the Hooded Bastard. But beneath the hood was a leather wrestling mask. The crowd rushed to the ring, past us, and the big man backed up. In the din, I yelled. "I'm not going anywhere. I'm going to find the guy who did it. And if it's you, then you better bring a real gun to poke in my back, motherfucker. Because I sure as shit ain't bringing a finger to a gunfight."

He rushed forward.

"Or help me find the killer," I said, before dropping his ring name. "TV!"

He slid in his Adidas, eyes wide. "You don't know shit, mark."

I walked forward. "Tell me where Finch is."

He growled. "If I knew, he'd be dead already."

"I can find him."

"You can't find your own ass with both hands."

Almost in punching range. "I found you out. I know there's a war on. I just need to know who fired the first shot. Help me."

He shook his head. "You're just another scavenger."

"No, fucker. I'm the last honest friend Robbie ever had."

Play enough bars and dives and you can read the eyes of an angry drunk. TV Psycho's wild green ones stared at me, hunting for trust. He wiped his nose.

"Trust me," I said. "Like Robbie did in Red Wing."

Red Wing. The place was as close to a badge of authenticity as I had to offer in this bullshit world. And it stung TV even through his haze. From behind me, a dimwitted voice came out of the crowd. "Hey! Hey, it's Max Carnage!" The wave that had crashed against the ring rushed by me.

TV growled, turned, and fled … taking the crowd with him.

Fuck.

Back in the ring, the Black Widow stood glistening under the spotlight, make up cracked, arm raised in victory, glaring.

Didn't need to be Professor X to read her mind.

You fuckwit, you stole my crowd, my payday, my autographs. I just sweat blood and tears through the goddamn stretchmarks and crow's feet for another shot at glory. How much of my life do you need to steal before you're satisfied, you whiny brat—

That daydream shattered. Her lip tar perked. She blinked, huffing, and kept her arms up. Smiling. Glad to see me.

I couldn't read her mind for shit.

Backstage was a coatroom. Seated and standing in various stages of undress were old timers and lost causes, Halloween faces eaten by open-handed slaps and sweat, bald spots competing with saggy tits and wilted arms and thighs. Muscle and fat clinching each other.

"No marks," said an ogre-faced man in silver singlet, built like a cheese puff on two toothpicks.

"Hush, Maurice," said the Black Widow. "He's smartened up. Works for Val in New York."

A sarcastic round of "Oohs" came from all the old faces.

"Ready for my close up, Mr. Easton."

"Make sure you get my good side," was followed by a protruding ass and wet fart.

"Where's Teddy?"

"On assignment sucking some New York balls," I said. Cackles and hoots followed.

"You getting a feature, Marky?" said a masked man.

"Better believe it. About time they put someone on the cover that sells. Unlike that peroxide twinkie Ric Flair."

"Whoo!" said everyone in the room.

Accolades for the main eventer came fast after.

"Great match, Marky."

"How can you still fit into that slim thong?"

"You'll get yours next time, you commie rat!"

She led me like a gold-winning athlete dragging their medal through the reporters stuffed into the Olympic Village. A small partition of Legion banners cut the room in two, but the stink was non-discriminatory. Blood, shit, and that creeping grey stink of the old made this smell worse than Time's Square on New Year's morning. The heat didn't help. Each hulking form was a space heater hot-boxing the room with fetid breath and leaking assholes. So much life lurching towards death. A wake before the carnival graveyard. One last taste of glory before it all goes hush.

"C'mon," the Black Widow said. "I want you to meet the *real* stars of the show, not the opening act for the big time!" The boos turned to laughter as the old grapplers pulled at their bootstrings. She hit the partition. "Knock, knock, Angels and Heels! I'm bringing in a journalist for an interview with your queen. So cover your bits and bites and clean up your foundation."

"Oh go fuck yourself, Katey," said a female voice. Weak laughter followed. Apparently, she had less pull with her own gender.

She pulled the partition.

There were only three wrestlers inside. Sitting on folding chairs. One chair was almost swallowed by the rump of a massive lady. Samoan, I'd say. Wild curls and dark skin that contrasted with fucking everything in this monochrome state. She wasn't even out of breath. Evenly proportioned. Just *big*. She had tossed a blue towel across her breasts. "A bit more warning next time, Katey."

Beside her was a spry thing, chain smoking, fists like little clusters of rocks, wearing a red flannel shirt. "Christ, why you bringing me jailbait? I need a man who has to shave every day, not one who just learned to read!" She and the mountain of woman beside her laughed together.

Opposite them was the blonde, working her spaghetti laces.

The Black Widow cackled. "You guys really need to take this work on the road, far away from my ring." The spry one gave her the finger. The big one a kiss.

The blonde one kept her head down.

"Hey, Jessie. I want you to meet … Val's main writer."

She'd brushed away my requests to talk with her until she finished her introductions and got dressed, saying "Going to bask in the glow a bit, we can talk about other things later."

I didn't want to. But I needed her.

"He came to see our match, Jessie," she said. "Can you believe it?"

The blonde picked away at her laces. "Uh huh."

"Well, don't you want to get dolled up for an interview?"

"Why don't you do it for both of us, Katey," she said, the grey roots in her peroxide locks easier to see in the makeshift locker room's fluorescent glow. "You do your best work on your own, anyway."

The Black Widow's arms went akimbo. "What the hell does that mean?"

Jessie looked up. Strong alpine nose. Cold eyes. Beautiful but distant. "We agreed. We'd work out the spots. I came here early because *you* wanted to work out the spots. And as soon as we're in the ring you're fucking improvising."

"I read the crowd," she said, leaning forward. "Or couldn't you hear the deafening silence when you came down the aisle?"

Jessie took off one boot, her beige tights torn. "You really think that was for me?"

Both sides of the divide silenced.

The Black Widow laughed. "It sure as fuck wasn't for me. I brought the crowd so *you* could get a payday because you lost your job as a butcher at Safeway."

The other boot came off. "You brought the crowd for *you*. Your ego. Your bank account. And they ran as soon as you won. No autographs. No kisses or dates. You're not the draw you think you are. You're a freak show for guys who jerk off to their first wet dream."

Shit. Jessie was a poet laureate. The Black Widow snickered. "Keep up the lies," the Black Widow said, "and I'll stretch you till you tell the truth."

Jessie shook her head, then stood. In stocking feet she was a head taller. Shoulders twice as broad. She was powerful and had kept in shape, built for war or athletics. A Scandinavian goliath. "Don't believe your own hype. You're no Johnnie Mae Young, let alone Mildred Burke. No one is making a movie of you. And I'm tired of your bullshit grandstanding. Pull rank again in the ring, I'm going to stretch *you*."

I stood behind the Black Widow.

Which meant I got hit first.

The Black Widow threw back her right hand so fast it smacked my eye socket like a knuckle ball.

Stumbling, I saw flecks of light. She did not look back. Jessie tossed up her block to protect her left side.

I slipped, dropped, and watched as the flip book of violence unveiled between blinks.

The Black Widow feinted with her right.

Jessie tossed out her right hand for a neck-grab. Those long-boat fingers clasped the Black Widow's neck.

The Black Widow lurched forward, into Jessie's breasts.

Then her neck was locked in in Jessie's taut arms.

The Black Widow's claws gored Jessie's stomach.

Jessie winced, but locked things deep.

The Black Widow's arms flailed, pulling Jessie down.

Chairs screeched behind me.

The two other Angels were up. Watching. One grin apiece.

I scrambled up like a wild thing, and the icy eyes of Jessie glared. I spat.

She moved her head.

Hands clasped my shoulders.

I had one second.

I tossed out my fingers, spread them in a V, and poked her eyes.

Two hands yanked me back into a seat.

As I landed, Jessie's hands dropped from around the Black Widow, and covered her eyes.

The Black Widow screamed.

The Samoan and her partner ran between them, but the Black Widow snatched Jessie's arm.

Jessie's body shook, as if sensing what would happen.

Teeth bared, spit of her lip, the Black Widow swung herself around Jessie.

One arm tied behind her, Jessie's shut eyes burst open.

Hoisted in the air, Jessie screamed. "Uncle! Uncle! Uncle!"

She landed on her knees, but the Black Widow remained at her back. Jessie's arm was locked in the chicken wing. But a real one. A real hammerlock. Worse, she was articulating it at three angles, including the wrist. Pain flushed the serene visage from Jessie. Wrinkles of pain turned her into a hag.

The Black Widow gasped. "Bitch. You work because I let you work. You get paid because I'm the draw. The only reason you ain't a cripple is that I chose it. Right?"

Jessie spat. "Go to hell—"

One flick of the Black Widow's wrist cut Jessie's tongue. The Black Widow licked her teeth. "Sorry, baby. Didn't hear you. Who's your fucking mamma?"

"… You."

"Who?"

"You are, Black Widow!"

The Black Widow shoved her, stomped on her twisted arm, then spat. "Don't you forget it, you second rate cunt." She glared at me. "You're driving. The stink of losers is getting a little heavy." She walked towards a back exit, yanked her coat and purse from a yellow bench, then belted: "Douglas? Get my check." I followed, then tossed a look behind.

The partition was filled with the heads of the male wrestlers, staring out at the carnage as if they were severed heads on a hunter's wall. Including Douglas, who looked like he'd just seen his favorite peep show. "Shit," said the masked man. "That was the best match of the night."

The main drag to the freeway was packed with mounds of snow on each side. Squalls drifted with phantom movement on the wind. We cut through them, scattering their remains, but they never fully died. Cigarette between her teeth, the Black Widow stabbed her index finger into the lighter, sweat and glitter from her opponent making her twinkle in the dark. "Goddamn that Viking princess. That crowd was lining up for refunds during her comeback. What did she want, to lose *more* money? I pulled them back from the brink. That's the art of it, kid. You leave them wanting more, not wanting to leave. But tell that to a goddamn housewife. I'm not Mildred Burke? She ain't Penny fucking Banner."

Rum. Wasn't sure if it was from her breath or the new orange air freshener. Rum was never my weapon of choice. Rat considered it beneath contempt. "Unless you're a pirate or from the goddamn Caribbean, anyone who drinks rum is an imperialist asshole." Granted, he preferred Irish Car bombs and Molotov Cocktails.

"Third rater. And just for the record, kid, I did not need your help."

"Sure."

The lighter popped.

"Don't say sure. It's weak. There's zero conviction. Want to suck a donkey's ass? *Sure.*"

"Okay."

"Okay is even worse. Was that match okay? I pulled off a god-damn miracle with that stiff jobber. You saw it."

"I did."

"Goddamn right." She took a deep drag. Held it. Considered it. Smiled. "I always wanted that." She exhaled. "Fuck the promot-ers. They hated if kids ever came backstage. But in my prime I had stroke and could have made it happen if it wasn't for your father." She sucked in smoke, buying me a second for a sentence with substance.

"What do you know about the policeman known as Finch?"

The cigarette poised by her lip, cherry pointed toward the shag ceiling, shook as we crushed snow lumps under the wheels. A mock pose with real fear. Her volume dropped. "Where the hell did you get that name?"

Squalls thickened before the onramp that would take us back to Dinkytown. "A source."

"Listen," she said, slow and cool. "Don't be an inscrutable Oriental who speaks in riddles. Where did you get that name?"

"I found a link. Between him and Robbie's death."

"And? What's that link?"

No way. Wasn't giving up Sasha. She may have been evasive but that Commie was the only one who had told the truth, shown me proof, and seemed to give a damn about reality in this fucking bullshit kayfabe world. "Later. First, what do you know about Finch?"

"That you're not supposed to know who the fuck he is." She shivered. "Christ. I've either underestimated you or you're messing around in shit you can't even fathom." Both. It was probably both. "Look, I feel weird even hearing that creature's name."

I shrugged. If there was one rule with her, it was: she wanted to talk. But it took two more Marlboros before she spoke again.

"He's mostly a rumor. The old promoters kept a couple of heavies around. Hookers, not shooters. Guys who kept order in the locker room. And …" she shook her head as if to get water out of her ear. "Just hearing you say 'policeman' like you think you know what it's like …"

"School me," I said.

Another stab of the lighter. "Hookers knew holds no one else knew. They were a small fraternity of carny types. Guys who fought for money, and guys who fought for real. They tore out eyes. They gored groins. And in some cases, they were sent to 'silence' a talent that had gone rogue."

"You mean murder."

"Rumors. Finch, he was one of them. Rough reputation. You only heard about him in cars and even then it was *a la* whispers. His name never entered a locker room. He was the closest thing we had to a boogeyman. I didn't think he was real until I went to Kansas City. Before you were born. Dangerous town. Lot of bikers, lots of Klan. I hated it. So, one night, the ring boys there took liberties with some of the ladies. Followed them to hotels, begging them for a fight or a kiss or both. Well, it was also the fake hometown of a heel. I won't say his name, because he doesn't matter anymore. He brought a gang of fans to the hotel and went "hunting" for angels and heels in the area. Like, with a knife."

Her eyes shut and the smear of eyeshadow made her into a skull. "Bettie was in that hotel. She was a top draw. Former gymnast, but a trick knee killed her Olympic dreams. A machine in the ring. Could do a sixty-minute Broadway and the fans loved how she screamed with every clothesline. She was tough, but this guy …

"She went missing. I knocked. Had the motel manager check. Clothes gone. No Bettie. Never sat right but sometimes girls just gave up. The road is cruel as a hurricane. I never judged. It wasn't for the weak. But Bettie *wasn't* weak. Wasn't until I got to Independence that it was clear she wasn't there. No one knew. And that's when I heard Bettie wasn't just an amateur. She had connections going back to the Trust. Thomas Bartlett was her great uncle."

I signaled, pressed the gas and got on the freeway. "NWA chairman in the fifties," I said.

She ignored being impressed. "He was sweet on Bettie. Whether that was a good thing or a bad thing, who knows. Hired a PI, who found her body in Arizona, her throat choked with barbies." Ash hung from her cigarette like a fuzzy Russian hat while she inhaled, head jutting from side to side. "PI looked for years. Bartlett just kept paying as he picked up clues. And eventually, it turns out the guy, the … suspect was now someone who mattered."

She swallowed smoke

"He was a rising star. Big in the West. Where he'd hid out. Handsome. Good worker. Charming." She cleared her throat, eyes still skull holes. She moistened her mouth, facial tremors moving with the cadence of a busted clock. "And after years of success, of drawing top dollar, he vanished, too. And like her, reappeared out of state. In his real hometown, Boulder. He'd been gored. Testes torn out. By hand. Shoved in his mouth."

My own balls retracted with the practiced smoothness of a sumo. "Holy shit."

"But that's not what killed that cowboy. Coroner said his heart gave out. Heart attack. What happened after was just insult to injury, boss's orders. He was gone." Tears welled in her eyes.

The West? Ugh. Her three letters from the road. Always about Cowboy Bob Thurston. One of ten thousand Cowboys in the world of wrestling. But the only one I'd heard of that was a friend of the Black Widow. A friend she'd accused of rape and murder and who had his cock and balls removed by the guy who I think killed Robbie. But her lack of memory was an asset. I played ignorant. "You ever see Finch?"

"There were policemen, but then there were Ghosts. You never saw a Ghost and, if you did, good night sweet princess. Why the hell are you digging that kind of dirt?"

"Think he might be involved."

"How? Why?"

"Can you identify him?"

"I just said he was a fucking Ghost, why don't you ever listen?"

"But you never said you never saw a Ghost. Honesty, remember? That's what builds trust. So have you ever seen Finch?"

The ash fell from the tip, crashed upon her tights. Sweat and rum and lady stink rose up to my nose as we carried on in silence. "Maybe."

I grinned. "Then let's get a good night's sleep. I'll need you in top shape tomorrow."

"Why?"

"It's Robbie's funeral. And I need you as a witness." And maybe a bodyguard.

FIFTY

KSTP EYEWITNESS NEWS

The following message is brought to you by the Reverend Edward Snow.

"Robert Frost was among the greatest poets in American history. Which is why I keep returning to him in times when our current history seems so tragic and bizarre. Because as Frost noted, taking the road less traveled has made all the difference. And there can be no road less traveled than the world of professional wrestling.

"This garish sport is not a sport at all, but a horrific spectacle of violence, sadism, and ignorance that continues to draw in more and more of our youth. And then take their lives.

"When I was eighteen, I joined the Navy to serve my country in the Pacific. I was no brave soldier but I did my part in helping my nation, contributing to something greater than myself. And I have observed with growing sadness that Frost was, in fact, wrong. There are too many less-traveled roads in this dirty decade. Ones that threaten to become the super-highway in which the future will travel.

"A reasonably intelligent American will have no trouble finding these issues scrawled across the evening headlines. Drug use. Satanism. Witchcraft and the Occult. Heavy Metal that appeals to the basest human instincts and drives chasms of difference between family members. The result? Unemployment, crime, and suicide. Not since the Great Depression have we faced such a foe on our own shores. I fear that our desire to remain free of Soviet influence has blinded us from the rot on our own shores that hides in plain sight: punk music, heavy metal, Dungeons & Dragons, movies about men who kill girls with machetes. When I was in school we read Chaucer in Middle English. Now we must endure the screaming of Ozzy Osborne, who is barely literate. The result is degeneration the likes of which were last witnessed during the fall of Rome.

"Instead of gladiators, we have wrestlers. And as much as I love my state, I have cringed every time one of its proud and good inhabitants has seen fit to cheer as grown men sell violence without consequences. How different are we from the Colosseum, where Christians were thrown to the lions? How different are we from the decadence which killed an empire by blinding the public with spectacle?

"If President Reagan is good to his word, he and the First Lady will do all that is in their power to untangle the web of hedonism that is stifling this country. And we must lead by example. I am asking all of you watching to abandon the world of wrestling that killed our city's son Robbie Varhooven. Do not attend the public displays that his promoter hands out like free narcotics. Ignore the celebrations. Vote with your dollar and your disdain and come to the All Faith vigil this Friday night, where the moral leaders of our community will lead us to a greater appreciation of the threat we face and how we, as a moral, Christian, and righteous nation can be."

FIFTY-ONE

WINTER HARVEST

FINCH.

I placed the index card way above Robbie's head.

String between my fingers, I wanted to make a direct connection … to New York City. But I'd said nothing about Sasha's indicators. And I didn't want to give up my source. The shower was sending out wet warmth that died before it could reach me. Behind its door, the Black Widow was singing to herself. Off key. *"Don't you call me a hobo, for that would make me explode. Don't you dare call me a hobo, I'm really a knight of the road."* I placed the string between FINCH and THE SWEDE. Both might as well be ghosts. I swung the string to NEW YORK. Which made more sense? Everything depended on Robbie's loyalty. Did he double cross The Swede. Or Little Cassidy Junior?

The string was equidistant between each possible backer. Maybe I had it wrong. Which one would hire a killer? The Swede had a rep for working stiff and taking liberties. Cassidy was capable of anything. He took risks. So many of the old-school promoters hated him. Maybe the Swede got smart to Robbie heading to New York. But Munchnick detested anything that would bring regular journalism into NWA territory. He loved Val. Or did Robbie inject dog urine into his heart to become an Olympic-sized grappler?

"You got more strings on that table than the Moscow symphony." Free of makeup, the Black Widow's miles were evident. The pink housecoat was tight on her thick legs and shoulders as she wiped out the wet of her red hair and hustled with slaps of her feet to the fridge. "And what has it gotten you?" A better idea of what made sense. A winnowing of possibilities. The light from the open fridge bathed her in yellow. "You hungry?"

"No," I lied.

A sound akin to piss against the tiles followed. "Good, because I haven't done shopping yet." Which was code for being broke until Douglas brought her check. She walked back, a black mug with a Wonder Woman emblem half-filled with box wine. "Whatever this is, we need to turn it into a proposal. Get it to an agent. Deliver when we get paid."

Her view of how publishing worked was hilarious. "Sure," I said.

"And I think your Finch theory, whoever gave it to you, is sending you on a wild goose chase. Might as well said Elvis did it, god rest his ass."

"You have a better theory?

She brushed me away with her mug-hand. Whatever warmth was in her eyes at the show was long gone. Mug down, she popped the top off a Sharpie and took a card, and then blew all the pieces away.

"Hey!"

"That spider web has caught nothing but dust. And I don't feel like waiting until you have a Eureka moment. Who had the most to gain if Robbie died?" She handed me the pen and card. "Oh, for fuck's sake. Are you going to soil your diaper? You need a mouthful of Gerber's? You said one thing of value on that ride home: we may see a person of interest at the funeral. Guilt is a powerful emotion, and most wrestlers are about as mature as a Toddler wearing a diaper for a crown."

No. I wasn't going to be pumped. "You knew him better than I did. Did he have any rivals?"

"Of course he did."

"And their names are …?"

"You don't get it. He was a cash cow. You don't kill the golden calf."

"Even with the old timers?"

"They knew who was filling the seats. It sure wasn't Ox Blood or Thunderguts."

"What about friends? Who was he close with? Train with?"

She took the mug. "Why don't you tell me? Your source, who told you about Finch, they must have had dirt on Robbie's buddies."

"We talked about Finch."

"Sure, but why?"

"I thought you didn't want to talk about him."

"Answer the fucking question."

"Answer mine."

She snorted. "My god, you are a little shit. And say, where's that girl in the leather who dropped your carcass off?"

Resisting the urge to cross my arms, I thumbed the belt holes in my jeans and tried not to look at the jacket with its stuffing. "She had to work."

"Fuck, there's nothing worse than a bad liar giving me shit about telling the truth. Wanna build that bridge? Take the first step yourself. Or I'm going to bed."

She took the last slug from the mug, wiped her mouth with the back of her raw red hand, and turned. Inside me, something hissed. "She's scared of me."

Halfway down the hall, the Black Widow turned. "Scared."

"I got in a fight."

The Black Widow walked back, silent, cautious. "With who? And best be the truth, kid."

My mouth became toast. "Jack Ripe."

Her head lifted, eyes narrow. "Jack Ripe, the carny creep? Runs a comedy shop that looks like a cult?"

I nodded.

Three claps were followed by cackles. "Well, fuck if that ain't bold as brass. You hit a guy who likes to get hit. How the hell did that go for you? No, don't tell me. He wouldn't talk."

"He talked. It's what he said that made me hit him."

"And made that pretty thing run from you? That must have been rich. What was it?"

So I told her. About dog piss and injections. About hearts growing like the Grinch, only instead of saving Christmas, Robbie had a heart attack.

The wrinkles of joy sagged until I was done.

"Bullshit," she whispered. "He worked for that muscle. He remade himself again when he came to the Swede. That boy was the most dedicated worker I've ever seen. He earned that body. He earned his spot."

"With your help," I said.

"Everyone uses contacts. What the fuck do you think, this world is a meritocracy? Maybe your father never taught you this, but the world is not fair, kid. But that doesn't mean everyone is crooked." She leaned back. "The Swede is covering his own ass with this whisper campaign. Drugs. Suicide. Anything that builds the chasm between him and a dead kid."

"So you think he did it?"

Her face puckered. "Didn't say that. You're jumping to conclusions. The Swede is in the business of making money. Wrestlers are a commodity. Robbie's brand of soup is tainted so he's getting it off his shelf as fast as possible. Never put a personal motive where a business decision fits."

I cranked up the dumb. "So was it Little Cassidy?"

"What the hell did I just say about jumping to conclusions?"

"Then Finch."

She coiled her fingers closed in the shape of a Muppet. "Mouth nap. Just … don't talk. Listen." Scribbles filled the index card. "Who had the most to gain from Robbie's death? Neither promoter wants a dead man's trail to their door. No one would send a ghost to snuff out a guy who made money. There has to be a different reason. Personal. A crime of passion. His sister still nuts?"

I shrugged.

Her Muppet hand opened. "Mouth nap doesn't count for questions."

"Penny's high strung. A speed freak. But unless he was pushing her into rehab, or stealing her stash, I doubt it. Did he …" I waited for her to assert dominance with her hand-puppet, but she merely glared. "Who else was close? Girlfriends? He must have had tons of ring rats throwing themselves at him."

The puppet became a hand.

"What?" I said. "What did I say now?"

Eyes at the ceiling, she shook her head. "God. How oblivious are you, Du-Pin?"

I grabbed my hair. "Then smarten me up, Sherlock."

She smiled, then giggled. "Better sit down, 'cause if you didn't know this is going to hurt like a wrecking ball."

Oh, shit.

"He was queer. Though he'd never say it. Queers have been in locker rooms forever, often hiding in plain sight. And I will tell you that the boys tend to look after their own. But there will always be those who look upon queers like abominations. They bully. They hurt. They abuse."

Something squirmed across my body. I snorted, swallowed, and focused. "Even when a queer is drawing money?"

"You should see your face, kid. Want to sit down?"

"I want to find out who killed my friend."

"Making you feel odd?"

"Stay on the fucking road," I said. "We've got one chance to identify who might have killed him. One. After this funeral they're going to be locked up tighter than Fort Knox, mouths shut, their future in any promotion on the line if they say jack shit. So don't worry. I don't care. I don't need to talk. I'm not weirded out. I've seen guys fuck each other on stage while bands played queer bashing anthems.

So spare me the high and mighty speech. You're not the first one to meet people who fuck themselves. So who was he fucking?"

She smiled. "You know what, I almost believe you."

"*Who?*"

She shrugged. "Wasn't part of our conversation. I'm sure he did the usual at men's bathrooms. But he wasn't out, kid. And honestly, if you asked me to rate him, I'd say he was a virgin. Dude was looking for someone to love, not fuck. And he found it with his fans. Best high in the world. Give me ten refills of that any day instead of …" She polished off the wine, slammed the mug down. "Where were we?"

"Friends? Who was his best friend? Here or anywhere else he worked?"

"Well, there was the clown he ran with in Mid-South." She grunted. "Guy had a mouth on him that never stopped."

TV. "Who?"

"Wrestled under Psycho. TV Psycho."

"Bernie Coombs. Wrestled as the Lumberjack for a while in Quebec before heading south. He's not on the Swede's roster."

"No." Silence. Watching her words now. "Though Robbie wanted it. Wanted them to be a tag team. God, the kid had no idea how good he was on his own. He didn't need that fast-talking idiot, but yes, they were friends. I could get Robbie a tryout, but the Swede didn't like TV."

"Why?"

She sighed. "It could be any reason. But the last time I heard any rumor, the idiot talked about starting a union. Can you imagine anything so dumb?"

"Why would it be dumb?"

"Listen, you start a union, you strike, you get replaced by two miles of scabs willing to do it for half the price. It hurts everyone, solves nothing. But TV talked loud about it for a while. The Swede didn't need that shit, I guess, so he was headed for another territory."

New York. And now he was here.

"He was Robbie's friend. And fucking unstable. He's just like his namesake, a TV that keeps changing channels every second and you never knew what he'd spout off next."

"Not a fan?"

"I was trying to protect Robbie's future. Sweet thing was easily influenced. And TV was a rotten influence. Of anyone in the roster, I'd say it was him." She picked up her mug, then remembered. "Funeral's at eleven. You're driving." She walked away, feet slapping the floor. The door closed tight.

I picked up the index cards and put them back in their order.

I put TV down on a new card. But I put it next to Hooded Bastard.

Why would a wrestler bound for stardom murder the man who would make him a star?

I had one day to score more data. See who I could see. Then report back to Sasha.

From the bedroom, the Black Widow coughed like a dying rat.

I showered, mindless, head sore from strings that stretched out and grabbed nothing. No towel, so in the misty air that smelled of cold cream and nicotine I dripped all over the floor and rummaged through her medicine cabinet.

Eyeliner pencils with blunt edges. Asthma inhalers missing their caps, gaping at the world like drowning fish shaped like boots. Fresh yellow vials of prescription codeine. Old orange bottles of tranqs with the pills half-chewed for later use. Rat would have called it a Winter Harvest. In the misty haze of the post-shower air, the world looked like an old TV show that was coming in on the wires.

Get some soap, Kid Kong. Right, now just touch it with your finger. Up you go … now, write a message for your daddy. When he takes a shower, the message will appear like invisible ink! A secret message just for him! B … U … M … ha! Okay, smart ass, down you go. Now, what will we do with a bum on the mirror?

Wipe it off!

Haze looked back. Nothing got clearer.

The funeral was my last move.

FIFTY-TWO

IN MEMORIAM

Robert William Varhooven (January 23, 1960- November 30th, 1983). Born in St. Paul, Minnesota, to Charles R. and Roberta Varhooven, brother of Penelope, and friend and local sportsman. Robert will be remembered for his contribution to local athletics, devotion to Christ, and the love he always had for his family. He will be buried in a private ceremony on Saturday, December 3rd, at Lakewood Cemetery. Please respect the family's wishes. No outside media. No sports fans or athletes. Donations may be made to First Lutheran Church of Minnesota.

FIFTY-THREE

TOMBSTONES

"That's what you're going to wear?" Three times. Three times I heard this in the morning, in the car, and finally en route to the funeral. Jeans. Converse. A nearly clean green button-up I'd scored off a preppy fuck who'd made the mistake of starting shit. At least now the food and blood stains had withered into indistinct shadows on the gut. She did a last round of dark lip tar, left hand on the rear-view. "How the hell do you come to a friend's funeral dressed like you got in a street fight with a salad bar?"

"I won't unzip my jacket. Perfect crime."

"Perfect insult." She puckered, smiled, tongue lashing her teeth. She was in a midnight-blue blouse, a feather-strewn winter coat, long black dress and her regular black work boots. Red hair pulled back hard, giving her face a hawkish countenance (one of Peter's favorite words for face). "When we get there, you go in first."

"Why?"

"Penny hates me. So you're my shield." The lipstick retreated into its container with a twist of nails the color of old blood. "You want honesty? You don't get to pick the truth you like."

"Fair enough. Also, your eyeliner's smudged."

"What?"

I turned right and passed the gates while she swore and dabbed her face. Down the winding path I saw an old enemy.

Cops.

Shit.

A lonely Crown Vic sat at the opening of the parking lot like a sentry.

"Probably a gift from the Swede," she said. "Give the family the peace it wants. Not a bunch of marks wanting to take a bone from his hand like a relic."

"I'd lead with that in your next fan club newsletter."

"I love the marks," she said, dead serious. "But I'm no fool. They can be the clingiest sons of bitches this side of a newborn infant."

I laughed. "I wouldn't know." Pulling up, I rolled down the window. The cold was comforting.

The guy's gray moustache was stained yellow at the fuzzy edges. Wrinkled, tired, clearly brought out and into the cold as a favor to someone. Best years behind him. Must suck to be a babysitter at a funeral.

"Morning," I said. "We're here for the Varhooven Funeral."

"Yeah," he said. "Name?"

"Sully Alexander."

From the dashboard, he yanked a pair of wire rim glasses that had been warming against the heating vent. Slowly, he put them on. "Uh huh." A clipboard emerged from his lap. "Yeah, okay. I got you down here."

"Great, thanks—"

"Hold on," he said, tougher. "Who's the young lady?"

The Black Widow cackled. "That's rich. I'm Katey Moskowitz."

He lifted his head, stared down his nose. "Oh. Well, that's a problem."

"Why?" I said.

"The family has very strict rules about who can go because, well, you know."

"And?"

"I only have Mr. Alexander down on this list." He took off his glasses. "I'm afraid the young lady will not be able to attend the funeral."

"*What?*" she said, and the walrus moustache cop dropped all emotion. "I am a friend of the deceased. You have to let me go."

"No ma'am," he said. "I do not. This is a private event. If you want, there's a donut shop around the ways where you can wait while your boyfriend—"

"My *boyfriend?*" she said. "You ignorant pig, this isn't—"

"Officer," I said. "I'm sorry. It's been a bad day. We will respect the family's wishes."

"Hell we will," she said.

I gave her a glare. "We understand you'll have to do what's best for the family. We'll circle the parking lot and she can grab a donut."

He nodded, I nodded, and the Black Widow fumed.

Window rolled, I pulled into the parking lot. K-cars with working class care taken against rust filled the lot. No limos. No Jaguars. Nathaniel Princeton was nowhere to be seen in his Bentley. The Swede's Royal's Royce, a favorite attraction of the Minnesota State fair, was also MIA. Respect the wishes of the family or serving to cut ties with a guy they used up and dumped ... or both.

"You've got no guts," she said.

"And you've got no brain," I said.

"Fuck your investigations," she yanked the handle. "They can't keep me—"

"You'll ruin it."

Her head turned slow. "Pardon?"

I stabbed the lighter. "This isn't about you. It's about him. If you show up, you'll make it about you. Cops. A fight. A screaming match. Your argument for being there. Penny likes me. I've done her a favor. You? Fuck, she might blame you for his death. Just sit. Watch. Look at who's coming in and coming out. Pay attention."

The lighter popped out.

She slammed the door. "Get out."

I did.

The sky was a wall of ash. No sun. No wind. Just cold that warmed as it sunk in an inch deep. Five-paces from the Pontiac, I was downright comfortable. Headstones poked out of the earth. Gray Lego. Some dusted, some buried, and some clean. Dates going back to the 1800s. English names. Irish names. Not much from Scandinavia. Robbie was buried above his station.

The long 's' of the road crunched beneath my sneakers. A procession in the distance featured a handful of cars and dark sticks against the white. I sniffed, but the snot was salty ice on my lip. I marched alone, but took in a panoramic view unscratched by the wind. Both sets of grandparents were dead before I was born, Dad's in Nebraska, and the Black Widow's in Jersey. Funerals were for cop shows. Cemeteries a place to get high. Peaceful. "The good thing about the dead, the kind that stay dead, the real dead, is that they stop being active." That's what Rat said one night in some graveyard in Newark he drove me to after our short tour of the state got cancelled.

Marching to Robbie's hole in the ground, I realized yet again that Rat was full of shit.

The dead stay with you. Drag you around. Possess you.

I looked back at the Pontiac.

Still there. Best I could gather, so was the Black Widow.

As I stood there sweating in the freezing air, the black sticks came into focus.

I passed a Bentley. Good shape. Swede buying distance and silence, perhaps?

Finally, I reached the somber party.

Penny's eyeshadow was thick and sharp. A blonde raccoon wrapped in black. Jaw clenched. Behind her were ten or so people clutching themselves. Old. Thin. Not one monster of the squared circle among them.

Except the priest. Fuck. It was the drunk Mom looked after. Shiny face in heavy vestments. He still looked like Solomon Grundy, but at least he wasn't swinging fists against invisible Japs. But that was it. Marks, every one. Jesus. I had *nothing* to bring back to Sasha.

My lip snarled until I saw a backhoe. The mechanical mastodon's jagged shovel hung in the air, shattered roots between the teeth. The earth was scuffed dirt, hard as concrete. A hole in the earth gaped and above it, balanced across a wooden frame, was a silver coffin that likely cost more than the Bentley.

Penny's pinched face approached. Last time I saw her she shoved me out of a window. Hands out of my pockets. "Sorry I'm late."

Penny hugged me like a junkie does a lost dime bag.

"I'm so sorry. I can't believe I treated you so bad. Sully, thank you. Thank you for being here." Her voice was measured, clear, and she made sure not to speak into my puffy green shoulder. So all could hear. I reciprocated the act. Because that's what it was for her.

"Don't mention it," I said, warm as her performance. "You've had nothing but bad days."

"No, you came to help. And I want to help those who help me." She pulled back, Oscar-worthy eyes on me. "You're the only friend of Robbie's I would let come."

She'd banned wrestlers. Or maybe the Swede did.

"That's a true honor," I said, then smiled.

She did, too, almost cracking her layers of white cosmetics that could be seen from the back seats of her theater. "Come. We don't want to keep the old folks out too long."

She introduced me, quickly. A fifth-grade teacher with red cheeks. Football coach chain-smoking Pall Malls, his broken arm in a gray sling, head wrapped up in a scarf. Five folks around my age. Penny's friends. From the theater. Extras. She brought extras to a funeral. She introduced me as "Robbie's friend." Three pretty girls with crimped hair and cherry lips. Two guys with sallow cheeks and thick manes. I shook hands with each guy and received three hugs that smelled like bubble gum and weed.

No Jack Ripe. No Davey. No TV Psycho. No Finch. No Swede.

I shook hands. Even with the priest. He nodded. "Very sorry for your loss, son."

I nodded. I turned to Penny. "Where's your mother?"

Penny nodded at the Bentley. "She said it was too cold." Compared to where we were standing, I bet she was right. Then the casket was before me. A massive silver attaché case hid his body. At one end was a wreath. In its center was a picture. Big goofy grin, canine missing. Bleach blond hair, wild eyes. He looked like a kid growing into a weird man. About a year before Red Wing.

"Sully?"

There hadn't been a viewing.

Penny pulled me back to the circle. "We should get started."

A string formed in my head. Wiggling with the other worms in my brain.

How had he died? Who had seen him last? Who the fuck was in that casket?

"Minister?"

The mighty priest that had fought the Black Widow until she knocked him out on his drunken ass said, "Let us pray."

They did. Eyes shut, mouths repeating the words he tossed from the good book. Penny took my bare hand in her black leather gloves, then bowed. The extras looked wholesome and solemn. The old folks moved their feet to keep warm, Depression era faces that looked tougher than a wrestling mat

Head down, I glared up. At the casket. At the picture. And around this strange commercial being broadcast from a cemetery. All the while words like Jesus and Spirit and Heaven followed the steam from the priest's mouth. The strings of my mind flailed and my guts sloshed. Acting. Ignorance. No cameras. No media. My neck itched like when I'd study in the NYC public library surrounded by the homeless. From the moment those stone lions stared until I got out, it felt like I was being watched.

Penny squeezed back. "Easy," she said, and I relaxed my grip.

The priest finished up and passed the honors to Penny.

She looked at me, squeezed my hand back hard, and smiled. Somewhere among the stones I swore I heard a director yell "action."

She stepped forward, stood beside the drunk man of god. "Thank you, Minister Clancy. And thanks, every single one of you, for coming out today. It's funny, Robbie said the cold never bothered him." Sniff. "Robbie used to say." Sniff sniff. "He'd run outside in the cold. No jacket, just gloves. He'd build a snowman so fast, and never stopped moving, it would be two boulders tall by the time I got on my boots." She smiled. The extras smiled. The old people's smiles flashed and retreated into gravity's tug. "We weren't very similar. I loved acting, art, and dance. I was my father's daughter. Robbie was meant for different things." Her eyeliner an old-school comic book mask like Robin or Kato or even the Atomic Kid, her blue eyes as dead as the white space of a blank page. "But he taught me many things. To live life big. To work hard and love your family. To serve others more than yourself. And to find salvation in a Christian life." My clawed hands coiled into fists. Mist from her mouth was steam from fresh and steady bullshit. "And now, I'd like to introduce Robbie's childhood friend." We met as teens. He'd betrayed my trust less than a year later and I'd ignored him for a decade. Her polished smile was colder than the tombstones. "Who knew him better than anyone." The extras vied for the gold metal sniffing award. "And who came all the way from New York just to say goodbye."

Fuck me.

"Sully?" She pouted, walked towards me, face wrinkling. "Oh, god. Sully, please?"

She held her arms out.

Receiving the hug, I returned the favor, but she snugged in tight. Lips on my ear. Sobs. Loud. Then a whisper. "Say nothing about wrestling. Or I will fucking kill you."

Choked up, she pulled away and stood amongst her friends. The snow crunched until I stepped on uneven ground made of grave dirt boulders soft as concrete. Looking out at the audience, I

realized it.
>This wasn't a shoot.
>This was a work.
>And I was on stage.

FIFTY-FOUR

TRUTH AND LIES

Troubling times for the gladiators of the ring. The State Athletic Commission has ended its probe into the alleged forfeits and fixes within the sport of wrestling. The allegations emerged from Jack Pfieffer, himself a wrestling promoter and best associated with the Greek sensation Jim Londos. According to Pfieffer, the major promoters have been working to forfeit matches in an attempt to grouse the public. "These promoters know well in advance who will win and who will lose, and they are eating the public out of house and home by selling these exhibitions as real fights! Trust me, I've done it myself!" Pfieffer's efforts have led to a hearing later this month that will include notable promoters Jack Curley, Ed White, Rudy Miller, and perhaps such vaunted starts as former Heavyweight Champion Ed Lewis.

"Londos has a wallet with $50,000," Pfieffer said. "That's dive money. At the rate things are going, wrestling will be as dirty as boxing."

After initiating a probe into allegations of malfeasance in the world of wrestling, The New York State Athletic Commission has called a halt to its investigations. Interviews with major promoters have revealed that the allegations of promoter Jack Pfieffer were "bunk from a promoter with an ax to grind." The Commission released the following statement to the News. "The allegations appear to stem from a business dispute between rivals, and all of the supposed evidence is hearsay and conjecture. Experts within the field have assured us that the wrestling matches are in fact athletic competitions. Mr. Lewis, former heavyweight wrestling champion, has also offered to wrestle anyone who claims he is not the best grappler in the world. Thus far, none has come forth to challenge his assertion. Unless claims can be backed by evidence instead of opinion, this investigation is at an end."

FIFTY-FIVE

BLOWN UP

The stuffing in my jacket hung out in two small puffs of cloud. The extras smiled at me like cult members proctoring a new convert. Penny grinned, but the edge of her eyes were sharp as a broken bottle. Brut wafted in my direction from the big priest's cheeks. The old people looked placed there from a box set. Thin smoke plumed from the backhoe. Guess the crew who dug it had to stay close, but out of sight.

Penny's smile pinched.

"Okay," I said. "I'm Sully." My hands pressed down to stretch out the jacket. "So, I met Robbie when I was thirteen." The backhoe was to the left. A good place to hide without having to crouch behind the jagged teeth of tombstones that stretched out to the horizon. "He wasn't as big as me. And where we met, things were tough." Penny nodded. "I think it's safe to say we saved each other's lives. And not in some stupid hippie way. I would have been in a casket like this one before my fourteenth birthdayif not for him," I said, then knocked on it. Fucking thing was made of iron. No echo. Damn thing could be as solid as a battleship hull.

A grey shape flittered from behind the backhoe. Like a ghost.

Penny's face widened.

"Yup," I said, knocking twice more and the shape came into view. Hooded Bastard.

I put my hand in my pocket. "Most of my stories about Robbie involve … well, we got into a lot of fights. Real fights." Penny's eyes relaxed. The extras followed suit. It was like a fucking wave. One that lashed me when I pulled my hand back. My fist was raw, cold, scratched. "The kind that hurt if you win. Hurt more when you lose." My fist popped out. "Real hurt. Not pretend. Not fake. The kind that stays *hurt*." Knock.

"Sully?" Penny said. The figure shot forward. Each knock yanked his chain. Wore grey. Blended in. His clothing choice was goddamn camo in a Minnesota graveyard.

I ran toward the net of bullshit artists. The dudes grimaced. The women soured. They all gave way. "Sully!" Penny screamed. "You cocksucker! Next time I see you I'm going to cut your balls off! Asshole! You fucking ruined it!"

The words stabbed my backside, then melted. All that mattered was the gray mass. The Hooded Bastard ran, fast, behind the backhoe and into a thicket of pine trees. I targeted tracks mashed by boot prints, hoping I didn't sink.

The yellow machine that dug the grave for a fake funeral sat like a frozen dinosaur while I rushed by. Cigarette butts were stamped into the dirt. Anorexic branches lashed my face. Hands, up, legs threshing, I kept my eye on the Hooded Bastard. Fucker moved like Rocky. Thick and fast. Sweat annoyed me, and stung my eyes. Penny's words stopped shooting adrenaline. The chased move fast. I felt like a cop. A fat, idiot pig. Snow ate my steps. I hustled out, feet in the air like a fucking music theater major.

The next step sucked my step like tar. I yanked, and my foot came out. My shoe was still buried. My arms pin-wheeled, and my ass sunk into the snow.

The Bastard stopped, turned. Two city blocks between us.

"Hey!" I said, soaked shoe dangling in the air, elbows two inches deep. "Nice hoax."

The Bastard huffed air.

"I know this is a work. And I'm willing to bet his body ain't in that coffin."

The Hooded Bastard straightened his back.

I yanked my Converse out of the snow pit I'd made, shoved it on. All feeling from my hands gone. I stood, lungs sore. "You killed my friend."

The Hooded Bastard crouched on bended knee.

"Which means I'm going to hurt you." I took a step forward. "I might even kill you." The Bastard hugged himself. "Know why?" Each step filled my muscles with sand. "That's who I am. That's what I do. I hurt people for real. So I don't care if you're a shooter, or hooker, or don't know a headlock from a padlock. You're going to hurt for what you did to Robbie. Because you're real. Not a ghost. Not a rumor. And because you're real," I snarled, "you can die."

I ran hard, ready for hell, my prey blurry in my sights. I cut the distance in half before he raised his arms. Then, a black mass came at me.

Snow exploded across my face.

The shock blistered, then vanished, almost no pain: the snowball was light. I gasped, stumbled, and fell on my hands. Like a dog or collegiate wrestler, I was on my hands and knees. "Fuck."

Laughter.

Shutting my eyes, I could see the halls. Smell the stink of bleach and blood. The hum of the lights. And that laughter. "Oh, shit."

The Grey Tumor took a few steps forward. "So close. So close," it said, muffled. "But close only counts in horseshoes and hand grenades."

I stumbled to my feet and sucked in air. "No."

"You always fought to the last," he said. "But you never win."

Anger swarmed my eyes. "Stop talking."

"Just like at Red Wing."

I ran.

Another crash of snow, this one denser. But I kept on.

Hands up, I charged as the Tumor ran out of ammunition.

A scream came from the funeral party behind me, but I ran forward. The Tumor bounced up and down, then started running backwards. He was in a track suit. Black shoes. Face covered by a white scarf. Big. "Look at you! Can you see your face? You're not even breathing through your mouth."

"Shut up!" But the fucker was right. Hard to breathe. Soaked. Cold.

"Love to stay and chat, but got a lot to do. Suggest you go home. Tell Val what he wants to hear. And sit back and watch the fireworks."

Close. Eyes were antic.

Iced blue.

Not TV.

Maybe Finch.

Maybe.

Never saw the last one coming, hard as a rock, deep into the socket of my left eye. Crashing, I ate dirt and snow. The Tumor turned, darted, and waved. "See ya around, Demon."

He shrank. Distant. Punching the air. Like he'd already won.

The world swirled as I rolled on my back. Lungs burning. The dark stalks glared down, twisting, spinning. They grew long. Inky scars. Strings. They strangled each other and snuffed me out cold … light flashed. Flip book momentum. In and out. Trees. Screams. Crunches. Everything wet and crisp. White and blue. Then red.

*

"Get up," said the Black Widow.

My guts wretched.

"Get it out of your system. Then get up."

One leg up and the tree strands spun like an articulator.

Then, gravity failed and I was up.

"Jesus, you don't weigh more than a sack of flour. So move your feet. Don't care if they are rubber. We're leaving."

Black boots crunched the earth in rhythm with ragged breath.

"That's it. Keep moving, Kid Kong. Keep Moving, Kid Kong. We'll be home before too long, we'll be home to finish the song, keep moving, Kid Kong."

Ahead, flashing red and blue through the trees, was the line of cars leaving the gravesite.

"Don't mind the motorcade. That was my doing. Though what you did to make that witch scream I have no idea."

Words mumbled.

"Don't speak. Hell, by the look of that shiner someone belted you good and you're on punch-drunk legs. So much for a quiet and tidy funeral. Serves them right for barring us."

Us?

Wanted to speak. About the hoax funeral. And the Grey Tumor. And that everything was a lie. But the only sound I made was "Muh … muh"

"Shh, you gibbering idiot. Let me do the talking."

Didn't have a choice.

Through the tree line the lights swirled. Could have been a dozen cops or one. She coughed, spat, and when we passed the last stalks she spoke at a volume that shook my teeth. "Thanks for the help, boys. You're real humanitarians, leaving me to drag him out myself."

"Put him down and come with us."

"Not on your life."

"Take him to jail!" Penny screeched from somewhere beyond the wall of cops. "He ruined our funeral!"

"Ma'am, relax, we have this under control." The one cop from the entrance. "Folks, you're going to need to come with us."

"Can't you see he was assaulted? We're going to the hospital. You want to drive a motorcade there, be my guest."

"Ma'am, you crashed a private funeral," said the cop.

"Not so private that some creep didn't bash him one. Show them your eye."

My hand dropped. Watery darkness gauzed my sight.

"Oh, my, okay. Boys, we'll finish this later. Ma'am, that's a serious shiner."

"And the monster who did it is out there in the woods."

"We'll send someone—"

"No!" Penny screamed. "You have to arrest Sully!"

Tears dropped from my swollen eye. "How much did they pay you, Penny?" I said, then lifted my head, which was still spinning. Penny's dark raccoon eyes glared back, the center of the vortex. She was biting red nails raw. "I hope it was a lot. But it wasn't enough. Because I *know*, Penny."

"Arrest him!"

My head dropped.

FIFTY-SIX

THIS JUST IN

"Local news now, and a strange occurrence at Lakewood cemetery. Reporter Tina Yoothis has the story. Tina?"

"This afternoon at approximately eleven AM, a private ceremony was held for local athlete and professional wrestling star Robbie Varhooven, who died tragically this week at the age of twenty-three. According to local police, a fight broke out just outside the funeral involving members of the procession and an unknown assailant. Police have identified the victim as Sully Alexander, a former Minneapolis resident and friend of the Varhooven family. While the injuries were minor, the Minneapolis Police informed us that they are still on the lookout for the assailant. No motive was given. We will update you with this story as it progresses. Tina Yoothis, WTCN News, Minneapolis."

FIFTY-EIGHT

SCHMOZZ

"Hospital? For a shiner?" the Black Widow laughed. "I think New York living has made you soft."

The sack of frozen peas sat in my right eye-socket. I refused the comfort of the couch. I had very little medical knowledge, but Rat had toured across the US with the Dead Kennedys, where Jello Biafra used to get bashed in the head from skinheads like a daily requirement of insulin. *"Dudes who get head injuries, man? They go to sleep, they don't get up. Slow Eddie Spaghetti knocked himself out by spinning his mic at Max's Kansas City. Hilarious as fuck, but they dragged him to the Green Room couch. He could walk, but he sat, and then he died. Land of Nod for life."*

"You don't need a hospital."

Mouth numb from the pill she gave me, I sipped a Sanka. The crystals that bred this sludge lit static in my head. "What if it's a concussion?"

The Black Widow pulled out a wooden chair. The legs screeched against the ground. "You still sick?"

"No."

"You dizzy?"

"No."

"Are there two women in front of you who saved you from making more of an ass of yourself?"

I dropped the peas. "Ass?"

"If you weren't mine and already beat like a mule I would have dragged you out by your ankle, hitting every stone on the way out. You disgraced yourself. You disgraced me. You—"

"Shut up."

She smiled, steepling her hands. "Excuse me? I couldn't hear you over the bitching and moaning."

"*Shut up.*"

She leaned back, crossed her arms, I half-expected a spotlight. "You're in my home, you ungrateful bastard. You tell me to respect the wishes of that hack speed junkie. You deny me a place at that funeral. *Me.* You have the gall to call me arrogant and then become the star attraction—"

"It was a work."

She cackled. "Please, don't use my language. It's just embarrassing and I have no idea if you know what it actually means."

Eyelid fluttering, I leaned against the table. "The funeral. It was a work. It wasn't real. It was staged. Like a dark match no one wants to see but they need to use to fill out the roster. I ruined it because it was horseshit. Who paid for the million-dollar casket? Who paid to make everything about it *not* about wrestling? Sure as fuck wasn't Roberta, who watched from inside the rock star Bentley. I ruined it to see what would happen to those pulling Penny's strings."

"And what happened?

"Someone came out of the woods. They were watching. I chased them."

"And didn't catch them. And who were them, anyway?"

"Dude wore grey. Track suit." Mouth dry, I sipped the coffee. Didn't help.

"Well? How does your theory wash out? Was it some old man who stretched you?"

World War III went off in my head. My lip shook. "It was your son. Your real one."

"What the fuck does that mean?"

"The one who replaced me at Red Wing."

"Oh god, I am not going to keep apologizing."

"Once you had him, we were the dead ones."

"This pity party better be closing soon."

"Kara almost died. Did you know that?" She locked her arms. Face puckered like her ass was thrust down on a pinecone. "Got bronchitis. She was out in the snow. Wrestling a snowman. Guess who she was dressed as?" Her leg bounced, tapping the earth for an SOS. "Dad drove like a maniac. We got her in a bubble. First time I ever stayed awake all night. Never left her side. Ever."

She shook her head.

"Probably happened around the time when Robbie came knocking. So fit. So strong. So eager to eat your bullshit."

"Quiet."

"Did he do everything you say? Excuse all the lies? Never talk back?"

"You best get quiet, kid."

"A fucking bootlicking fan. The perfect son for a lying, no good, mommy dearest piece of shit."

The blade of her hand cut the distance between us and though I saw it coming I couldn't predict the pain, staggering dusty sparks eating my sight and spinning wild like firecrackers in a locked chest, twisting me as the pain sought out my nerves, riding them, burying inside me until gravity calls back—

"Oh no."

My collar tightened as her fist turned my shirt into a noose.

"You can't fall. Blame me for this. Blame me for everything. What kind of man are you?"

Copper tickled my mouth. "I'm your little monster."

The noose tightened. "Yeah. Monster is right. You want to know why I walked away?"

I spat on the floor and it came out red. "Enlighten me."

"Smart mouth words don't hide what you are. Shit, blame me? I don't hurt people. I could, but I don't. I never hurt anyone in the ring. Ever. I made everyone look good. I could have broken those Barbie dolls in half. Shattered their wrists. Crippled them for life. I could have and they knew it. So they took no liberties and I made them look great and we all made money. No one got hurt.

"You? I could see it. The way you looked up to me. The weakness you got from your dad. The way between us was clear. Violence. Power. Attention. You *were* a monster. What you did to that kid … you should have stayed in Red Wing."

I bit her hand. Hard. Nicotine and cream was bitter in my mouth.

She screeched. One punch dropped my jaw.

"Get up! You fucking monster."

I gripped the table. "Why?"

"I said get up."

"Why did you bring me back? Why did you bother? What do you think I have that you need?" I stood.

Her fist flexed while she rubbed my bite. "Hardest thing to come by in this world. The truth."

"About what?"

"Robbie. Everything stinks about it. His death. You being here. That funeral. The Swede on lockdown. Promoters never see disaster as a failure, but an opportunity. Yet here … it's like his body has the plague. It's not right. It doesn't make sense. No promoter would turn down the opportunity to make a death a success."

"Unless someone else orchestrated the hit."

"Finch? Was that who beat your ass? You see his face? He warn you not to keep digging up the old graves?"

Rubbed my mouth. "Nuh uh."

"Then who was it?"

I blinked. "Did you ever see the body?"

"What? I told you, I was not invited."

"Me neither. Just the burial."

"So?"

"Who said Robbie had died?"

She glared, then blinked. "A doctor in the AAW."

"Who?"

"Henry McAllister. Dirty old WASP. He's been with the Swede for years."

"Know where he lives?"

"He won't turn."

"Even in a chicken wing?"

Her hands dropped. "What are you getting at?"

"I don't care about the law. Like you, I want the truth. And only that bastard will know."

"Know what?"

I smiled, wiping my lip. "Really? You can't put the strings together? Let me use your words. Ahem. Robbie's death? It's a work." Her nose flittered like I'd farted in church and she was curious and repulsed. "They're trying to out-Kaufman Kaufman. It's a stunt."

"For who?"

"Whoever Robbie is working for, Cassidy or the Swede. The NWA is too old to know what to do with this stuff. But both GWA and AAW are breaking into the mainstream. They just need a revolutionary moment. What hasn't been done in wrestling?"

She grimaced, eyebrow high. "… A savior."

I grinned, nodding. "When he comes back from the dead he'll make millions for whatever company can have him. That's the angle. That's the work. It's fucking genius. Which means Robbie didn't come up with it."

"You think he's *alive*?"

"Fuck yes! Who do you think threw that rock? Who called me Demon? He's going to pull a Jesus and be bigger than wrestling."

Hope and fear played in her mind, you could see it in the near tears "No. This kind of strategy is beyond his paygrade."

"Is McAllister loyal?"

"Sure, but he's also old and has a penchant for call girls he can't afford. Cassidy solves problems by throwing money at them. We won't know until we get him."

"You know where he is?"

"Hell no."

"I might."

She snickered. "Really?"

I walked to the door, everything on fire. "You're driving."

"Where?"

"To the only ally I have."

She pushed past me, and I marched to the door, the leak of my right eye made of pus and tears.

FIFTY-NINE

AMAZING WRESTLING PRESENTS

NOVEMBER TO REMEMBER ISSUE: JAM PACKED WITH WRESTLING ACTION, 1983

Every year, fans all over the world wait with bated breath for us to reveal the *Amazing Wrestling* 500, the only official and globally recognized hierarchy of excellence in the squared circle, only brought to you by *Amazing Wrestling*.

This year is no different! This December, we will reveal who are indeed the greatest wrestlers of all time working in promotions around the world. Who will be number one? Who will be left out in the cold? Will your favorite make the cut?

While our deliberations are top secret, we've included your predictions from *Amazing Wrestling*'s dedicated fan base. We hope you enjoy these Criswells of Grappling! Carnacs of the Squared Circle! These Prophets of Professional Wrestling! Send in your predictions by mail and we'll select the most engaging letter for this fan showcase.

This is Ric Flair's year. He's survived a plane crash and made a name for himself as the best wrestler in the world, no matter who his opponent may be. And the figure four is the deadliest submission hold in the world. WHOOO!

Doug L., Nebraska.

If you don't give the number one spot to Terry Funk this year I'm going to burn your Yankee operation to the ground like Sherman in Atlanta. He's a legend and you've looked him over too long because of your Liberal bias, which is evident by your almost zero coverage of the amazing Dick Slater. The South Will Rise Again!

Mary Jo Blithe, Daughter of the Confederacy

This is the year of the Atomic Kid. He has the moves, the strength, and the charisma. He's really good and he will be champion before the end of the year. I hate Nathaniel Princeton. Thank you.

Kara A., New Jersey.

SIXTY

BATTLE ROYALE

I shot toward the dash in fast forward. The belt caught me, but shook sweat through every pore. The car rumbled. "That's for the silent treatment, kid," said the Black Widow, reversing into a parking spot on the street. Sasha's house was swathed in night. No lights on a street surrounded by illuminated homes. And it was only 7:30. Not cool.

"Shit," I said, then barreled out.

"Hey! The engine ain't off!"

The ground fought back as I slid toward the steps, then the path, the drugs in my blood fading into the throb of my eye socket. Fifteen feet felt like three blocks in Times Square. "Come on," I said to the Black Widow, to myself, to the world. "Come on, come on, fuck."

Skating on black ice, I slid toward the door.

I pulled. It opened easy, almost smacking me. The wood around the lock was mangled.

"Move," said the Black Widow, shoving past and pushing into the dark. "Stay behind me."

I did. "End of hall. Downstairs." The door's outline shimmered with light through the hinges. I stumbled in the wake of the Black Widow. Blinding light washed against the dizzy dark in my skull. Her form was consumed by the maw of bright and I tagged along like a fan to a backstage murder. From the maw came the scream of fans so loud it was static. Down the hard, stone steps after the cannonball of the Black Widow, there was a crash.

Into the light the Black Widow ran, out of sight from the top steps. The floor was swimming with tapes. Tables turned upside down. The immaculate archive was smashed into a trash dump, and in the center there sat a hurricane of limbs that the Black Widow crashed into.

"Gah!"

By the middle of the stairs they splashed onto the floor, wrestling match in a box of giant Lego. The TV blasted a black and white match between a mastodon of thickness in Greco Roman dominance over another man. On the floor, though, a hooded man straddled Sasha, hands around her neck. Even if it was a house, this was an apartment fight. "You did it!" the man screamed.

"No!" I screamed

The Black Widow clocked back her hand and open-palm slapped the side of his head. The impact made him stumble. He barely moved, but his choke softened, his shoulders drooped, and she slid her arms around his neck—a blood choke, for real.

He stood, lifting her on his back, then flipped her into the tapes. Just like me.

And magnets in my guts yanked. I jumped the last steps.

But the Black Widow twisted in the air, coat opening like a top, and landed on her boots. From the ground, Sasha's ballet slipper gas-pedaled the guy's balls.

"Jeuh—" he grunted, elbows locked at his side.

The Black Widow turned. Fury. Deep hate etched every wrinkle a half-inch deeper. Yet she looked timeless, as her elbow swung hard and cracked the hood in the temple.

I landed as he fell, splitting my legs so I didn't stomp his hood.

Beneath it was a mask.

"You," he said, shooting his arm up. I smacked it with my hand. Fucking thing was like concrete, but it moved.

"Time to talk," I told him.

The outline of his mouth frothed. "You don't get it. They killed him." He reached for my leg. I kicked it back while the Sasha pulled herself up from the wreckage of the tapes. The Black Widow killed the volume and took smart steps to keep herself grounded as we circled the large man on his back.

"This the jobber who tossed you?" said the Black Widow.

"Depends," I said. I looked at him. "Get your mask off."

"Slow," said Sasha.

He hissed, but his ice blue eyes were glassy. Fingers shaking, he tore behind the hood and peeled off the mask, straps like stray tentacles of a space alien.

Then, the mask was in his hand. "They killed him, don't you get it? For real. It's a war. *A war.*"

At our feet was TV Psycho, Robbie's best friend.

The women got him in a folding chair. Sasha worked a red scarf into a knot around his wrists, and fetched two more for his feet.

"Jesus, *this* is what you're into?" The Black Widow said.

"Shut up," I said.

Shaggy bangs crept over a moist forehead bumped with a fistful of scars from blading. His ears were cuffed but not the hard cauliflower of veteran grapplers. Handsome. Big teeth and smile. But those eyes were wild. "You're helping them. I fucking know it. You're all in on it, just like I thought ..." TV didn't shut up. But he also said nothing. Repeating vague and smoky assertions.

"You two, upstairs," Sasha said. "He can talk and move, but he won't escape."

"Confident," said the Black Widow. "You must be the subby. Figures."

"Focus," I said, and marched up after Sasha.

The kitchen had no smell of cooking. Just bleach. The dumplings a day-old memory erased from the room. Like it had been reset for opening night. "What happened?" I said.

Sasha's neck was starting to bruise. Potato sized marks. Fucker tried to strangle her. "He broke in while I was in the basement, looking for evidence of Finch."

"Oh god," The Black Widow said. "So, this is your rumor monger?"

I crossed my arms. "This is Russell Muldoon."

And for a second, the Black Widow was speechless. She turned to Sasha, then me. "The *Wrestling Dirt* bastard? You found him?"

"Just followed the strings," I said. "I know you're impressed. Try not to gag on the excitement. Sasha, do you think he followed me?"

She shook her head while the Black Widow sat in disbelief. "No. He's vulgar, cunning, but not smart. He has been trailing you, but unable to follow, so he started breaking fingers until he got data he could use. I suspect your connection at the Galactic Circus is probably in the hospital. Or worse."

Shit. Davey. "What did TV want?"

"I have yet to ask, and he's been making little sense. He realized who I was when he saw the tapes. Then anger took over. I think he's been drunk and high for the past three days. And, TV likely suffers from a variety of mental health issues. It makes him engaging for the viewers-"

"Cut the editorial," the Black Widow said, massaging her hands. "We need to know the whereabouts of Dr. McAllister. Give us the dirt and you can do what you want with the broken TV in the basement."

Sasha focused on me. "What did you find at the funeral?"

I gave her the short version.

"The funeral was a hoax," she said. Not a question.

"Oh god," said the Black Widow. "You people are worse than the UFO freaks. What next, the Loch Ness Monster was in the casket? Elvis in the woods?"

"No, Robbie in the woods."

"Shut up with that theory."

"I don't think anything was in the casket." The Black Widow huffed. "Robbie's alive. Someone fixed his death as a publicity stunt. And I think I owe that fucker a black eye."

Sasha's face was passive. "Interesting theory."

"It's delusional unless we have evidence," the Black Widow said. "Do you know where McAllister is being held? The company doc? Where has he fucked off to?"

"Nowhere we can get him."

"Says you," said the Black Widow.

Sasha smiled. "The Swede's training compound in Duluth."

The Black Widow's face shook, then calmed. "I see."

My fists flexed. "Damn it."

The Black Widow stood. "Let's go. Being this close to a smark is giving me a rash."

I waved her down. "That's what I got, Sasha. What about you?"

The Black Widow shook her head and muttered swears before taking the chair. Sasha placed her hands on the table. They were scraped and bruised. "I found Finch."

The Black Widow raised her chin. "Jesus Christ," she muttered.

"A match. Against the Swede. I found it before TV arrived. But there's only one. He'll be older, but you won't mistake his face. "

"He'll be in his eighties!" The Black Widow said. "We need to hit the road to Duluth

"No. We need to talk to Robbie's best friend

We all went back down to the basement. TV's head was slumped down in slumber. The actual television was soundless static. I pressed my middle finger against the tip of my thumb, coiling strength and anger, held it before the bangs that hid his trenched forehead, then released it in a hideous flick.

Quick as shit, his face snapped up and he chomped the air. "You fuckers. You dirty rat fuckers."

Pulling my hand from behind my back, I took a deep breath. "TV. I want to ask you something."

His teeth were wide, snarling under a smile. "You can do

whatever you want. Don't change the fact that you're all going to get it. Huh. Yup, all of ya."

"Who did it?"

He laughed. "You think you know, don't you? Listen to the mark, talking like he knows shit about shit. You're an ignorant worm, chasing something you will never find and you barely get, so take a dollar out of my pocket, tough guy, and buy yourself a clue."

Before the Black Widow could say a word, I barked. "Who faked Robbie's death?"

And the jabber jaw of TV Psycho hung like a draw bridge. "Nah. No way. No goddamn way." He shook himself forward. I moved back. Sasha stood behind him. The Black Widow watched static. "You miserable fuck, I will break your goddamn neck for that shitass lie."

"He's alive," I said.

"No way, no goddamn way. We were going to New York."

"I know. You got there first. Setting up an angle.'

He snarled. "Stop talking like us."

"He was supposed to follow after he finished his run with the Swede."

"You don't know shit."

"Because the Swede was never, ever going to give him the belt. Not unless he could bank on him for a long time. And as good as he was, he wasn't Gorgeous George. He wasn't Lou Thesz. He wasn't the Swede. Not yet."

Everyone looked at me.

Nerve-touch down.

TV's head rolled back and forth "Whatever. Whatever."

"So the question is, who was he going to screw over?"

Head rolling. "Don't go down this road, hobo."

"The Swede or Little Cassidy?"

"Mary had a little lamb."

"So he could die."

"Little lamb," TV said, but the anger slackened. The tight ridges and handsome face became a mask he'd wear into his eighties.

"And be reborn. Wrestling's first messiah. The call of a revolution. The AAW and GWA are going to war, TV. You said so yourself. And the Atomic Kid was the prize."

"Little lamb."

I kneeled. Eye to eye. But his were closed. "But Robbie wasn't smart enough to orchestrate it. You know it. He probably learned half of what he needed to do in the ring watching you. He was … a great mimic, but not an original idea in his goddamn head. It had to come from a top guy. Fed it to him. Made him believe it was his own grand idea. The angle with you might have been the first one of a civil war. You as TV Judas. Him as Atomic Christ. But he never told you."

"He told me everything."

"Like injecting hormones."

He shook his head. "That was just once."

"Now, I may be a mark for a third-tier wrestling mag. But I know you're smart, TV. And you've seen things I haven't. In AAW and GWA. So, turn on your mic, TV. Tell us what you know. Maybe we can find Robbie before he really does get himself killed."

He shook his head, then his whole body quaked. Sasha raised an eyebrow, hands behind her back. The Black Widow was punching the buttons on the VCR. Gulps of air came out of TV. Then snorts. Then … cackles of laughter. He threw back his head, bangs splitting. "You need a jacket to hug yourself all day, my friend, because you're as batshit as Charlie Manson on ice."

"You didn't say I was wrong."

"It would take too long to kick down the doors of stupid you just put up, so here's what you got right." He spat, and my hands shot up two seconds too late. "Nothing! You're so close and you can't see you're being played. We are *all* being played. And Robbie, he got it. You say he's alive? Then tell me this, hero. Who the fuck did I see in the morgue yesterday, huh? Before I went looking for you? They shove just anyone in that body bag?"

But he wasn't looking at me. "Katey!"

The Black Widow turned.

"You know he didn't die on his own. I've been hunting the god-damn hooker all around town. I finally caught him."

The Black Widow said nothing.

Cold fear sharpened his green eyes. "I slowed him down, but, hell, I'm a shooter. Broke his arm, but he almost got me," he said, then swallowed. "I think he let me live because it was one body too many. Plus, who the hell is going to believe a pro wrestler about anything?"

Broken arm?

Arm in a sling. Smoking Pall Malls at the hoax funeral.

The light of the TV cast the Black Widow in shadow. Behind her, a wide-faced man with thin hair, wearing simple black trunks, neck thick as a Michelin tire, had his wide hand raised in victory.

"Finch," she said.

The doorbell rang and everyone flinched but Sasha.

"Remain quiet," she said, then turned to the Black Widow. "I wish we could have met under different circumstances, Katey. You were the one who inspired me to become part of this world."

But the Black Widow's glare was back on the TV.

The door upstairs closed.

"Katey, cut me loose," TV said.

"Tell me where he is," I said.

"I'm going after him one more time."

"Where is Finch?"

"This time I'll finish it."

I cracked his jaw with my palm. "You're talking to *me* now. Where did you see him last?"

He shook away the pain as if I'd hit him with a sock. "He's probably leaving town. He just needs to get paid. I know where."

"Where?"

TV Psycho stared at the Black Widow. "She's the only one he fears."

The Black Widow cut through cassettes of a thousand dead matches with the grace of a ballet dancer. She stood before TV. "Why?"

Eyes pleading, he kept on. "He'll be gone soon. Just untie me."

"Why did you come here? Why would you attack a dirt sheet editor? What did she know that you didn't want out? And so much as think of trying to sell me a work I will bust your hide until your balls pop off."

TV looked like he was going to launch into another breakneck speech. "Look, the one thing this mark said right, the only piece of truth that came out is that there's a war on. Robbie died. I came out here to find out who started it. Because he's no messiah, he's a casualty. I tried to talk to the boys. But the Swede, the fucking Swede gave them marching orders. Anyone talks about the death, they're done. Wrestling bingo parlors instead of stadiums. Only some of them don't care. Because they know the war is already on."

"With Little Cassidy?"

Contempt dripped off his head. "No, with Little Caesar's Pizza. Robbie was the lynchpin and he got snuffed. That heart attack was no accident. But you know some old timers, they can stretch a guy and send him to the ring sick as a dog but he won't know until ..." He glared. "Finch fixed him. But who hired him? I thought, look, maybe Muldoon the Dirt Shit hack might know. That rag gives away more truth than anything even it hurts the business and, well, Glen or Glenda be damned, turns out she wasn't a he and damn near took my head off."

"Serves you right, you fucking idiot," said the Black Widow. "You committed a felony. You'll be lucky not to get life in prison if she presses charges." An unlikely event, if I figured Sasha right. I expected this place to be in flames before we closed the door. Soviet burn operations. No evidence but smoke. "You say Finch is here?" said the Black Widow. "Where is he hiding out? He doesn't stay in motels. Never leaves a goddamn trail. And he's too old to be sleeping in his car."

"Untie me and I'll tell you."

She sighed. "He's lying."

"I am not!" he said, thrashing in his chair. "Am not am not am not am not!"

"I know where he is," I said.

Everyone turned. TV in shock. Sasha bemused. The Black Window doubtful.

"Anyone here like the theater?"

SHOWING LIGHT

SIXTY-ONE

THE PROGRAM

The Minneapolis Young People's Theater is proud to present the next exclusive three-week run of *James and the Giant Peach*, featuring Penelope Varhooven as James! The classic from Roald Dahl continues to be a favorite of audiences worldwide, a treat for the holidays, and the critics are agreed that Varhooven's performances is:

"Spirited!" (*Star-Tribune*)
"Captivating!" (*Telegraph*)
"Completely and utterly sincere!" (*City Pages*)

Enjoy fun for the family before tickets sell out at MYPT!

SIXTY-TWO

SHOOTING GHOSTS

"It's your choice," said the Black Widow, taking her car keys in her hand. The dim light of Sasha's basement seemed weaker with the adrenaline drop. I wanted a coffee and a donut and codeine crushed in my molars and Dr. Pepper sipped through a straw. Instead, we were headed out to the theater. Me and the Black Widow.

Sasha looked at me. "I think you should decide."

"Bullshit," said the Black Widow. "He hurt you. We can handle the rest on our own."

I didn't believe her. But I didn't believe anything now. Other than what I saw. What I thought. What I felt. And there was a worm in my stomach that grew dark and oily when I thought of Finch … and the snowball tossing ghost

Sasha read me like a cheat note. "I think you should take him. If Finch is there, if he fixed Robbie, you'll need him." As she undid TV's straps, the Black Widow's contempt for everyone raised the temperature by ten degrees. She wouldn't look at me. Because it was my fault we needed extra muscle. If I was a better monster, a deadlier creature, then she would have an ally she could trust. One who could do the job. Or maybe she needed no one. And thought

Sasha a weak member of the stronger sex. Either way, she clearly wanted to go alone and yet somehow she needed us.

TV grunted, rubbing his wrists. "Katey, I—"

She jabbed his nose. It broke. Two red lines made an inverted V coursing down his face. "Listen here, idiot box. I call, you do. If it is Finch, you got lucky. But you're the only tool I have to work with that means a damn."

"Thanks, Auntie" I said. "Now if you don't mind. I'd like to talk with Sasha. In private."

"The less you talk to me," said the Black Widow, "the better we'll all be. But I ain't waiting." TV followed her upstairs, snorting red bubbles into his nose then spitting it on the ground.

"He's dead," TV said. "Whoever Jedi mind-fucked you wasn't him."

I shrugged. He grumbled a series of swears low and dirty.

The door closed. I had seconds.

"You're going to vanish," I said.

Sasha smiled. "Wrestling has taught me, Sully, that reality is a malleable thing. People vanish. They reappear, and they're not the same. Heels become Faces, and back again. It depends on whose reality has the most capital." She held out her hand. I took it. In her palm was a roll of quarters. "Finch may be going blind in his right eye. If you need to hit him, come from behind him on the right." Her hand pulled away. "Your mother will need you. Finch is a monster. And I hope your friend is alive. The one you remember, anyway."

Upstairs and outside, the coughing fit of a Pontiac in the cold drove me up the steps. I did not look back, but held the quarters like a winning lottery ticket.

Opening the front door, there was the Pontiac peeling away.

Fuck.

Off they went. Into the darkness. She'd left me behind, again.

Behind me, an acrid scent. Fire and plastic.

I ran. Turning right on the street, I did Rat's old trick of pulling car handles to steal change and shit. It could take hours. The stink of smoke rose. I pulled. Nope. No. Fuck no. Shit-

Fuck. A Chevy Nova popped open. I slid inside. Pepper carpet cleaner stank up the joint. I yanked out my home keys. The jagged edge wedged between ignition chrome and plastic neck. Fucker was tight. I bashed my fist with the quarters down—

Bam. Jackpot … until the paper wrapper in my palm split and the quarters spilled into the dark. "Shit." Jaw clenched, I went to work.

Fifteen seconds later, the streets in the rear view were glowing with orange light like a thousand Jack O' Lantern filled with napalm. Wires sparked. I dropped into gear and hit the gas. Behind me Sasha's house was a white-hot chimney. Chasing the red brake lights of the Pontiac, I kept moving forward. Thinking forward. Dragging my past into the future.

The Black Widow drove 80 mph down ice-laden streets and I barely knew where she was going beyond following hard turns, quick lefts, and one-ways. She had an allergic reaction to stop signs. Suburban traffic fucked off when they heard her horn and engine. The Chevy never got closer than eight cars. Losing me. That's what she wanted. Here I was. Chasing her again.

Her and Robbie.

"Enough," I muttered.

I gunned it.

Closed the distance.

Just went straight.

50, 60, 75.

She pulled further away as we approached an intersection shaped like a T.

The fender nudged forward. Her bumper dipped down my line of sight. That space I could never judge. Where things are close, but hidden, and then you smash them against your will.

She pulled away.

Distance made her safe.

Me from her, her from me.

The T approached.

I eased off the gas. So did she. Then red brakes and a decision.

The car fishtailed as she turned left, recovering, and I turned right.

She's going to the theater.

She took what I dangled on the string. I'm went to get Penny.

Fifteen hard miles later and the TV crews and their vans were gone. Chasing the next tragedy. I parked opposite the apartment and could hear the insane volume coming from next door. The goofy kids who saw me fall? They were practicing louder than a jet engine at takeoff.

The quarters glittered on the floor of the stolen Chevy. "One, two, three—" I counted on as I picked them up and shoved them inside my fist. Maybe five bucks. Half-power. Still better than my stupid keys and way less obvious.

I ran. A disintegrating Yellow Pages was propping the door open.

Someone was in and wanted others in, too.

One step, and the stairs creaked. No surprise. So I ran up.

I knocked on Penny's door, eyes adjusting to the weak bulb above the frame.

Knock-Kock.

"Penny?"

Nothing.

"I'm sorry about the funeral. Can I come in?"

A grunt.

The knob was warm as I twisted.

Inside, shapes jutted in darkness but remained frozen. A Rorschach test I resisted. "Penny?"

A haughty grunt from her bedroom. Where I'd never been.

"Look, I know. I know what's happening."

A laugh. High and disdainful.

"Where is he?"

I pushed open the door. Darkness.

"Where's Robbie?"

I hit the light.

A boulder of a man sat on the bed. Gray hood on. Sweats. The Grey Tumor was giggling.

"Welcome to my nightmare," he said, then pulled down the hood. "Demon."

Robbie's smile was wide. His eyes manic. Speed or acid or something you could only get from a rock star's pharmacy. Old makeup covered his eyes. The aroma of shit stains and fast food trash reminded me of 53rd and 3rd.

"Fucker," I said.

"I know, I know." He nodded hard, like a wheezing cartoon dog, then put his thick index finger to his lips. "But it's a secret. And it has to stay that way. Which means we need take a trip. Somewhere no one will find or see." I backed up.

My back hit something.

I jumped forward, and spun.

The old man from the funeral, one arm in a sling, stood in the doorframe.

Finch.

Robbie stood. He had to be close to three hundred pounds of rock shoved into sweats. "Think it's time for a nap, Demon."

Window. Take the window.

Robbie shuffled to the right and blocked the straightaway. "Oh, Penny told me about your last exit, flyboy. God, you were always nuts, weren't ya?"

"This coming from a guy who faked his own death."

He pounded his chest like King Kong, and laughed without a sound. "God, I've missed you, Demon!"

Finch took a step forward. "Get going," he said, low and bored. "Or leave it to me. No time to fuck around."

"Easy, Birdie," Robbie said. "Demon here is my best—" Robbie took one step forward and I swung my five-buck punch—

—it tagged his Frankenstein jaw and he stumbled around on the bed. "Whooo damn!"

An iron arm slid around my neck. I tucked in my chin before

the choke closed. Finch was slipping a sleeper deep, yanking back. Total command. I struggled, but he wouldn't budge, his arms frozen. Left hand reached up for his eyes, but I couldn't find them. Air pulsed through my nose while spit crawled out of my mouth.

Finch pulled back, arching my back. was clenched hard and rough. I threw punches. Each one weaker until my fists felt like balloons. Flies filled my vision. My legs kicked, and I lost balance. Finch's arm slid deep. Pressure dropped, then expanded.

Robbie spun around, blood running from his mouth, eyes dark as coal.

I threw another punch … and stray quarters flew out like stars.

His jaw dropped. Joy filled his eyes. "You hit me … with a foreign object? God, you are such a good heel. That's enough change for a few rounds of Pac Man! But it's time to go to sleep." He lifted my arm high. I couldn't stop him.

He dropped it. "One."

He lifted it, then dropped it.

"Two."

Darkness flooded before he said three.

Two rotten eggs dipped in pepper and steak sauce were shoved up my nose. The rusty hinges of my lockjaw gasped open while tears turned me into a gasping baby. Dark trees shot up around in me at weird angles. Iced wind whispered. Everything sucked. Tears hissed as they hit snow. "Morning, sunshine."

Blue starlight gave Robbie's form a radioactive glow, part magic, part Chernobyl. His massive back looked stuffed with three hundred pounds of starched clothing shoved into one used gray sack. If Finch was here, it was out of sight. Somewhere in the trees. "Great night. God, this cold makes me feel alive."

The trees slowed their spin cycle. His back was all that seemed stable.

"Robbie."

"Can you see it, Demon? Can you see the lights at lockdown?"

Lockdown.

Jesus.

I rolled on to my stomach, which then shot out of my mouth. Steam misted from my last meal as it ate into the snow with a hiss.

"I know, I know. Not a lot of good memories. But it's where we met. Where AK was born."

Palms touched snow. I pushed up. The world shook. My neck craned.

The clearing was surrounded by trees on one side. But where Robbie stood was an edge of a hill. Below him were caged boxes surrounded by wire, blue moonlight and searchlight caressing the thick snow. The Gulag of Minnesota. "Red Wing," I said. "You brought me to Red Wing?"

Hands on his hips like Superman, Robbie took a very deep inhale, them let out steam. "Yesssssssss, and a very good reason too. So much history. So many secrets. So much we don't talk about."

"It's a fucking crime scene."

"Yes, and it seemed fitting."

"Fuck that 'yes, and' improv talk," I leaned back, knees in the snow. "This is me you're talking to."

"And who are you, Demon?" He turned. The grin was wide and malicious. "Are you my friend?" He crunched one step closer.

"I've been trying to find out how you died," I said. "Sound like an enemy?"

"You did it for Val's mag. So you did it for money. Sounds like a whore."

"Sure, but I found the truth."

He smiled, revealing his missing canine. "Did you? What's the truth, Sully?"

"You're not dead."

"But we buried the body. The only one who saw me was you. So, you're the only one to see me alive." His eyes popped open. "See what I'm saying?" His accent took on a southern drawl, like Dusty Rhodes and Dick Slater, "Why don't you lay down some more truth, Demon? See where it leads ya. What else is true?"

Snot hung off my nose, swinging like a spider's pendulum. "You're starting a revolution."

He sucked in air, eyes shut. "Ohhhh, well, ain't that a fact?"

"That will spark a civil war."

"Mercy, mercy, mercy me this sounds epic."

"Until … only one promotion remains. GWA or AAW. Because the only angle no one has tried … a resurrection angle. First one to bring you back from the dead wins."

He clapped once, the accent gone. "Brilliant, Demon. You get it. You get that the truth is in the secret. And the secret is the truth. That's something Katey never got."

Fresh sick splashed the back of my teeth, leaking out. My hands melted a layer of snow. Hard brush revealed itself before my hand went numb.

"Yeah, about Katey." He squatted. The earth seemed to shift under his weight. "I read Penny's letters. I get it. You have every right to hate me."

Tremors lit my elbows. I clawed my hand into the earth until it made a fist. "Shut up."

"But you understand, right? I didn't really have a choice but to become you, or a better version of you."

The dirt was hard in my palm. Better than a roll of quarters. But he was still too far. Goad him. Be pathetic. Lure him like a loser. Resting my weight on my knees, I pulled myself up and leaned back. That face. Crinkled like a relief map of Afghanistan. Buried in it the boy I met at Red Wing. The Robbie that *I* had known? Dead. "Don't. Don't talk about her."

"You should really get over your Mommy issues, Freud. You know, before it's too late."

I huffed. "And who's going to make it late? You or Finch? Where is that crippled fuck?"

He slapped his knees. "Good. Good. That sounds like you, Demon."

"I bet it's him. He'll be the one to end me. Not you."

"Tell me why, Demon! You were always the smart one. The violent one, too."

My hand was ice. I smiled, then snickered. "Simple. You're just a fucking wrestler." My laughter was genuine but it hurt to breathe. "You ain't been in a real fight since we were *here*. You're fake, Robbie. A phony. You're a fucking joke." His smile crested, then sagged. So sensitive. He got closer. Each time I spoke. Misting breathe coming for me. "I fucking deduced your plan and you know what? It's a joke. This war you say is going on? You're going to be the first casualty. For real. One wrestling promotion means you're chained to that ship until it sinks or sickens of you. You're not free. You're going to be a slave to either the Swede or Little Cassidy Junior with nowhere to run. They'll love you till you're useless and then they'll toss you like a dead horse at the glue factory. They'll own you until you're homeless. So the question that's left is what kind of dick you like to suck."

He swung.

I shot out an iced jab.

His chin was pay dirt and he fell on his back.

Two seconds later, I was up. Spinning my head, all I saw was trees. Then, a dark road of freshly cut tire tracks in the white. Dirt dripped from my hand as I hustled, lungs scratched and blowing. The shaded shimmer of old headlights stared out of the dark path. A jeep.

"Woohoo!" Robbie cried. "That was a hell of a shot!" I turned. He snapped up back to his feet like a gymnast Frankenstein and I gunned it toward the jeep. "But you're in a handicap match, Demon."

The green jeep sat like an antique. I clawed at the door.

Pain splashed my spine. Everything choked. Knees buckling, I turned.

Finch wore a wool coat. In his good arm was a shovel. He stood in some kung fu wrestler stance. Left side closer to me.

Breathless, I tossed a right hand.

The shovel smacked my face.

Ass hit the ground.

"Now *that's* what you call a foreign object," Robbie said, cackling. "A Moldovian with a gardening tool."

"Pick him up," Finch said.

Nothing worked. Breathing was a full-time gig, but each breath shrunk and expanded my skull with a nauseating thrum. Gravity clawed but Robbie caught me and then I was in his arms, like a horror film queen being kidnapped by a river monster. "Sorry it had to end this way, Demon."

They marched me into the darkness, trees raced by like telephone poles on a car ride. But the bruise on Robbie's lip was swelled like a boil.

"You're going to be a tool," I said. "And then a casualty."

"You sound like TV."

"He's right," Finch said.

Robbie smiled like a smug bastard. "Doesn't matter."

"Like the truth doesn't matter?" I retorted.

"What truth do you want? How about the truth of Red Wing."

"What's that, Robbie? What should I take with me when the light snuffs out?"

His nostrils flared. "You would have died in there without me. Raped more than you were raped. You were weak unless you got the first shot. I took a hundred blows for you until you learned how to fight back"

I grimaced. "Right. I was the violent one. The one they were going to kill. But you? Sweet, innocent Robert. You were just a spaz. But in there? You became a hero."

"Now I'm doing a heel turn."

"Shut your mouths," Finch said, voice like tin.

"No one can hear us, Birdie" Robbie said. "He could scream for an hour and the worst you'll do is scare a deer."

"You're both making me sick," Finch said. "Shut it."

"Make me!" I yelled.

Finch turned, holding the handle near the blade. "Drop him."

"He's just being himself," Robbie said.

"Won't say it again."

"Fuck you!" I said.

I hit the ground.

"Stay down," Robbie said. "Trust me."

"I'm putting him to sleep," Finch said.

"Not yet. We're not done with the show."

"Don't give a shit about the show," Finch said. "I'm finishing the job. Step back."

"Taking orders from a killer?" I said. Flashes of pain popped against my guts. "You really are a heel. A shit heel."

"Shut up, Demon," Robbie said. "The big deals are talking."

The ground pulled me against action. Then I saw it. Dirt mound that had been vomited up from the earth. My second grave in one day. This one dug by a one-armed murderer. Jesus. How long did that take? Legs stiff, lifeless, nowhere to run. And on the rim of the horizon, the horror of my past was the backdrop to the nightmare of my ever-shrinking present. Would I swoon, like some shitty Poe character? Because there was no goddamn way I was making a comeback. Two guys. One killer. One stronger. And anger wasn't ammunition. It was blanks.

"Leave," Finch said.

Before I could mutter a useless, "Who, me?" Robbie stepped over me. "This is my angle. You go."

"Not part of the deal."

"Fuck the deal, you one-armed bandit. This is my angle. You can finish him but I'm not missing this for the world." He towered over the thicker old man by a foot.

"Last chance," Finch said. "Go, or I'll make you."

"You know what, Finch?" Robbie said, poking the guy's chest with each word. "Why don't *you*—" Robbie dropped to his knees, seething so loud night birds jetted. Finch's paw-like left hand contorted Robbie's wrist and mangled his fingers. "You broke my wrist!" Finch tugged and Robbie silenced against the gentle wind.

"Ain't broke. Yet. You ain't shit. And if you don't get in that jeep and scram, I will make you piss blood every day until your Jesus moment. Don't care who you complain to up the ladder. Don't care if you die. Get gone."

He released Robbie's hand, which the big man cradled like a dying child.

"You fucking relic!" Robbie said. "You have no idea what we're doing. I can't believe I have to work with a dinosaur who doesn't know he's extinct—"

Bullet-quick, Finch's spider digits pinched Robbie's neck.

Robbie fell hard, eyes wide and then closed. Out on his back.

Finch spat. "Fucking marks."

His awkward steps on thick boots gave him a waddle. But he never let the blade drag. "Up."

I tried.

Fell.

Craned my neck. His hammered nose looked high as the tree-tops. Crowned by stars. "Up."

"Just kill me."

I couldn't hear him breathe, but he strained his neck as if the words were a weak punch.

"Just do it. Cut my head off with a shovel. Break my neck. Strangle me again. Go ahead. I fucking dare you. But I won't make it easy, you old fuck."

Steam trailed from his large nostrils. "You? I like you."

The shovel dropped.

I thought of Val's office. Where it began. Of Teddy handing me the Black Widow's business card. Of how sick I was of this shit.

I stood, turd sliding out my ass. I had one move. And it wouldn't work. Still, I cultivated the saliva and blood and vomit in my mouth, packing it in my cheek. This is how my flame went out. In the snow above Red Wing. A mystery for Dad to grieve. Another member of the family that abandoned Kara. And the Black Widow getting her final wish. To be far, far away from her little monster.

Finch blinked. That broken mug narrowed his eyes. "You look. You look like." He swallowed his thought. "Jesus. I'm shooting with ghosts."

"You ever do a job, Finch?"

His mauled face lifted a chin. "Only for pay."

"Fuck, all I got is a story."

"Then you ain't got shit. C'mon, mark. Try me. You earned one last chance to lose. Again."

I raised my arms. Fists tight. Took a bullshit stance.

Then spit.

Watching the bullet of gore, I swooned. Wet, birthed from my lip, the loogie launched itself into the air. Bear-sized hands from both arms cut the air in front, trying to catch it.

They missed.

Splat went the hoark against Finch's one good eye on the right.

Blind. For a one swipe.

I dropped, grabbed the shovel, and swung for his knees.

Thunk.

The lumbering beast bared his teeth: little stained tombstones bright with spit. His good hand wiped his eye as I chopped again.

He teetered, then fell on me. Dude was made of cement. I swatted but the shovel fell out of my hand. He leaned down, breath like a dead rat, and balanced himself by shoving his good forearm against my cheek. "You're going to hurt before you die." I swatted again, and his knee cracked into my ribs. Like flicking the switch on an amp, the juice in me went cold. But the pain flushed awareness into my prone form. His forearm dropped twice. I let it. No choice. Pain bounced through me. Useless, I looked up, his forearm bracing me against the ground. Finch's jaw hung open. "Shit bird move."

I spat blood, muttered "Fuck you."

He leaned back and gripped my neck. One hand grabbed his wrist, then dropped. He squeezed my throat shut. Drowning in air, my eyes inflated. Finch grinned. "At least you fought. Unlike your daddy." Wordless, my eyes screamed. Daddy? Who the fuck ... then

Mom's words came in. The Cowboy. Her good friend.

"Didn't know, did you," he said. "When you go south of heaven, tell old scratch Finch says, hell—"

A crack of thunder shook the world as Finch's head broke into a thousand red pieces, the puzzle of his face scattered across the blue sky, vanishing like smoke in the winter breeze. Rain dropped in red, hard bits as his body fell to the side. The rain stopped. I drank in the copper air, penny-flavored gasps, then my torso popped up like Frankenstein.

Smoke rose from the hand of the Black Widow. A snub-nosed .36 shone bright. Behind her, TV Psycho held his ears. Silence washed over the gore, the gunshot fading in the howl of wind through trees, all of which punctuated through my gasps and snorts.

"Get up," said the Black Widow as her hand slowly descended, pistol nose pointed at the dirt. "TV, get that guy in the ground. We're leaving."

The shovel. I grabbed it. Used it like a crutch. My throat felt pencil thin, each breath more like a gag.

The Black Widow glared at Finch's headless form, but it eased as she mouthed words lost to the pulse jackhammering my ear. A prayer. An apology. I spat the dead man's blood from my mouth. Dad's green jacket was spray-painted Finch. And I had no more puke to surrender. I trudged over to her, shovel's blade tapping the ground. "How was the theater?"

She raised the gun like she was going to slap me with it. Then closed her eyes, shook her head, and dropped her hand. "You lied."

I took on the authorial voice of Columbo's nephew. "Nah. When you ditched me I realized he'd be hiding in plain sight. But then again, for that to work, you had to believe he was alive."

TV grunted, lifting Finch by the feet, dragging the remains behind him.

"Lucky guess," she said.

"Like knowing where he'd be?"

She looked in the direction of Red Wing. "The tracks were easy."

"That's not what I meant."

Her eyes softened. "Part of him is still here. All those hours in the ring. In the gym. It was to destroy something here. Even in this stupid idea of coming back to life, I think it's to leave this behind."

Empathy. It frosted every word. Poor Robbie. He worked so hard. It wasn't fair. Boy, he tried hard. So much to regret. If only she could have done more to save him. Not one word that her wrestling son had tried to kill me. That there was an open grave Finch had dug. She was still his mentor. His mother. I wiped the gore onto my green sleeve. "Better go wake up your boy."

I walked toward Finch's jeep, shovel tapping the ground, sneakers crunching.

"Where do you think you're going?"

"New York."

"Not looking like a horror movie."

"At the Greyhound station? I'll fit right in."

"We need to talk."

I reached the door. "No, you do. *I'm* going home."

"What about Robbie?"

"Fuck him. Leave him. I don't give a shit."

"I can't believe I saved your worthless hide and you're going to leave your friend—"

An ember of anger flared and coiled and I swung around. "He was going to kill me! That's what your boy was going to do. He was going to get Finch to do it. It was his idea. The hoax funeral. He believes that shit. He believes his resurrection will start a war that will make him the greatest wrestler of all time. He's worked himself into a shoot and was going to kill me to make it happen. He's batshit. So save him, nurse him, fuck him, I don't give a shit. Just don't be surprised when he snuffs you out while you sleep."

And that's when I noticed the gray beast that was Robbie was on his feet.

TV was a lump on the ground. Silently broken like a monster toy next to the open grave. Robbie stepped over his prone body and waved to my so-called mother. "Hey, Katey."

The Black Widow's arm snapped down. "Jesus, kid," she said. "You scared the piss out of me and for what?"

Robbie raised his hands. "I'm so sorry! I know it looks crazy, but I've worked it all out. It's time for a revolution. I've got it all planned."

"You worked with Finch." Her hand shook. "You worked with a killer."

"I had to. He was the only one who could make my heart stop for the gimmick. That was non-negotiable."

"With who?"

He smiled, taking small steps closer. "Kayfabe, Katey."

"Fuck kayfabe," she said, elbows bent. "Who put you up to working with him? The Swede? Cassidy? That clown Lawler?"

He made a lock motion on his mouth. "Crossed my heart, and hoped to die. But you did me a favor. I needed to use Finch. He's the last of the hookers who can make a guy's heart stop … but not for long. But he's a ghost anyway. And no one will miss him. So you freed me of the need to end him."

I cackled. "Fuck, I did a better job whipping his ass than you did and I stunk."

"Is it true?" said the Black Widow, as she pointed the gun at me. "Was I interrupting an execution?"

"Sully doesn't get it," he said, getting closer. "Katey, I was just going to scare him to keep his mouth shut. But Finch, he was going to kill him. I tried to stop him but, god, the guy knows moves that are older than the pyramids."

"Bullshit," I said, lurching forward on the shovel. "Can't you smell it?"

"Why would I kill the guy who gave me the courage to be all I've become?"

"Because you're fucking nuts."

"Shut up!" she said. I did, but we both kept walking.

"Katey, he doesn't get it. You do. I'm going to turn the wrestling business inside out. It's all planned. I just need you to believe me.

And we'll all get what we want. You can get the treatment you need."

The Black Widow's gun hand rose towards Robbie. "Silence."

"How long do you have?" Robbie said, face worried.

Silence followed.

"Your insurance must be running out."

She swallowed, and the barest glimmer of wetness lit her eyes. "It won't matter."

He inched forward. "You don't know that. I know doctors. Rich ones. The kind that save people that cancer normally kills. I want to help, Katey. They change lives. Do what other doctors cannot. Why do you think I have this incredible body?" He flexed his bicep. "You know all I've ever wanted was to pay you back."

I trudged forward. "Don't believe him."

"You just have to trust me." He reached out his hand across the distance. "Give me the gun. I can save you."

"Don't do it!"

She swallowed. "Promise?" she said, so tired, so weak, so hopeful.

He nodded like a dog. "You know I keep my promises. I never told Sully you were alive. You trusted me then. Trust me now, and I can make it go away."

She handed him the piece. "Fucking knew it," I grumbled, and hate gripped my skeleton Lightning from his hand produced a thunder that knocked me back a few steps. The Black Widow crumbled backwards as if kicked by Bruce Lee. "No!" I screamed, and ran.

Robbie smiled, watching me coming, then raised the pistol. "So long, Demon. Thanks for giving me the life you could never have!"

Click.

I seethed. Finch's blood like electricity across my face. I tasted hate. There was nothing left but the name he called me. I ran harder.

Click, click, click.

I cut the distance, then turned around to see those stupid wide eyes finally lit with terror. "No fair!" he said. "That's a foreign object!"

The blade of the shovel cleaved into his blocking hands.

Fingers dropped and he screamed. "No! My punches! My punches are the best!" He tore his eyes from his severed hands and growled, body shaking, like he was about to make an epic comeback. "You can't stop me, Demon! I'm the Atomic Kid!"

The blade cleaved into his skull. His eyes went cross watching it bite into his own head. Then everything twitched until I yanked it out.

His back hit the ground, shoulders on the snow. One, two, three … No bell rang. But the snow stained dark as the ghost in his body hit the showers somewhere the fuck else.

I dropped by the Black Widow, pulling her head back. "Hey! Hey, wake up." Her mouth was slack. "Wake up, Mom! Mom, wake the fuck up!" Tears I didn't want swelled and bled down my face. "Fuck."

She coughed. "Goddamn it."

Then, I got it.

Smoke rose from her gut where she'd been shot. But nothing leaked. I touched the wound and felt heat, no blood, then something stiff.

"Vest?"

Her pained face looked ten years older. "I'm a goddamn professional. Who walks around with a gun and no vest? That makes me smarter than all of you fucking rubes. Now get off me. We need to move or no matter what we'll be dragged into the limelight."

No thank you. No apologies. No explanation. On her feet, stumbling a bit in her boots, she woke up TV and got him to work. Then she saw me, leaning on the shovel.

She walked back, shaking her head. "Stand up straight, we need that."

She gripped the shovel.

I held it firm. Until everything shook. Our eyes met. All I saw was death. And all she was, was a killer. She sighed. "Come here."

I couldn't. I'd fall.

So she stepped forward. Arms slipped around me.

The shovel dropped. Heavy snow fell. The temperature dropped. She held my weight.

"Come here, Kid Kong. Mommy's little monster did good."

SIXTY-THREE

SCREWJOB

Amazing Wrestling continues to mourn the passing of the Atomic Kid. To honor his memory we would like to dedicate the following Photo Issue to the memory of one of the brightest stars in our favorite sport and includes some of his greatest feuds, like with Dusty Rhodes, Dr. Death, and TV Psycho. We have no doubt that he would have been a leading light and champion.

We are also proud to announce the appointment of Teddy Filkers as our new Writer-in-Chief! A fan favorite for his magic photos and witty puns, Teddy will be leading the bullpen into a new age of action, access, and adventure here at Amazing Wrestling. Congrats, Teddy!

Val Easton III, Editor-in-Chief.

SIXTY-FOUR

PARTS UNKNOWN

Seven days. That's how long we waited in the basement. I bought take-out Chinese from a place called Gong-Time. Charson, our delivery guy, wore a vest over his winter coat that had a karate guy kicking a gong. "I drew them," he said. I told him they were badass. He nodded like he didn't need me to confirm a known fact.

The Black Widow made phone calls in her room, door closed, and never said anything when they were done. We never spoke of what happened at Red Wing. But we knew that when the snow thawed things would be different.

We tossed the string and index cards into a garbage can and set them aflame. But the ones in my mind were branded there and would never go away.

I'd figured something out.

I was right.

I got to the truth, or at least part of it, and no one would know.

Unless I wanted jail time.

We watched the string and cards churn in the can. White and blue going black and orange. "I'll give you a ride to the Greyhound."

"Thanks."

"You need some money?"

"Still got a handful of Val's cash."

"You going to keep writing for him?"

I nodded, knowing I was fucked. "You need anything?"

She lit a cigarette. "Nah. I'm good."

We both smiled.

The ashes swirled in the rusty bucket like snow climbing a vortex.

"I could tell Val I'll be back a little later."

She nodded, then shook her head. "Nah. You got a job. Focus on that. But, uh, could you do me a favor?"

The burn flared. "Sure."

"When it's a good time, could you, uh … could you tell Kara? You know, about, well, about me." She buttoned her lip, and ashed her cigarette. "No rush."

"Yeah," I said. "I will."

She nodded. "Well, last redeye to Jersey is in an hour. Suspect there won't be a line up."

The Pontiac cut through the fresh powder, tires wet and sure. In daylight, the Greyhound station was like a strange theater. Everyone buying a ticket to a one-way show away from Minneapolis.

She pulled out up front, honking and swearing at a hotdog vendor whose silver box was steaming like a dying engine. "Move it before I break your goddamn neck and pretzel your balls!" He obliged.

She pushed the cigarette lighter. "Bus is leaving soon."

I took the hint, then grabbed the door handle. "Thanks."

She smiled. "You did good. You did good, Sully." She sniffed away a tear. "Say, I gotta ask. Before you go. Who … who do you think … who put him up to it?"

I let go of the handle. "I don't know. But I think we'll find out."

"Oh yeah?"

"He was right. I think a revolution is in the air. And most revolutions have a fail before they take off. The Atomic Kid was a test. And he failed. Whoever gets it right, they're building on his bones. They're the ones who turned him into a loon. Whoever wins killed our boy."

She nodded. The cigarette lighter popped out. "Best get going. Don't want to be late."

We both froze until she grabbed my neck, and pulled my head over her shoulder with the strength of a lioness. "You're good. You're a good son." She let me go before I word could beat my tears. "Now get the hell out of my car, I need to go job hunting."

I laughed. "Okay."

I opened the door. It was so heavy. But the cold made me move. I shut the door and walked on, the Pontiac's screeching tires and the Black Widow's honks and screams filling my backside like a hug.

In line, feet an inch deep in slush, green and ripped jacket reeking of bleach like a janitor's slop bucket, I unslung my bag. I had stowed away a single Gong-Time egg roll for the trip but couldn't bear to let it sit there.

Unzipping the top, I unpacked the paper towel damp with grease. But beneath it was a lump.

A shoebox.

God. She was giving me mementos. News clippings? A piece of her championship belt?

I opened it.

Paper. Notes. Letters. Old. Her life. On top was one of my index cards.

"Sully: for when it makes sense. For you and Kara. I did my best. You've done better. Take care of your sister. Remember me. Love, M."

ACKNOWLEDGMENT

This novel was written in fits and starts while working five-to-seven jobs in five different cities. I stole time at lunch, while monitoring study hall, while on the BART or the Google Bus, and on weekends while renovating two houses. You know, the lazy life of an artist.

I would not have finished it without the love and support of the following people: My wife and family, RJ Hill, Michael Slembrouck, Nick Mamatas, Kate Alice Marshall, Elizabeth Hand, and Chad Dundas.

Thanks to everyone who understands why WrestleMania is a "high holy day" at our home.

Jason Ridler is a historian and writer. He is the author of nine novels, including ***Dead in the Ring***, ***Harvest of Blood and Iron***, and ***The Brimstone Files*** series for Nightshade Books. He is also the author of ***Undefeated: Stay a Writer Against the Odds***, a strategy and creativity guide for new writers.

A former punk rock musician and cemetery groundskeeper, he teaches history at Johns Hopkins University and creative writing for Greater than the Sum, vendor for The Arts at Google. Visit him at: www.jasonridler.com

ABOUT
SHOTGUN HONEY BOOKS

Thank you for reading ***Dead in the Ring*** by Jason Ridler.

Shotgun Honey began as a crime genre flash fiction webzine in 2011 created as a venue for new and established writers to experiment in the confines of a mere 700 words. More than a decade later, Shotgun Honey still challenges writers with that storytelling task, but also provides opportunities to expand beyond through our book imprint and has since published anthologies, collections, novellas and novels by new and emerging authors.

We hope you have enjoyed this book. That you will share your experience, review and rate this title positively on your favorite book review sites and with your social media family and friends.

Visit ShotgunHoneyBooks.com

SHOTGUN HONEY
FICTION WITH A KICK

www.ingramcontent.com/pod-product-compliance
Lightning Source LLC
Chambersburg PA
CBHW011925050726
47591CB00009B/2342